JEREMIAH BLOOM

AND THE

AMULET OF OSIRON

JEREMIAH BLOOM
AND THE
AMULET OF OSIRON

By
STEPHEN WREN

Blackbeard Books
Tennessee, USA

For information or permissions, please write:
Blackbeard Books, P.O. Box 2015, Mount Juliet, TN 37121-2015.

First Edition: January 2009

Blackbeard Books titles may be purchased for academic, business or promotional usage or special sales. For specific information, please write to Blackbeard Books, P.O. Box 2015, Mount Juliet, TN 37121-2015.

Visit our website at www.BlackbeardBooks.com
Visit the official Jeremiah Bloom website at www.JeremiahBloom.com

Publisher's Cataloging-In-Publication Data available

ISBN 10: 0-9819021-0-3
ISBN 13: 978-0-9819021-0-4
Library of Congress Control Number 2008906151

Cover art/illustration by David Sourwine
Interior book design by JustYourType.biz

Text type set in Garamond
Display type set in Caribbean's Treasure and Captain's Table

For Tyler and Noah, my two pirates

ACKNOWLEDGEMENTS

For Marlo Garnsworthy, an amazing editor with a keen eye and a brilliant way with words, it's been exciting and an honor having you work with me on this series. Your understanding and feedback has been priceless. I'd like to thank my family and friends for their reviews of the manuscript, even when it was in its initial, unpolished stages and for all their inspiring and constructive criticism and feedback: Marian Wren, Lora Wren, Stephanie Wren, Ryan Wren, Cindy Poole, and Christine Goodno. I'd also like to thank the first two age-appropriate reviewers that gave their opinions of the book: Malcolm Miller and my own son, Tyler Wren. And lastly, I would like to thank some of my friends who are well versed in the areas of the paranormal: David Doughty of TN Paranormal, Julie Adair of NC Paranormal, and Todd Bates, host of Haunted Voices Radio. Our many hours discussing and investigating all things strange and unusual inspired some of the different elements in this series.

CONTENTS

1721,

THE BRUBAKER INN

I t was old and dilapidated. Its shutters teetered helplessly from their hinges and its roof was caving in. Most of the window-panes were shattered or missing and it was missing boards throughout its two-story walls. The Brubaker Inn was a ghastly sight indeed.

It had survived over a hundred years. Nestled lonely against the bay and unshielded by any other buildings, it outlasted every ocean storm that tried bringing it down. Many of the other build-ings in Gordington Square were at times nearly destroyed by the ferocious storms, but for some reason, the Brubaker Inn always sur-vived unscathed. It was one of the most frequented places in town and there was always something strange and mysterious about its mere presence. Its visitors didn't seem to care about this though, or the mustiness and rat infestation it was dealing with.

Standing on the front porch of it was Ebineezer Drake, the innkeeper. He smiled devilishly at the storm moving in quickly from the east. He loved the ocean storms — the lightning illuminating the forbidden sky, the cold ocean winds blowing past his face, the rain pelting onto the cobblestone streets, and the taste of salt upon his lips — he couldn't think of a better combination.

His chubby cheeks creased inward as he puffed on his pipe and he took a sip of brandy from his old pewter tankard. This was the life for him — no bothering visitors and a good storm to enjoy his pipe and brandy.

This was one thing that made him different from the rest of the locals. He would sit back and grin smugly when they'd hit, knowing that while he found them absolutely fascinating, everyone else found them absolutely terrifying. For many years he was the one that waited them out, while most everyone else fled, and he found a sense of self-gratification in that. And though this storm was not one of the more terrifying-make-you-want-leave ones, it was a strong one nonetheless and put a wicked smile across his rounded face.

He was nearing fifty and his health had been declining. On top of the fact that he was particularly stout, he was a heavy smoker and drinker, and in the past few months had developed a horrid cough. With any significant amount of exertion he would become tight in the chest and quite short of breath.

He had taken his complaint to the local physician, Doc Hazleton, but Hazleton blew it off as some sort of "bronchial dysfunction" and sent him on his way with a wacky concoction of Elecampane root and molasses. Ebineezer saw the questionable doctor's medicine as a bunch of "hockey pock", and had no intention on taking such nonsense. The way he saw it, if smoke and drink were going to kill him, then they might as well go ahead and do it — for those were his two favorite things in the world and he wasn't about to give them up.

He gazed down Banyard Street. It was a cold, dreary night and the streets were desolate. Everything was closed and boarded up, except for the Wharf, a small tavern that rarely closed. A heavy fog hovered over the cobblestone streets. "Very peculiar," he commented. Banyard Street seemed a little stranger on this night than he had ever seen it before.

He yawned and scratched his balding head, noting a large ship appearing in the middle of the bay. His eyes followed it, trying to get a clearer view through the spectacles resting on the end of his nose. Its shape looked a little unusual to him, but not too unusual, for Gordington was constantly seeing new ships come from what seemed every corner of the globe. He watched as it moved in slowly, until it eventually sat motionless in the small harbor.

His attention was drawn towards the sound of hooves, echoing from the depths of the fog. He saw nothing though. The ferocious storm had subsided slightly, but the relentless fog made viewing anything virtually impossible. There typically wasn't too much traffic during this time, but if there was it was usually someone headed to the inn or the tavern across the street. The sound was right upon him and through the dense mist it appeared.

It was an elegant, black, gentlemen's carriage. The two Clydesdales pulling it were massive and they created a rhythmic sound against the stone as they approached. The driver was hunched over, trying to find refuge from the storm under the coat he had draped over his head. He pulled towards the inn and stopped directly in front of Ebineezer.

"Evening, Ebineezer," he said.

"Templeton Shrevehouse. Didn't recognize ye under that coat on yer head. Yer out a bit late tonight, aren't ye?"

"It's been an odd sort of night. Can't explain it. Things seem a bit curious tonight for some reason."

"Doesn't get any better than this," Ebineezer quipped sarcastically. He smiled and pointed to the stormy sky.

"Oh yeah, I forgot. You actually like it. What do you make of all this fog?"

"A bit odd," Ebineezer commented. "Can't hardly breathe in it and the wind doesn't seem to be affecting it in the slightest."

Templeton turned and pointed to the carriage behind him and whispered, "Other things have been a little odd tonight as well."

"Oh yeah?" said Ebineezer. He leaned down and peered inside the carriage, but couldn't see what the driver was referring to.

"Ebineezer, what is that?" Templeton asked. He pointed out towards the bay.

Ebineezer looked. There was a small lifeboat rowing into shore from the ship that arrived just minutes earlier. It was moving rather quickly and a large silhouette of a man was controlling it. "Now that's not something you see every night."

The fog rolling across the bay filled it completely, soon covering everything. They couldn't see him anymore.

"Not a good night to be coming ashore, eh?" Templeton said.

"Not a good night to be on the water either," Ebineezer commented.

Ebineezer opened the door to the carriage and peered inside. There wasn't anyone seated on the bench. "Hello?" he called, but there was no answer. He began to shut the door, but noticed something. Cowered beneath the rear seat was a runty, little man. He appeared to be in his mid-forties and he looked extremely malnourished. What little clothing he wore was torn and tattered. His brown hair was dirty and matted and he lay on the floor, trembling.

"Sir, are ye alright?" Ebineezer asked hesitantly.

"Where am I?" the man asked in a low, frightened tone.

"Yer at the Brubaker Inn."

"Is it safe here?" he questioned, still trembling.

"I assume so," said Ebineezer. He looked up at Templeton. The driver shrugged. "Let me help ye out."

Slowly, he scooted out from underneath the bench and climbed out of the carriage. As he stepped out, he reached back in and grabbed a large leather bag, his only possession, and tucked it tightly under his arm.

Ebineezer reached to him. "Would ye like me to get yer bag?"

"NO!" he snapped, turning the bag away.

Ebineezer pulled his arm away and gazed up at Templeton again. The driver had endured enough. He gave Ebineezer a tip of his hat and whipped the reins, letting the horses know to move ahead.

As he disappeared into the depths of the fog, Ebineezer stood alone with his passenger. He turned back to the shivering man standing beside him. "I'm Ebineezer Drake, the innkeeper. And ye are…?"

"Daniels."

"Well, Mr. Daniels, sir, let's get out of this storm and get ye a room."

"I'd be obliged," Daniels said, shaking.

They walked inside. Water dripped on the wooden floorboards and two enormous rats scurried along the walls and disappeared into the darkness.

Ebineezer watched Daniels standing just beyond the entrance, looking about the room questioningly. He shuffled behind a small bar. A single candle sat on it, flickering helplessly from the draft.

"What's yer likens?" Ebineezer asked, holding two bottles of liquor high in the air. "Whiskey or rum?"

"I don't drink anymore. Please, I don't mean to be rude, but I'd just like to be shown my room." He seemed desperate.

"Of course," said Ebineezer. He was just trying to be hospitable. That was his nature. He loved a jolly ole sit down with his guests, but didn't much care for the non-sociable ones.

He grabbed the candle off the bar and led his guest to the dark, vacant stairwell leading up to the second floor.

"Alright sir, here we are. Room one." They stopped at the first door at the top of the stairs. Ebineezer pulled a small skeleton key out of his pocket and inserted it into the rusted, iron lock. The door let out a horrendous moan as he pushed it open.

The room was chilly and obviously neglected. There was a small, rod iron bed with a worn-out mattress in one corner and an old wooden desk in the other. There were holes in one of the walls from missing boards and the cold blew in between them. The room was painted a dark shade of olive; however, most of the paint was cracked and peeling from the wall. The shutters to the windows were closed, but they shook violently from the force of the storm on the other side.

Ebineezer hurried over to the desk and lighted the wick of a nearly melted candle.

"I know it's not much, but it's the driest room in me place."

"It will do fine," Daniels said as he reached into his pocket and pulled out a coin. "This should cover the cost of the room for the next few days."

Ebineezer took the coin and dropped it in his pocket, not thinking to look at it. "There should be extra candles in the desk. Is there anything else I can get ye?"

"No," Daniels replied sternly, showing him to the door. "I would like to be undisturbed the rest of the night if ye don't mind."

"Of course," said Ebineezer. He had endured all he could from this guest. And he didn't have any intention of revisiting his room anyway. He proceeded downstairs as he heard the door locking behind him.

Daniels placed his leather bag on the bed and opened it. He fumbled around for a moment and pulled out three, cloth-covered objects. They were wrapped in white linen and wound numerous times with a thin string. He held them, only for a moment, and returned them quickly to the bag. He breathed a sigh of relief knowing they were still there — safe and unharmed. He continued searching through the bag and pulled out a quill pen, a bottle of ink, and a small, brown leather journal. It was smooth and thick and had nothing printed on its outside. He carried them over to the desk and sat down with them, opening the journal and uncorking the ink. In the flickering light of the candle he thumbed, page by page, to the last entry and then turned the page once more. As he sat there trembling, he dipped his pen and began writing:

> November 19th, 1721
> I feel I am reaching the end. I feel
> him getting closer. Over the next few
> days I will take what I have obtained
> and see if I can locate the Di...

Ebineezer refilled his tobacco pipe. The storm was nearing its peak and the inn creaked loudly as the winds hurled against it. Alas, maybe the rest of his night would run quietly. He peered out the front entrance — he could see a clearer view of the ship that arrived earlier.

It was a bit 'odd' looking. The shape of the boat itself was different from anything he had seen before. It appeared to be dark in color and the sails looked square and rigid. The small lifeboat he watched earlier was empty and bobbing helplessly next to one of the docks. He looked around, trying to see its owner moving about in the fog.

"Hmm, he must have gone to the Wharf," he mumbled.

Lightning lit up the night sky and the thunder cracked as the immense wind forced itself through the front entrance, flushing the life from his candle. He threw his pipe down and slammed the door shut. He grabbed the candle and fumbled in the darkness, trying to find his tinderbox. "Stupid thing! Where ye at?" he barked.

He thought to look for his pipe, but as he turned, the sight before him froze him stiff and sent a chill from the top of his neck to the base of his spine. He stood there staring, his hands quivering with utter fright.

Standing there in front of him, his head nearly touching the ceiling, was a monstrosity. He was easily seven-foot-three and his shoulders were as broad as a brigantine. He had on a black waistcoat and a pair of muddy boots. His head was covered with a large, sopping hat and his long, black, tangled hair descended from beneath it. His scraggly, unclean beard grew from just below his eyes to the middle of his waist. His eyes were dark and piercing and his mouth looked rotten. On his side he sheathed a cutlass and on his chest he harnessed three pistols. He stood there eyeing Ebineezer, breathing heavily.

Ebineezer didn't know what to do. He just stood there, trembling. The man reached down and rested one hand on his cutlass and with the other he removed a pistol. His breathing became heavier and in a low, deep tone he said only three words.

"Where is `e?"

Ebineezer pointed upstairs. His finger shook nervously. He didn't want to show him, but feared it would be himself if he didn't show the fiend where his guest was. At least he assumed it was his guest he was searching for. The beast walked upstairs, slowly — his frame filled the stairwell completely. He inched up the staircase, causing the boards to creak and pop as he went.

Daniels finished his journal entry. Unknown to him though, his doorknob was turning — slowly. Just as it was turned to its limit, it popped, and at the same time the storm blasted in from the outside, forcing the shutters clean off their hinges. Daniels jumped from his seat and watched as the lightning defined the man standing in his doorway.

The brute standing before him took his pistol, tipped the barrel into the air, and slid a lead ball inside it. He looked at Daniels and his breathing became heavier again.

"Bloody thief," he moaned. "Where's it?"

Daniels didn't say anything. He looked towards the bed.

The man pushed his ramrod down the barrel, pointed the pistol at Daniels and pulled back the trigger.

Daniels threw up his hands, "PLEASE! NO!"

BOOM!

The force of the blast threw Daniels's body up against the wall. As he lay there, lifeless and bleeding on the floor, the man advanced through the lingering smoke towards the bed. He ripped open the leather bag, took out those same three items and placed them in the deep confines of his waistcoat. He walked towards the desk and picked up the journal, eyeing it closely. He crumpled it with his enormous hands and threw it across the room, where it landed between the wall and the old, iron bed.

Downstairs, Ebineezer paced. Unsure if the gunfire was going to be on him next, he grabbed his hidden pistol from behind the bar. He loaded the pistol and hunched down, moving stealthily towards the staircase. The lightning jolted the night sky and created quick flashes of light throughout the inn. He was having a terrible time — trying to adjust his poor vision in the quick flashes of light. He looked up the staircase and could see the open door to room one. Everything was still and he heard no movement coming from the room. A horrid stench lingered throughout the entire place. He covered his mouth with one hand and kept the gun pointed with the other.

As he reached the room, he peered around the corner. Daniels was lying there, dead, and the mysterious swine that killed him was gone. There was only one way out from the second floor — down the stairs. And he had not exited that way. The shutters to the windows lay on the floor and rain swept into the room.

Ebineezer went to the window and looked outside. The fog had completely cleared. The lifeboat was gone and the ship was moving slowly from the bay. Dumbfounded, he stood with one hand in his pocket and stared outside. He felt the coin Daniels had given him earlier and pulled it from his pocket. As he opened his hand, he gasped. In it sat a gold doubloon.

CHAPTER ONE

A PEASANT BEGINNING

The idea of constructing coffins was, for most, a morbid and dreadful living. Coffins symbolized the final stage of existence, the reality of death, and a means to 'the end'.

But for fifteen-year-old Jeremiah Bloom, it was coffin-building that put food on his plate and the clothes on his back. For the last two years, he had worked at Dobbit's Casket Company, seven days a week, alongside his father. They would arrive promptly at daybreak, sweat laboriously over the caskets all day, and leave at sunset every evening.

And this scrawny, brown-haired, peasant boy was very good at the coffins he made. He had developed quite the touch to the wicker willow caskets and the old pine coffins that he worked with such detail upon. He even created an ornate, wooden piece that he placed on the outside of the pine caskets that, to him, appeared unnaturally plain. He felt this 'decoration' gave them the extra touch they so desperately needed. However, there was something ironic about these pine caskets he made day after day.

Many of them were exactly like the one he buried his mother in just two years prior. Following a deadly bout of Winter Fever, she was placed in one very similar to the ones he made before being buried in a small cemetery a short distance behind their cottage.

You see, she worked at Dobbit's Casket Company for years and immediately following her death Jeremiah was forced to stop his schooling and work alongside his father. It was the only way they could afford to survive. His parents never planned on him having to endure such a living, but after her passing, there weren't any other options for him. Building caskets *was* the only option.

Besides the constant reminder of his mother and the dreadful day that he laid her to rest, he didn't mind the job really. What seemed so grim and unpleasant to so many others was an every day way of life — as far as he knew. The sight of a casket didn't bother him in the slightest, but the idea of a body inside of it was a completely different story.

He couldn't bear the sight of a corpse. In fact, he could barely even stomach the thought of it. And the idea of what would happen to it after it was buried beneath the earth was a whole problem in itself. The thought of worms and bugs gnawing their way through the casket and munching on the body for years to come was positively dreadful to him.

For the most part though, Jeremiah was proud of the work he did. And Mr. Dobbit, the owner, was quite pleased with the caskets he created. He had been programmed to do the same monotonous tasks week after week, without the smallest hint of a change — except on this day.

It was nearly noon when Father, looking around confused, popped the question. "Son, have you seen Mr. Dobbit today?"

Jeremiah was placing the hinges on a drab, pine casket when he looked up, realizing too that it was very out of nature for Mr. Dobbit not to have made his typical, early morning appearance.

"No, Father, I haven't. That's strange. Mr. Dobbit is always here early. Suppose everything is alright?"

"I don't know."

They both looked in the direction of the building's front as they heard the door opening. Mr. Dobbit walked in.

"Ah, we were just talking about you," Father chuckled.

Mr. Dobbit was a portly fellow, always sporting a leather hat, a huge smile, and rosy cheeks. But on this day he didn't arrive with his typical grin.

"Mr. Dobbit, is everything alright?" Jeremiah asked.

The large man took a seat. "No Jeremiah, it isn't. I need a moment to speak with the two of you."

Jeremiah and his father stood in front of Mr. Dobbit, anxiously awaiting his news.

"I'm afraid we're going to have to close up shop — immediately."

"I'm sorry, what did you just say?" Father asked with large, open eyes.

Jeremiah felt his heart skip a beat.

"Jonathon, I am terribly sorry. Competition a town away has forced us out of business and I have a sister that's dreadfully ill that I must visit tomorrow. I don't even have enough to pay the two of you your wages for this week's work."

"But what are my boy and I supposed to do?" Father asked tearfully. "There's no other work here."

"I'm sorry," Mr. Dobbit said, shrugging, "I hate this just as much as you do. I really don't have any other choice here. I've seen this coming for a while, but was hoping I could get it turned around. And I was worried to tell the two of you. I know how hard the two of you work and how much you need this job. I know there's no other alternatives for the two of you here."

Jeremiah was at a loss for words. His stomach started tying itself up in a large, tangled knot. He felt his father's hand grab his shoulder and lead him in the direction of the door.

"Jeremiah, wait," Mr. Dobbit said. "Before you leave…" He reached up and pulled the leather tricorn hat from his head and placed it on Jeremiah.

Jeremiah's face lit up. "You're giving me your hat?" He couldn't believe it — he had always admired Mr. Dobbit's hat and yearned to have one just like it for himself.

"That's not all, Jeremiah. Wait here just a moment." Mr. Dobbit shuffled to a room in the back before quickly returning. "I also want you to have this," he said, handing Jeremiah a pistol.

"Oh, no sir, I couldn't possibly…"

"He's giving it to you as a gift," Father said.

"You were much better with this than I ever was. You've got a special talent, Jeremiah, and I've told you that for a long time. It pleases me greatly to give this to you."

Jeremiah held the pistol and rubbed his hand up and down the barrel. He couldn't believe it — he had wanted this gun for such a long time. Ever since he began working at the casket company, he would practice shooting behind it with Mr. Dobbit. They would always shoot simple things such as boards and tree stumps, but no matter what the target, he could always hit it — and with incredible accuracy.

They said their goodbyes and Jeremiah and his father sadly walked out to their wagon.

At dinner that evening, Jeremiah received his usual helping of potatoes, turnips and broth. Father pulled the kettle from the fire and scraped it down to the very last drop.

As they began eating, Jeremiah noticed his father looking up at him, then back to his food, and then up at him again.

"Is something wrong, Father?"

"Well…" Father hesitated. "Son, we've already had such terrible news today, I don't know how to share any more with you."

"Go ahead, Father." He felt his heart sinking again.

"You know we're out of food and money," Father said as he gazed at the small turnips sitting on his plate.

"Yes, sir."

"Mr. Dobbit was right. There's no other choices here for us. I've given this a great deal of thought and the only choice we have is to move away. There's a shipping town a couple day's ride out and it's said to be rich with job opportunities. Our old neighbor Mr. Wiley went there a year or so back and started his own fishing service. I'll see if I can get a job with him. And maybe even you too."

"Are you talking about Gordington Square?"

"Yes," Father answered, not looking up from his plate.

"Father, for years we've been hearing rumors of people coming up missing from there or dying unexpectedly. And you know most of the coffins we made were shipped directly to that town." Jeremiah was extremely unsettled by this.

"I know of the rumors. And I know where our coffins were shipped. But we have no other choice. And there's one other thing," he sighed, "you know we're out of food and money."

"Yes, sir. I was wondering about that," he said, his heart pumping furiously.

Father looked up. "All we've got left is the horses."

Jeremiah gasped, "No, Father. Please!"

"I'm sorry boy, but they're all we've got left. The way I see it, Jonah is the stronger of the two. We'll only sell one of them. I'll let it be your decision, but Jonah will last longer and can probably pull us by himself. We will have to lighten our load — only take what we need. I'll take the musket and we'll bring our clothes — everything else stays. Mr. Dobbit told me weeks ago of a peddler that came through these parts and noticed Arien. He apparently showed a liking to her and left his name should we ever be willing to sell her."

The horses were the only things left from what his mother had given him, besides a small, leather necklace she'd made. On the necklace was a wooden cross his father had whittled from a piece of birch wood. Jeremiah rarely removed it from his neck.

He stared at his plate and stirred his potatoes slowly with his fork. "I guess we'll sell Arien then, Father." He wouldn't look up. The idea of it was sickening enough.

"Boy, I know this is a hard thing for you to stomach. I wish there was something else. You know your strong-willed mother would have done the same."

"Yes, sir, I know."

"We'll leave at daybreak. Finish up that food on your plate and get yourself a good night's rest. You'll need it."

Jeremiah finished his supper and stretched on his cot in their tiny, two-room cottage. Father was already asleep in the room in the back. Hopelessness flooded his veins and he felt empty inside. Sleep was the last thing he could think about doing and he stared around the dark, quiet room, praying that another solution would present itself. He thought of Arien and the idea of having to sell her to some stranger. How could Father do such a thing? He started becoming angry at the thought, but was quickly distracted by an unusual, tapping sound on the shutters.

It wasn't the typical sound of the wind scuffling the branches against them, but rather a light, scratching noise. And in the thin, little crack between them, something started glowing. The room was as black as coal, but the glowing was so intense, it began lightening it.

Could it be a firefly? No, he knew right away it couldn't be that. Never before had he seen one that glowed with this intensity. It didn't appear threatening and he quickly rushed over to the shutters and unlatched them.

What an incredible creature! He had no idea what it was, but watched in amazement as it hovered just a few feet away from him, suspended a couple of feet off the ground. He watched as it pulsated — growing to twice its original size and then shrinking to something smaller than a firefly. It grew again — back to its original size and then darted off out of sight. Maybe it was just his overactive imagination, but he swore he thought it looked like a small man — with wings!

He ran to the front door and hurried outside, scanning the air for another glimpse of the creature. But it was nowhere to be found. The night was still so dark he struggled see a few feet in front of him. He heard the horses in their stall and walked over to Arien.

Even in the darkness of night she was a beautiful sight. Jeremiah stroked her mane and ran his hands down her white, shimmering coat. She turned her head towards him, nudging him in the chest.

"I'm sorry, girl. If there was any other way, I wouldn't let Father do it. I hope you'll understand," he said, wrapping his arms around her neck.

She looked back at him, her tail swishing from side to side. Her large, brown eyes showed a warm and innocent glow. He felt a terrible sense of guilt knowing that he was about to play a part in the selling of her. How would Mother truly feel about this? She loved Arien just as much as he did. Would she really allow her to be sold even though they were without money and food? He was torn about whether to stand up against Father and refuse to allow him to sell her — or allow her to be sold for the good of their family. He closed his eyes as he nuzzled against her.

"It's alright Jeremiah. This must be done," said a comforting, female voice.

He jumped back. "Huh?" He looked around — no one was there. He looked at Arien. She was still and watching him. "Was that y—? Nah..." He knew his stress was getting the better of him. Arien licked the side of his face and he turned to go back inside. He knew he'd need the rest before he embarked on the dreaded journey to Gordington Square.

CHAPTER TWO

Primeval
Thicket

When he awoke the following morning, Jeremiah had an awful feeling churning and cramping his stomach. He knew it was probably the thoughts of selling Arien that had haunted his dreams all night. He also knew this was the day that he would have to say goodbye to one of his most beloved friends. He tried desperately to come up with an alternative to selling her — if only there was another way. Realistically, he knew there wasn't, but he couldn't bring himself to think about letting her go.

Father came tromping through the door. He had his musket on his shoulder and he was empty handed. "No luck this morning. Sorry boy. I know you're probably hungry and we should be at the peddler's by late afternoon. Hopefully, he'll have a hot plate for us when we get there to sell Arien," he said.

Jeremiah sat quietly. Eating was the last thing on his mind. He would have gone the entire trip without a single bite if it could have made a difference in selling his horse. But Father stayed firm on his decisions — he rarely swayed from them.

They packed up their things and Jeremiah removed the horses from their stall. He looked upwards, scanning for any sign of the creature that visited him the night before. He didn't dare tell Father about it though. He figured he'd never hold with such nonsense.

"Come on, you two," he said as he led them towards the wagon.

After hours of riding down the long, barren road that would lead them to their destination, Jeremiah noticed a single, large patch of forest nearing them. The trees appeared gargantuan as they approached and there was little he could see through them. Their presence sent a cold chill down his spine. They slowed as they neared another thin, dirt path.

"I think that is it," Father said hesitantly. "He is said to live within Primeval Thicket."

"That's where we'll be taking Arien?" Jeremiah asked, horrified at the thought.

A small sign was posted to the edge of the dirt path. It read:

PRIMEVAL THICKET

~ ENTER AT YOUR OWN RISK ~

"Father, I'm not too sure about this."

"It'll be fine, son — no worries."

But he saw that Father was worried. How could he not be concerned about entering a dark and forbidden place that looked like it was waiting to devour them? They turned off the main road and steered down the narrow crosscut towards the thicket. Their wagon barely fit the dirt passage between the waist-high weeds on both sides. As they neared the entrance, they could easily see how it obtained its name.

Thick, dark vines encompassed the mammoth trees on the thicket's exterior. They webbed across the entrance and inter-tangled with one another, shutting out any hope of daylight. A cold breeze blew from within and the air carried a stagnant smell. If it weren't for their desperation for food and money, Jeremiah knew they would have turned immediately back towards the main road.

Father grabbed the lantern and handed it to him. "Hold onto this," he said, as he leaned over for his musket. "This might be an opportunity for you to use that pistol too — keep it close."

They proceeded slowly, barely fitting through the opening of the vines. Jeremiah looked behind them as they entered and his eyes widened with fear. The opening was closing completely — with more entangling vines that moved rapidly.

Jeremiah's heart raced. "Father, look behind us!" he whispered frantically.

Father turned, but did not comment. His hands gripped his musket tightly.

Jeremiah was amazed to see that as they advanced further in, the thicket started changing.

The ground was mostly moss-covered, and it continued to open up, revealing smaller, normal-looking trees, elephantine mushrooms and even some gigantic purple flowers. Though it appeared like a dreadful, closed shell from the outside, there was a large opening in the top center of the thicket that allowed the light of the setting sun to penetrate. Jeremiah saw small lights fluttering about far off in the thicket.

"Look at those little lights. How unusual." Father commented.

Strange noises resonated further in beyond their sight, and Jeremiah shuddered as to the thought of what could be making them — they weren't noises he recognized.

Jonah seemed nervous and hesitated with his steps, but Arien displayed complete comfort with her surroundings. She pulled forward quickly, as if she knew exactly where to go.

They approached a cottage on a small hill in the thicket's center. A thin, curling stream of smoke puffed up from its chimney and the air seemed to lighten as they drew closer. As they pulled up, the small, oval door on its front swung open. An elderly man stepped outside to greet them.

"Oh, the Blooms! It so wonderful to finally have you as guests!" said the man with excitement as he walked down the three steps from his door.

His hair was long and gray and his white beard reached down almost to his knees. He wore an old, brown robe that scraped the ground as he moved. Despite his apparent age, however, he moved with relative ease.

"How did you... oh, never mind," Father said. "You must have recognized Arien from the village back home."

"Hello Jeremiah. I'm honored to have you," the man welcomed heartily. Jeremiah didn't ask any questions, though he was curious as to how this man knew his name. "By the way, my name is Ozron... I am a peddler." He walked around the front of the wagon and stood beside Arien, stroking her mane. "I know it must be difficult to make such a decision. I promise you — she'll be in good hands." He looked into her eyes and she looked back at him, her tail swishing from side to side. "She's different, you know?" He moved around to help Jeremiah step down and as he reached up, he stopped.

He stared into Jeremiah's eyes intently, as if he was probing into his soul. "Oh... well... it appears you're a little different also." He grinned smugly. "Now it all seems to be coming together."

"What do you mean?" Father asked.

"Oh nothing," said Ozron. "My old age seems to get the better of me sometimes."

They entered through his oval door and Father ducked to avoid bumping his head on the upper frame of it. The atmosphere within was intensely welcoming. The interior as well appeared very old, as if it had been there for many centuries. He had books, scrolls and trinkets lying neatly about on the floors, walls, and the many shelves throughout the rooms. Their age seemed to be even greater than that of Ozron. There were paintings on his walls, mostly of ships at sea, and Jeremiah was instantly drawn to them. He drifted towards one in particular, a brigantine with a pastel-orange sky, examining its every detail.

Ozron pulled him away. "Young Jeremiah, why don't you go to the room in the back so I can have a talk with you? I'll find your father a nice, comfy seat while we talk." He directed Jeremiah towards a room in the rear of the cottage while he pulled a large, woven chair up for his father. He sat it directly in front of the painting Jeremiah was drawn to. "Mr. Bloom, why don't you have a bit of a rest from your long ride? I'll let you have my most comfortable chair."

"That would be great, but…"

"Oh, there'll be plenty of time for business momentarily. I'd like to talk with your son for a moment and console him over the… um… horse."

Jeremiah walked away, but watched the two of them from the back room.

"I guess a brief rest won't hurt," Father commented, settling back in the oversized chair. "This will be a pleasant change from that uncomfortable wagon bench." Ozron reached over to a cup of liquid sitting behind him and dipped his finger in.

"Stare at the picture, Mr. Bloom. It will make you feel as if you're right there," he instructed him.

Father gazed at the painting.

As Ozron walked away, he flicked his finger towards the image of the ships. A single droplet of water landed at the top of the painting and sat there, only for a second, before it slid down the front. As the droplet reached the water below the ships, it stopped. The droplet began melding with the entire painting, bringing it alive before his eyes. Father was transfixed.

"Ah, it's amazing, isn't it Mr. Bloom?"

Father said nothing. His eyes were fixated on the image in front of him and he had no other awareness.

"Perfect," Ozron snickered, walking towards the room where Jeremiah waited.

"That painting —" Jeremiah commented with wide, open eyes. "It's alive."

"Don't you mind that now," Ozron replied. "I did want to apologize for the dramatic entrance-way though."

"Entrance-way?" Jeremiah asked.

"My thicket —"

"Oh yes, it was a little disturbing," Jeremiah agreed.

"It is necessary to have it appear that way to keep out intruders... and to protect the inhabitants."

"Inhabitants?"

"Yes, the creatures living inside. I think you met one of them last night in fact..." He turned to a wooden box and opened the door to the front of it. A small, winged creature walked out, glowing. "There are many others that live here... though most of them won't come into view unless called upon."

"Yes, that's him — I saw him last night!" gasped Jeremiah.

"I thought so," said Ozron, frowning intently at the small creature. It looked up at Jeremiah — and to Ozron. It shrugged and bowed its head, obviously knowing it was in some sort of trouble. "I have explained to all of my neighbors that their survival is dependent upon staying within the thicket." He opened the window next to them and let the creature fly out.

"What was that?" Jeremiah asked amazed, watching it fly away.

"His name is Nefron. And he's a nisse."

"A nisse?"

"Yes, young one. You may have heard of them as pixies, sprites or such."

"Oh, of course. But… I was always told such a thing didn't really exist."

"That's what we want them to believe!" Ozron chuckled. "Nisse are easily, though rarely, seen. Other things require a special 'eye' to pick them up. Ever seen anything else you thought not to be real, Jeremiah?"

He thought for a moment. "Not that I've noticed."

"Well then, let us discuss your horse, Arien. What do you see when you look at her?" he asked, pointing out the window towards her.

"A horse?" Jeremiah answered, trying to be respectful and keep from laughing.

"Oh, bother! It appears that you haven't quite tuned in yet. I know you have an eye for it — I can see that. Look behind you and get me the chest below that stack of books."

Jeremiah fumbled and searched for the chest underneath a stack of old, dusty books on the floor. He picked it up and handed it to Ozron.

Ozron held the chest and felt around in the pockets of his oversized robe. "I know you're in here somewhere, you silly thing."

He pulled out a small silver key, roughly the size of one of his fingers, and inserted it into the box. He opened the lid and Jeremiah leaned forward to look inside.

"Rocks?" Jeremiah asked.

"They're more than rocks, Boy. I refer to them as my 'special stones'. These will aid you in 'seeing'... Ok, let's see here..." Ozron sorted through them all, pulling out one in particular that showed a brilliant shade of blue. He held it up to a burning candle and examined it closely. "Yes, this one will work just fine."

"What is that?" Jeremiah asked.

"This is indicolite. It will help you 'tune in' to those things which are not typically seen by others." He handed it to him. "Now hold this in your hand and close your eyes. Try and quiet all other thoughts in your mind and take some slow, deep breaths for me. Try and think of nothing else but your breathing."

Jeremiah held the stone and closed his eyes. He paused for a moment, breathing deeply.

"Very good," said Ozron. "Now open! Go look out the window."

Jeremiah walked closer to the window and peered outside.

"What should I be seeing?" he asked.

"Look towards Arien. Tell me what you see now."

Jeremiah looked out the window towards the horses. Arien had her back to him with her head down, but quickly rose up and turned towards him. Jeremiah gasped. Between her eyes and midway up her forehead, was a twisted silver horn — nearly a foot long. "She's a uni —"

Ozron interrupted, "Ah, now that's better."

"But, how?"

"Never mind that. It's what is and is supposed to be, young one. She is happy here... and she knows she is home now."

Jeremiah couldn't take his eyes off of her. She appeared more beautiful than ever.

"Thank you, Jeremiah," a warm, pleasant female voice said.

"That voice — I've heard it before!"

"Well of course you have," Ozron chuckled. "She does have the ability to speak with you — only mentally though."

"And Jonah?"

"Just a simple horse," Ozron said, smiling. "He knows nothing different... only the companionship he had with Arien. And speaking of Arien, who was it that chose that name?"

"I did," Jeremiah replied. "Why?"

Ozron scanned the room with an outward finger. "Where's it at? Oh yes… there it is." He pointed to one of the scrolls sitting on a shelf. "Hand me that scroll, young one."

Jeremiah picked it up — it too was quite dusty. He handed it to Ozron, who blew off the dust before unrolling it.

"Alright now." His eyes scanned down the old parchment. "Here it is. *Arien*. Do you know what this name means?"

Jeremiah shook his head.

"Arien's name means *enchanted*." He looked up from the scroll. "Kind of fitting, don't you think?"

"Enchanted," Jeremiah repeated. He grinned. "Yes, that's amazing, Ozron."

Ozron rolled up the scroll. "Now, you keep that stone I gave you. Always keep it close, for it will serve you well in your future days. Let us go now and wake your father and help you two on your way. You're only a short ride away from Gordington Square."

"But, how did you know where we were going?" Jeremiah asked, surprised as ever.

"I'm just a simple peddler," he snickered. "Just a simple peddler with a little bit of knowledge."

The two walked to the front room where Father was still completely transfixed by the painting.

Jeremiah felt worried at the sight of his father, who had wide, open eyes and was still gazing upon the painting without even a hint of a blink. "Is he alright, Ozron?"

The old man chuckled. "Of course he is." He snapped his fingers and Father immediately detached his gaze from the painting.

He looked around the room and at the two of them. "What the — I just had the weirdest dream," he said as he rose from his chair. Ozron winked at the boy.

"This is for Arien," Ozron said as he handed Father a small bag of coins. "And don't you worry, Mr. Bloom. Arien will be in good hands." He reached to a table to behind him. "Here's a bag of my best bread. Take this with you."

"Oh, thank you," said Father. Jeremiah's stomach rumbled painfully and he knew his father was just as hungry.

"Well, you two must be on your way now. I know you want to get there soon and your destination is just a short ride away from here."

CHAPTER THREE

GORDINGTON SQUARE

"Good morrow," said Ebineezer Drake, nodding to Mr. And Mrs. Otterstein. They were the elite of the town's upper class citizens and they loved to flaunt it, walking down the busy streets — she in her pristine dresses and elegant damask shoes, and he in his Ramillies wigs and gentleman's clothing that was always neatly pressed, down to every crease. They walked past him and didn't acknowledge his greeting, as always. After all, he wasn't part of their social class. Ebineezer wasn't the slightest bit daunted by this, but actually grinned as they passed, knowing exactly how they'd act when he greeted them.

It couldn't have been a better day. The sky over Gordington Square was as blue as the southern Caribbean waters and there wasn't a cloud to be seen. The bay was full. Several ships had made port and were lined up neatly — their masts pointing to the heavens and their sails white and crisp.

It was a typical morning on Banyard Street. Busy and loud — just as always. The iron carriage wheels against the cobblestone streets created quite a noise amidst the hustle and bustle of the usual morning flow.

Ivan Flick, son of the owner of the local paper, walked around yelling, holding the morning paper in his hand as he tried to sell the most recent gossip.

Two doors down, at the Tinsel's Coffee House, people trafficked in and out, conducting their daily business, sipping on the finest coffee and tea in Gordington Square.

Johan Burdett, the local butcher, stood at his booth serving a long line of waiting customers. He was out there at seven o'clock every morning, not a minute after, setting up his outdoor table that was covered by a small, wooden canopy. He served some of the freshest meat and poultry around — beef, pork, chicken, and some of the tastiest fish ever brought to the mainland.

The privateer ship *Nante* just arrived from a grueling, three months at sea. It looked rough and ragged and probably needed a good cleaning. Barnacles grew up its hull and the sails looked ripped and floppy. Its crew began unloading, one by one, until all seventy-three of them were either in town or making their way down the pier.

They were a rough looking breed. Most wore breeches or pantaloons, all beyond repair. The whole lot of them came ashore barefoot, though some of them did have shoes — most of which were the high-buckled, leather type worn by their kind. They were dirty from not bathing in weeks, and their hair was long, sticky and tangled. The majority was shirtless; however, some did have on upper garments that were light, made of cotton, stained and ripped.

Their captain, Van Russel, led the group. Unlike his crew, he was dressed in his best. He always came ashore in his finest garments. He paraded down the pier, with a sway to his walk and hand on his sword, like he had just come home from a victory of war. He loved to show off, doing whatever he could to capture the attention of the townsfolk — primarily the women.

His hat was a dark shade of blue, like the deepest of the oceans, and he had positioned a red, fluffy feather off the tip of it. His coat, waistcoat and breeches were all tailored from the same crimson damask. His coat was trimmed in gold buttons and on his wrists and neck was some of the finest French lace to be found. His shoes were nicely polished leather, dark and brown, each highlighted by a large silver buckle. Rumor had it that he dressed so finely to draw attention away from his face — something that wasn't so pleasant.

Years back he had lost an eye in battle. Now it stayed covered by a black patch secured around his head. On his face he had scars from his torturous days at sea. His hair was long and brown, always neatly combed, along with his beard. He had a full mustache and he twisted the ends, hook-like, towards the sky.

On his shoulder sat Blessie, an African Grey parrot he had acquired in a game of poker shortly after losing his eye. She positioned herself on his right shoulder, the same side as his bad eye, and did a remarkable job at keeping him informed on what he wasn't seeing.

He paraded, with sissy-like steps, directly towards the Wharf and the remainder of his crew followed close behind. There was no doubt what their intentions were. It would be just as it always was — a drunken fest for the captain and his entire crew, celebrating their safe return to Gordington Square. The townsfolk dreaded the time that they'd make port and create havoc during their stay, but never argued with the fact that there was always a great deal more money spent while they were there.

Ebineezer watched Mrs. Otterstein stop stiff in her tracks, just past the Brubaker Inn, when she noticed them coming down the pier.

"Disgusting breed," she remarked nastily.

Ebineezer heard this and couldn't hold back. "Aye, they may be a bit on the rough side, but let me tell ye lady — they know how to throw quite a party. You ought to go by and celebrate with `em." He smiled at her, devilishly.

She snapped away from him. "How dare you!" She grabbed her husband by the arm and stomped off. And he turned around and gave the innkeeper a hateful look.

"The two of ye have a good day now," Ebineezer laughed, waving at the two of them. He took a draw from his pipe. "Aye, it's a fine day... a fine day indeed."

Business had been slow, but it was about to pick up. With Van Russel and his crew in town, Ebineezer knew he'd be busy until they set off for the water again. They always stayed at the Brubaker, many of them anyway, and he always enjoyed their company. After all, he had been just like them years back. He loved to hear their most recent stories as they'd tell all, staying up until daybreak every night, drinking and recalling adventures.

At the far end of town, a wagon slowly entered. Jeremiah couldn't believe what he was seeing. He pointed. "Oh Father, look!" He motioned towards the ships docked in the bay. He pointed to the elegant carriages driving up and down the streets. He looked over the side of his seat. He couldn't believe the streets even. He had never seen roads made of pure stone. As they came closer to the ships, his mouth dropped. He couldn't believe their massive sizes. They looked so majestic — sitting there with their long, straight masts pointing to the sky and their sails so full and elegant. They were taller than the biggest oaks he had ever dared climbing back home. He wondered that, just maybe, this town wasn't so bad after all. He breathed a sigh of relief. "Well," he whispered, "this may have been worth the trip."

They rode slowly through the middle of town. Though it was quite different in many ways from the village back home, Jeremiah saw some similarities. He could tell who the peasant folk were. One woman walked from a stable, a yoke stretched across her shoulders as she balanced two pails of fresh milk. There was a blacksmith, just like home, and the sounds of banging iron rang from the building's open front.

Jeremiah was impressed with the coffee house. They didn't have one of those back home. The ornate sign hanging on its front was quite appealing to him. He smelled the warm, delicious aroma of fresh coffee that lingered in the air around it. How badly he yearned to go inside and try out a cup for himself. He watched the patrons through the open windows, chattering the morning away with one another as the steam floated from their cups.

Father stopped the wagon and asked one of the townspeople where they could go for lodgings. One man pointed in front of them, "Straight ahead… the Brubaker Inn."

"Thank you," Father said, and they rode the wagon up to the front of it.

Jeremiah looked at it, his mouth hanging open. Luckily for Jonah though, there was a full trough of water sitting in front of it. Ebineezer stood out front as they pulled up.

"Good morrow," said Ebineezer, "Can I help ye?"

Jeremiah was still looking the place over in disbelief.

"We…uh…we're looking for a place to stay here in town," Father said.

Ebineezer smiled. "Aye, ye couldn't have chosen a finer establishment." He looked at the two of them. "I know. I know. It doesn't look like much, but let me tell ye… ye won't be disappointed. How long ye plannin' on stayin'?"

"Well, I'm not quite sure yet," said Father.

Ebineezer pointed to the last of Van Russel's crew as they mobbed towards the Wharf. "Not to put any pressure on ye or anything, but see that large group of scours walking down the pier? Well, when they come to town, they fill me place up — completely — and every other place in town. Ye might want to decide quick cause they'll be here soon... after they hit the Wharf, of course."

Jeremiah noticed Father wasn't at all pleased to hear this. And another night in the back of their wagon was most definitely out of the question.

"It doesn't look like we have much of a choice now, does it?" Father sighed.

"No sir, unfortunately it doesn't. Aye, they look a bit rough, I know, but they're a good group — most of them anyway."

Jeremiah examined them closely as they walked down the pier. He had to ask — curiosity was getting the better of him. "What are they? Pirates?"

Ebineezer was taking a long draw off of his pipe, but nearly choked. He regained his composure, smiled wide and showed a mouthful of missing and rotting teeth. "Pirates, ye ask? Oh no, boy! Pirates don't come ashore here. After all, piracy is illegal. Ye'll get yourself a hangin' if ye try that one. That group of men there is what we here call 'privateers'."

"Privateers?" Jeremiah asked excitedly.

"Boy, quit asking so many questions," Father insisted. "You can ask this gentleman that later."

"Oh, I don't mind," said Ebineezer, "I actually like talkin' 'bout it. Lad, when ye have time later and if it's all right with your father, of course, I'll tell ye about the privateers."

"Really?" Jeremiah was ecstatic.

His father shook his head. "I guess we'll take a room then."

"Good choice," said Ebineezer. "Aye, a good choice indeed. I think the first thing ye might want to take care of is your horse. He's looking a bit weary and thirsty. There's a stable down the street that will board him and they'll hold on to the wagon for ye."

After they paid for Jonah to be boarded, they walked back to the Brubaker Inn. Father opened the small bag Ozron had given him and counted the remaining coins.

Ebineezer was still standing out front as they returned. "Running a bit tight, are ye?" he asked.

"Yes," Father replied, embarrassed.

"Don't ye two worry about it. I'll let ye stay here all the same." He thought for a moment. "I'll make a deal with ye. If you let... What's yer name boy?"

"Jeremiah," he answered proudly.

"If ye let Jeremiah hang out for a while and let me teach him about the privateers, I'll let ye stay for free. After all, it's been a bit boring around here lately. I miss having someone that's willing to listen to me adventurous stories and I can tell Jeremiah would be a great pupil."

Jeremiah grinned widely. He didn't have many friends back home, and he felt that he had already made one here.

"Well then," said Father, "I guess we can't pass up a deal like that."

"If ye don't mind me asking, sir, what's ye business here?"

"I'm looking for work. Actually, I came here looking for some-one that I was hoping would get me a job. I even thought about get-ting my boy a job with me."

"And who might ye be looking for?"

"A man by the name of Wiley Barnum. He should have a fish-ing boat here. Have you been acquainted with him?"

"Hmm." Ebineezer pondered as he propped his arm on his large, protruding stomach and scratched his chin. "Don't think I know of anyone by that name. I know most of the folks here, but that's not to say he isn't here." He continued thinking. "Nope, don't know that one. Let me tell ye who would though." He pointed across the street towards the Wharf. "There... in the Wharf. Everyone knows everyone there. I don't hang out there much anymore and I wouldn't suggest taking your boy... it gets a bit rowdy."

"No... um... I wouldn't take him there," said Father. "That crew that just came in...?"

"Captain Van Russel's crew."

"Yes, Captain Van Russel... how long is he typically here?"

"No one ever knows... it's never the same. Sometimes they stay a few days. Sometimes they stay a whole lot longer."

"A lot longer?"

"Several weeks," Ebineezer said, smiling.

"Oh, God."

"They're really not bad. I assure ye that. You'll probably like them once ye meet them. Don't ye hasten over that now. Let's get ye

a room." He patted him on the back. "It's a pleasure to have ye. I'm
Ebineezer Drake, the innkeeper."

Father held out his hand, "I'm Jonathon Bloom."

"And of course, I've met ye boy. Ye must be Jeremiah
Bloom."

"Yes sir," he said proudly.

They walked inside and looked around. The floorboards
creaked as they moved across them. Jeremiah said nothing as he
watched the scurrying rats.

"Don't ye worry, Jeremiah. Looks a bit frightful for those that
haven't ever had the pleasure of stayin' in me place, but I promise —
both of ye will get used to it." Ebineezer patted him on the back.

"Where are the rooms?" Jeremiah asked.

"Up there," Ebineezer said, pointing to the dark stairwell.

Jeremiah shuddered. He had looked forward to resting in a
bed after spending the last day in the back of a hard, wooden wagon.
At this point though, the wagon seemed like a better alternative.

"Do you mind if we see our room now?" Father asked.

"Of course," replied Ebineezer, "I'll show ye two yer room."
When they reached the top of the stairs, he paused for a moment
and looked down the narrow, darkened hallway. He seemed uneasy.
"Hmm," he said. "Let me see which one would be the best accommodating for the two of ye."

"Is someone staying in this one?" Jeremiah asked as he reached
for the doorknob of Room One.

"Oh! No, boy... how 'bout we choose a different one," he urged. "No one has occupied that one in several months — it's probably dirty."

"Dirty's alright," said Father. "If you don't object, we would prefer to stay in this one here. It has the closest access to the stairs. I'd prefer to be close to the exit... should we need it."

Ebineezer sighed. "Well... alright... if ye really want this one." He reached into his pocket and pulled out his skeleton key and inserted it into the iron lock. The mechanism in the door un-latched as he turned the key and, slowly, he pushed the door open. Its moan echoed throughout the inn as he pushed it... just a tiny bit. He peered around the edge and looked inside. A small bead of sweat trickled down from the top of his forehead to the tip of his nose.

"Are you expecting someone?" Father asked sarcastically.

"Oh... no..." said Ebineezer, clearing his throat. "Just check-ing out the place for ye."

It was dark in the room, except for a thin ray of sunlight that pried its way through the middle of the two closed shutters. Ebineezer unlatched them. It looked as nothing had been touched for years. The old, iron bed was positioned against the wall and the wooden desk had a nearly spent candle sitting on its top. Jeremiah and his father looked around, noticing the olive colored paint crack-ing and peeling from the walls.

"What's that?" said Jeremiah. He pointed to a couple of large, dark marks on the wall and floor closest to the window.

"Nuttin… I don't guess," said Ebineezer nervously. "You'll see all kinds of imperfections around me place. It's old all over. I'll let ye two get settled in. If ye need me, I'll be downstairs." He shuffled quickly towards the door and scanned the room once more before exiting.

"Well, what do you think?" asked Father.

"Gordington is great. This place… well, I'm sure it'll be great too when I get a little more used to it." Jeremiah walked about the room and was immediately drawn to the dark stains on the wall and the floor. "These spots are a bit odd, don't you think, Father?"

"I'm sure it's nothing." Father moved over to the bed and sat on the edge of it. "I'll let you have the bed tonight. I'll make a place on the floor."

"Are you sure?"

"Yes. By the feel of this bed, I don't know that it would be any better than sleeping on the floor anyhow. I'm going to go down to the Wharf in just a minute to see if I can track down Mr. Wiley."

"Can I go with you?" said Jeremiah.

"No — I don't think it's a place that I should be taking you."

"I can take care of myself," he assured him.

Father smiled, "I know you can, but you heard the innkeeper… it gets rowdy down there and it's probably not the best place for you. You can check out the street if you like… just meet me here later."

CHAPTER FOUR

STRANGE ACQUAINTANCES

Jeremiah acted upon his father's request. He noticed a candle shop on the way into town that sat a couple of doors down from the Brubaker. He was curious to go inside and take a look around for himself.

The sign on the front read:

MADAM KARLA'S CANDLES

He peered through the front window. It looked interesting enough. He walked up a couple of steps to the entrance and opened the door. The many scents inside rushed out, slightly overwhelming him.

"Whoa," he said, backing up a step.

"A bit strong for ya, eh?" laughed a voice from the back of the shop.

"Um… yes, yes it is," he replied, looking for the source of the voice.

"Back here," said the woman waving from behind what seemed to be a thousand candles. They were sitting meticulously on many tables throughout the shop. There was every shape, color and size imaginable.

"Come on back," she said. "What might you be looking for today? I've got the best of everything — spermaceti candles, bees-wax candles, bayberry wax candles, candle holders, candle snuffers — anything and everything you might be looking for."

"Um, no ma'am. I am not looking for anything. I was just looking around."

"Well, that'll be fine young man. You look around all you please. Everything here I've made myself… even the iron snuffers. Well, maybe not the snuffers completely. The blacksmith helps me with the shaping of them… I did design them though."

"They look wonderful," he commented, holding one of them in his hand and examining its detail. He looked at her. She had a pleasant air about her face and her long silver-black hair was pulled back in a bun. She wore large, thick mitts and was holding an iron pot over a wooden stove. He assumed this was Madam Karla.

"Do you mind if I ask what you're making?"

"Of course not." She smiled warmly. "See that large bowl of grayish-green berries sitting on the shelf next to you?"

He nodded.

"Well, those are called bayberries. They come from the Bay-berry Bush. I am boiling them as I make wax for some of my most popular, sweet-smelling candles."

"Oh," he said, scanning the room. On a near table was a single candle. It was short and dark green... and he was instantly drawn to it.

"You must be new to town. I haven't seen you around here before."

"Yes ma'am. My father and I arrived earlier today," he replied, still staring at the green candle sitting by itself. "Can I ask what that one is?" he pointed.

"Which one?" She rose and looked where Jeremiah was star-ing. "Oh, you mean *that* one."

"Yes ma'am."

"Why do you ask, child?"

"It looks interesting to me."

"Does it now?" she asked, moving closer to him. "What about that candle interests you?" she asked again curiously, nearly in his face now.

"I don't know," he said, backing up from her.

She was directly in his face now... and looking him over close-ly. "You're different — I can see that, but I find it very unusual that you would pick out *that* candle from all the others in my shop. That candle is a very special candle. It is a salvia candle, made from the pure extract of the salvia plant."

"I've never heard of that plant."

"The important thing to know is that this candle... this very special candle... can cause marvelous things to happen when used under the right conditions. Most never ask about this candle..." She leaned back and looked him over carefully, crossing her arms. "I'll tell you what; I am going to give you this candle... something inside me is telling me to do so."

"That's not necessary," he replied.

"On the contrary, young man, I think it is," she smiled. "Well, you take this now and let me know if there's anything else I can do to help you. It's time for me to get back to my candles now... before these berries go bad."

Jeremiah took this as his cue to depart and he placed the candle in his pocket. She walked with him to the front of the shop and just as she was about to close the door behind him, she grabbed his arm and whispered with large, open eyes, "Remember — use it only when you think the time is right."

"Thank you ma'am," he said. He wondered if the trip to the candle shop had been a good idea. After all, she seemed a little odd. He decided to do some more investigating down Banyard Street. He turned back towards her shop and saw her watching him from the shop window. She flipped her door sign to "closed" and quickly disappeared.

Meanwhile, Father had just arrived at the Wharf. It was packed full of patrons and sailors and a rumbling, hollering commotion burst

from its interior — infecting the air down Banyard Street completely. He walked through the front entrance and was a little taken back
by the commotion inside.

At the front bar sat a long line of Russel's crew. With bottles
in hand and their arms around one another, they sang a shanty:

Yo ho, yo ho!
A sailor's life for me
We drink all the rum
We slave in the sun
As we live our lives at sea!

Yo ho, yo ho!
We tend to ship and sail
We mend all the rips
And we scrub off the ships
As we drink that tasty ale!

As they finished each verse, they tipped their bottles straight
up in the air — a sure sign that they intended to finish them all —
down to the last drop. Soon their words became scrambled, off cue,
and slurred. The liquor was working its evils upon them all and they
seemed to find humor in it. They finished with rolls of laughter.

One man swung back and forth across the room on the chandelier, taunting three of his shipmates who stood on the tables,
swinging at him with their cutlasses.

At the table below him, an intense game of cards was underway. Van Russel was ahead in a game of Spades with five of his best men, slowly winning the money back that he had just paid out on the ship.

"Belcher!" Van Russel yelled, "I'll carve yer gizzard and fry it for me supper if ye don't watch what yer doing!" He shook his finger at the little man on the chandelier. "Thars a lot of money exchanging hands down here and I'm not gonna —"

Suddenly, the brackets holding the chandelier began popping from the ceiling. Belcher came crashing down, right in the middle of the table, and cards and coins flew in every direction. The candles from the chandelier smashed on the ground causing the room to darken slightly. The commotion startled Blessie and she took off in a torrent, flying in circles around the room. "Now ye've done it! Now ye've done it!" she cawed repeatedly.

"Blimey! You blasted ninny!" the men screamed. "Belcher, we're gonna rip out yer liver! We're gonna dangle you from the foreyard! We're gonna send ye to the scuppers!" They chased him around the room and over several chairs and he darted out the front door next to Father. Patrons burst out in laughter as they watched little Belcher running for his life from Van Russel and his mob of angry drunks.

Father jumped out of the way as they bolted through the front door and down Banyard Street. Captain Russel stopped at the front door and screamed to his men, "Get him crew! Bring him back to me when ye catch that nasty vermin! Men, collect my money off that thar floor! I'd better not catch any of ye trying to pocket it either!" He stopped for a moment to catch his breath and looked to Jeremiah's shocked father standing beside him. "I think I need a drink! What about ye?"

"Well," Father said, "I, uh…"

"Sure ye do," said Van Russel, "Everyone needs to drink tonight!"

"What's one little drink?" said Father, following Van Russel to the bar.

"What be yer poison?" asked the bartender, an extremely large man with a long, gray beard, a nasty pair of trousers and no hint of a neck.

"Two whiskeys," Van Russel replied. "And me bird. Blessie, where are ye?" He looked about the room intently with his one good eye. "Blessie, come here!" She flew to him upon command, landing upon his arm. "That's me girl." He reached into his pocket and pulled out a piece of dried apple for her.

"I'm your girl! I'm your girl!" she cawed. "Gonna get Belcher… Gonna get Belcher!"

"Enough!" yelled Russel. "We'll deal with him later."

The bartender placed two grimy-looking shot glasses on the counter and filled them with an amber-colored ale. He pushed them in front of the men.

"Here's to luck and a fair wind to ye," said Russel. "Arrgh… may there be a lot of it," he chortled.

"To a lot of it," followed Father, downing his shot and nearly choking.

Van Russel slapped him on the back. "Don't get yeself choked, landlubber! Ye don't take a swig often, do ye?"

"No," coughed Father. "It's been a long time."

"But ye felt like comin' by for one today though, eh?"

"Actually, I came looking for someone."

"And who might ye be looking for?" asked the bartender.

"A man by the name of Wiley Barnum. He should have his own fishing boat here."

The bartender laughed — his beard bobbing and his belly jiggling violently. "Old Wiley? Ha! His own boat? He works for me now — on one of my boats! He lost his boat to me in a game of cards months ago."

Father shook his head sadly. He looked around — the rest of the patrons in the Wharf were watching him.

"Do you want me to tell you where to find him?" asked the bartender, still amusing himself.

"Please."

"Go down to pier three. Walk all the way to the end until you see a boat named *The Majestic*. That's mine. He should be there now as a matter of fact — scrubbing her deck! His fishing boat?" he laughed again, "that tickles me insides. Nope, that's my baby now!"

Father shook his head in disgust. He had heard enough. He thanked Van Russel for the drink, and headed for the door.

"You tell ole Wiley that I sent you now, alright?" said the bartender as he left.

Father walked down the piers until he found number three. He walked the full length of it, amidst the many boats lined on both sides. When he reached the end, he saw it. *The Majestic* was a large boat, big enough to hold a crew of fifteen to twenty, and obviously worn from use. Several large nets were hanging in various spots and the sails had all been taken in and neatly rolled.

As he walked nearer, he saw Wiley. He had his back to Father and was scrubbing the deck on his hands and knees. "Get to work, old man!" Father yelled. Wiley stopped immediately when he heard the familiar voice.

"My land — now that's a voice I'd know anywhere." He stood up and turned around. "Jonathon Bloom. How the heck are ya? Better yet, what the heck brings you here?"

"Work... I actually came looking for you. I remembered you said you'd have a fishing boat here in Gordington Square. Dobbit's business went under."

"Sorry to hear that, Jonathon. That's bad considering it was the only work back there for the two of you."

"Yes... I know," sighed Father.

"As far as the boat is concerned, I had a bit of unfortunate luck a while back. I uh —"

Father cut him off. "I already know."

"You know? What do you mean you know?" Wiley paused for a second. "Oh, never mind… you found out the same way the whole town has found out. The fat man in the bar?"

"Yes, the bartender found it quite humorous when he found out I was looking for you."

"Disgusting lard… I bet he did." Wiley rested his hand on the side of the boat. "Yeah, I got a bit inebriated one night and lost her in a game of cards. Spades, if my memory serves me right. He renamed her right after winning her. He owns just about every one of the boats down pier number three."

"He win them the same way?"

"Yep, he's a real treat. He waits until real late… you know… when his customers are fully crocked. He finds the new, unsuspecting ones and asks them to play cards — only if they have something worthwhile to bet, of course. He's as dirty as they come. If I was willing to bet, I'd say he cheated on most of his wins. Who'd know? He only plays and bets with the drunkest of them. Kinda makes you wonder now, doesn't it?"

"Then why are you working for him, Wiley?"

"No other reason except Bonilla."

"Bonilla?"

"My boat. Rather, the boat… his boat. She's my gal. She always will be. And I couldn't part with her. I needed a job anyway. Especially when I lost her to that man. He does at least pay me as he should."

"I don't know what to do now," said Father, rubbing his head.

"What do you mean?"

"I'm needing work, Wiley. I was hoping I could get on with you."

"That shouldn't be a problem, Jonathon. We'll go talk to Adams — the crooked bartender. He's needing a couple more good men anyhow and I'd love to have ya on. Welcome aboard the... uh... welcome aboard *The Majestic*." They snickered together.

CHAPTER FIVE

GHOSTS, GOVERNORS & GOODBYES

Van Russel couldn't remember a meal so delectable. He knifed through the salted pork slowly, holding it in front of his mouth before chewing it daintily — as if it was the last bite he'd ever take.

He gazed up at Blessie poised on his shoulder and began humming a shanty. She watched him, without interrupting. It was a nonsense hum, but one that made him happy, nonetheless. He was eating this scrumptious meal alone with his bird and he was going to take pleasure in every last minute of it.

His cob of corn was next. He picked it up, placed it in front of his mouth and sang as he moved it back and forth. Van Russel loved toying with his food and he imagined he was playing a great musical instrument with his salt-laden cob of corn. He closed his eyes, sunk his teeth into it slowly and…

Knock! Knock!

He looked over to his cabin door. He threw the corn down, wiped his mouth on his sleeve, and stood up. "Come in."

"Captain, I was hoping I would catch you at a convenient time," the man snickered.

"Governor Addison! Yes… err… welcome." His employer, the governor, had a knack for knowing when the most inconvenient times were for the captain, and he always showed up then — just like clockwork. He brushed the doorjamb with his sides as he squeezed his way in. He was five feet tall and almost as round. His head was covered nicely with a long, blonde, curly wig. No doubt he wore the wig as his sign of authority, but Van Russel was just sure he did it to keep the strong, mid-day sun from reflecting his ample bald spot. As always, he pulled down on the lower front edges of his coat upon entering a room — as if proving some level of high dignity. "Mind if I sit down?" he asked, proceeding to take a seat before Russel could respond.

"Of course," said Van Russel.

"I was curious to see how we did on this last voyage… Captain."

"Mighty well, mighty well," replied Van Russel. "I've got a hull full of sails, some linen, some candles, and of course, quite a bit of brandy. If ye don't mind though sir, I'd like to keep a bit of this for me men. Ye know… as a reward for all their hard work. As ye may be inclined, three months at sea isn't a bit easy and it'd be my way…

and of course yours… of extending the additional "thank ye" to me crew."

"Yes, I am aware that three months on the water is a bit of a struggle —"

"A bit of a struggle?" Van Russel looked intently at the governor while working a piece of corn from his teeth.

"Don't mock me, Captain." The governor glowered.

"Oh, no… sorry sir… I wouldn't dream of that," he followed, sarcastically, as he removed the piece of corn from his teeth and, grinning at the governor's disgust, fed it to Blessie with his mouth.

"Is that absolutely necessary while I am here?" asked the governor, disgusted.

"Oh…sorry, sir. She's a bit hungry too, ye know?"

"I'm sure," sneered the governor.

"So, I'll have me men unload it all for ye and deliver it to the same place they typically do. When they get back from the tavern, of course. And if ye'd consider letting us having some of the looted brandy, we'd be —"

The governor interrupted. "I've already thought about it Captain, and the answer would be a firm 'no'. If you would, have them unload it all, with the rest of the supplies, and bring it to me." He gave the captain a snide smile. "Well, I have other things I must tend to." He rose and squeezed back out the door. "Idiot," he muttered under his breath.

"Stupid wig," Van Russel muttered back at him.

Van Russel and Blessie watched the governor from the cabin's window as he exited the ship. When he knew the governor was safely away he reached down and opened a large chest on the floor next to his leg.

"Who's the idiot now? Who's the idiot now?" cawed Blessie as she and Van Russel looked down at the twenty-three bottles of brandy stashed away in the trunk.

Later that afternoon, at pier number three, Jeremiah stood on the dock and watched his father preparing to board *The Majestic*, along with twenty other crewmembers. They were converging for a two-day fishing voyage. Jeremiah was unused to being without him and, as he watched, he felt the same emptiness he had when they'd left their home.

"Father, please don't go this time. I don't have a good feeling about it."

Wiley was standing near them and spoke up. "Jeremiah, everything will be fine. I've been out on this same boat many times and she's perfectly safe — even in deficient weather. She was mine once — and I trust her. Your father will be fine."

"It's alright, son," Father added, "I'll only be gone for a couple days. I want you to stay close to the Brubaker and Mr. Drake. I've already spoken with him and he's promised to help keep an eye out for you. And be careful around the 'rough' ones. Promise me…"

"I promise, Father." Jeremiah gave him a quick hug. As he began boarding with the crew, Jeremiah called to him, "Father!"

"Yes?"

Jeremiah removed the wooden cross necklace from around his neck. "You and Mother made this for me, and it's always protected me. Please wear it until you get back."

Father smiled. "Of course I will — now go!" He laughed and tied the necklace around his neck. "I'll see you soon!"

"Yes, Father." Jeremiah turned towards to the inn and didn't look back again — as much as he wanted to. He couldn't bear the thought of the risk involved, even though this was an everyday way of life for many of the other people in town.

When he arrived back at the Brubaker, Ebineezer put his arm around him. He patted him on the shoulder. "It'll be ok, Jeremiah."

"I don't have a good feeling about it."

"It's only 'cause this is all new to ye. *The Majestic* has been on the water for weeks at a time and not a single incident has resulted. She's a good fishing boat and ye father will be back with ye soon. And it gives us time to visit," he said cheerfully.

"Yes, sir, it sure does," said Jeremiah, smiling.

"Up for a stroll through town?" asked Ebineezer.

"Sure! But, what about the inn?"

"Ah, it's pretty self-sufficient. And there's nothing in it anyone would want anyway."

"I understand," Jeremiah giggled. "So, you were going to tell me of Captain Van Russel and the privateers."

"I figured that'd be one of ye first questions. What would ye like to know about `em?" he asked. "Better yet, let me just explain how it all happens to be and then ye can ask questions. Agreed?"

"Agreed."

They began their stroll down Banyard Street. Rolling carriages and busy patrons surrounded them on the crowded cobblestone walkway.

"Ok… regarding the `P' word ye brought up," he whispered.

"The pirates?"

His voice lowered, "Aye, the pirates. Let's not say that word too loudly around here."

"Why?" Jeremiah asked.

"Piracy is illegal boy. If ye be convicted of such a crime, they'll send ye to the gallows."

"Gallows?"

"They'll hang ye boy… straight from the neck until ye are dead."

Jeremiah gasped.

"Aye," said Ebineezer. "Or they'll hang ye body in a metal cage. Down that alley there — towards the water," he pointed. "Do ye see the cage hanging?" he asked.

Jeremiah strained to see the cage. He could see some form of mass inside it.

"That's a body, boy. A little unrecognizable at this point `cause the birds and insects have been munching on him for weeks now."

"Ugh." Jeremiah couldn't take his eyes off the cage. Though disgusted by the thought, he would have loved a better look if Ebineezer had been willing to lead him closer.

"Ok...ok... let's keep moving, boy." Ebineezer hurried Jeremiah along. "Now, regarding the privateers ye inquired upon... Privateers are a legal group of sailors hired by those in charge of the towns...or sometimes even the countries themselves. In the case of Van Russel's crew, well, the governor of Gordington, Governor Addison, made them legal. They've been issued a license, or special certificate, of sorts, to plunder other ships — legally. We call it a *Letter of Marque*. A percentage of what they obtain goes to the governor and the... um, governor."

"Plunder? You mean rob? That would make them pirates!"

"Shhh!" scolded Ebineezer. "I said not to use that word too loudly around here!"

"Did I hear you say the word pirates?" laughed the town's blacksmith. Not noticing, they stopped directly in front of him during their conversation.

"Hello Boswell," said Ebineezer, irascibly. "This is me pupil, Jeremiah. He and his father are new to town."

"Oh yeah... I think I watched you come in yesterday. Well, welcome to Gordington, Jeremiah."

"Thank you, sir," said Jeremiah.

"And regarding the word 'pirate', I use it myself all the time. No worries there — they won't hang you for saying it," he laughed.

"Ebineezer, calm down a bit — you get yourself too worked up and worried over such a thing." They stared directly at one other.

"Do I now?" asked Ebineezer.

"Well Jeremiah, it was a pleasure meeting you. Come by anytime," said Boswell. "And Ebineezer is a great teacher."

Ebineezer nodded to him and they went on their way.

They strolled the entire length of Banyard Street before heading back towards the inn. Once inside, they noticed Van Russel standing there, waiting.

"Van Russel! Welcome back!" Ebineezer greeted heartily.

"Aye, it's good to be back," Van Russel replied. They shook hands.

"Ready for a room?"

"Not yet." Van Russel seemed a little confused at Ebineezer's question and peered over at a small wooden clock mounted on the wall behind the bar. "Do ye know what today is, Ebineezer?"

He started, "Well, it's a perfect Monday and…"

Van Russel cleared his throat. He gazed at the clock again and then motioned his eyes towards the innkeeper's cigar room in the back. There were others moving about, though it was dark and they were shadowed.

Ebineezer gasped. "Oh! Aye, I didn't realize the day was already upon us. Jeremiah, why don't ye run along… but stay close and I'll be back with ye in just a while. I have a meeting that's requiring me to be in attendance."

"Certainly," said Jeremiah. Van Russel looked at the boy standing before him and grinned. As Van Russel and Ebineezer walked to the cigar room in the back, Van Russel whispered to him, "Ye told me ye wanted me here... what is..."

Others were waiting and he could hear some talking, though it was muffled and difficult to decipher. Jeremiah watched as another entered from a door on the other side of the inn, which accessed the poorly lit cigar room directly. He strained his neck and stood on his tiptoes as he struggled to see what was happening in the room near him. Ebineezer promptly shut the door.

The day was early still but had taken its toll on him. He figured that, since he had nothing better to do, he might as well take a nap while he waited for Ebineezer to finish his furtive doings, whatever they may be.

He entered his lonely little room and went straight for the bed. The afternoon sun was on the other side of the building, providing just a hint of light through the closed shutters. This made the atmosphere better for sleeping and he left the shutters as they were, despite the mustiness of the room and the fact that some open air would have helped in that regard.

He closed his eyes. He rolled on his back. He tried lying on his side. But it was no use — he had so many thoughts running through his head that sleep at this point was virtually inaccessible for him. He sat up, propped his back against the wall and looked around his room.

As he scanned the room's interior, he noticed every imperfection, much more than he noticed when they first arrived. Although it was a bit on the repugnant side, it was a step up from their two-room cottage and the back of a hard, wooden wagon.

He could not take his eyes off the stains that eerily penetrated the wall and the floor. He tried to rationalize as to what could have caused them, although no scenario he mustered made a lick of sense. He thought about asking Ebineezer about them again, but he readily avoided the subject the first time and would probably do so again. They were extremely dark in appearance and he knew they couldn't be from paint, mold, food, water or anything else he had ever come across. And why hadn't anyone tried to clean them up?

Jeremiah's eyes were immobilized by the spots, but after a long while sleep began to work its way upon him. His eyes were nearly closed when something caught his eye. Was it the moving light of the setting sun? A shadow? It couldn't be the sun though… the shadow moved just over the spots themselves — nowhere else in the room. Jeremiah froze and his breathing slowed, to a deep, irregular pattern. The hairs on his arms and the back of his neck stood up. Something was terribly wrong and he knew it was more than his imagination.

He looked across the room; his father's musket was propped against the facing wall. His pistol was nowhere close and he grabbed around him, feeling for something to use for protection. The shadow, originating from the stain on the floor, rose slowly and Jeremiah's heart raced as he watched it form. The shadow was unlike a typical shadow though — it was pitch-black with almost some solidity to it. It was gimpy and deformed and stretched taller, until it rose to about seven or eight feet in height and stood perfectly still. Jeremiah barely discerned the shapes of a head, arms and legs. It continued to stand motionless in this final state... as if it were watching Jeremiah.

Fear overcame him. He was anchored motionless on the bed watching the thing manifest before him. His heart continued racing and his palms were sweaty. He glared back at it, unable to move his eyes to anywhere else in the room.

"Please help me," Jeremiah heard a male voice say.

A minute passed with both of them unmoving. "Please help me," it pleaded again.

"Are-are...y-you talking to m-me?" Jeremiah gasped.

"Aye," it said.

Jeremiah's eyes widened and he felt his heart pounding out of his chest.

"Please... don't be afraid of me."

"H-how can I hear you?" asked Jeremiah. "You have no-no m-mouth to speak from."

"Because you have the ability to hear me, and to see me, we all know that. I don't mean to frighten you, that's why I tried to come slowly."

"Who are you? What are you?" Jeremiah asked, his pulse rate and breathing slowing slightly from the visitor's encouraging words.

"I was just as ye once... don't let my appearance frighten ye."

"What do you need from me?" asked Jeremiah.

"Help."

"What kind of help?"

"I need ye to share some information. Look beside the bed," it instructed.

Jeremiah looked around. "I don't see anything."

"Between the wall and the bed… it is there."

Jeremiah reached down, but could not feel anything. He climbed off the bed, pulled it from the wall and noticed something lying on the floor, crumpled and dirty. He picked it up and saw it was old and worn. "A journal?" he asked.

"Correct. I need ye to share this information with the appropriate persons."

"I'm confused," said Jeremiah. "How am I going to know what to do… or what to share?"

"Please… I don't have much time… it's nearing time for me to go. Read the journal… ye will know who to find and where to go," it urged.

"Do you have a name?" asked Jeremiah.

"Daniels."

"Ok… I will do what I can…" Jeremiah replied, hardly believing himself that this was actually happening.

"Thank ye… and please hurry. There's not much time and more will suffer… I have to go now."

His shadow shrunk straight back into the stain. Jeremiah, a little calmer now, walked over to the spot on the floor. He moved his foot over the top of it; almost in disbelief that yet one more thing happened he once thought impossible.

He opened the shutters and allowed the last of the day's remaining light to penetrate while he sat down at the small desk with the journal. He blew the dust from the book's cover and opened it to the first page.

> September 29th, 1721
> My naval captain, Captain Mather, notified me today that my presence has been requested before a special group, or society. Though they were vague in their wording as to what this meeting would entail, I strongly believe it has something to do with the offshore occurrences and the recent disappearances of many ships. My current stint with the ship Contender is over tomorrow and I will head out some time during the breaking of dawn and will meet with this assembly in several days in Tortuga for further instructions.

Jeremiah read Daniels's first couple of pages about his stint aboard the *Contender*, but it was making him drowsy. He was relaxing and his nerves were calming; sleep was close. Ebineezer was in a meeting and his father was absent on the water, so there wasn't much more to do besides sleep and hope time passed quickly. He tucked the journal underneath his arm and curled up on the small bed.

"Jeremiah, wake up. Wake up, boy," urged Ebineezer.

"Yes, sir?" he asked groggily.

"Ye've been sleeping for nearly two days now… ye must get yerself up!"

Ebineezer's words sunk in and his eyes opened hugely. "Two days? Oh my, how could I have slept so long?"

"I believe it to have been related to exhaustion, sir," said Ebineezer.

"Father!" Jeremiah exclaimed.

"Due to be back anytime now…" said Ebineezer. "If ye want, I'll walk with ye down there."

"Yes! Let's go!" said Jeremiah. He tucked the journal underneath the mattress and followed quickly behind.

"I checked on ye every little bit," said Ebineezer as they walked down to pier number three. "Ye must have been plum drained!" he laughed.

"I guess I was," said Jeremiah.

They walked down to the docking spot on pier number three where *The Majestic* was due to arrive. It was empty, dark, and no one was around. Jeremiah's heart sank.

"They could be here anytime tonight… depending on what they may have encountered weather-wise on their way back. There was only one small storm that we know of and *The Majestic* is rarely late. I'm sure ye father and the others are fine."

Ebineezer's words were comforting, although it didn't change the inner voice that had been chattering away since his father left. Maybe it was just his own insecurity and fear playing games with him. They sat down on the edge of the dock with a lantern at their side. They dropped their feet in the water, watching in the darkness as they waited for *The Majestic* to return.

CHAPTER SIX

CATASTROPHE ON THE CONTENDER

First Lieutenant Bradford peered over the side of the *Contender*. The young, sandy-haired officer watched an unusual flow of fog settling in over the water, completely surrounding the naval brig. He grabbed a lantern and held it over the side — it appeared only about six feet above the water, but didn't settle in as fog typically did. He spoke to the midshipman standing behind him. "Bernard, go get the captain."

"Aye, sir."

The breeze carrying them slowed, and he gazed up at the sails. Their fullness began to drop in the partial light of the moon.

Captain Mather came up from the deck below. "Bradford, what's the problem?" he asked with a look of concern.

"Sir, there's an unusual fog surrounding the ship and we are slowing rapidly. You might want to come over here and take a look at this." Captain Mather and the first lieutenant walked to the side of the ship and held the lantern over the port side. The fog wasn't moving, but had now risen to about twelve feet above the surface of the water.

"How unusual," commented the captain, "It's low and not moving at all."

"Only upwards. What would you like to do sir?"

"Go get the navigator."

"Aye, sir." He hurried below deck to fetch Solomon, the ship's navigator. The captain noticed that the air had chilled and he could see his breath.

"Doesn't make sense," he noted. "This night hasn't been cold enough for this." He looked around at the other officers standing on deck near him. They too had a mist coming off their breath and were looking at each other — confused as he was.

"Looking for me, sir?" asked Solomon, the young navigator.

"Yes, son... please report."

"Sorry sir. I've been spending the last bit trying to figure it out for myself. The compasses are all off and I tried to get our bearings from the astrolabe, but the North Star can't be seen tonight. The best I can make of it, there's some sort of magnetic interference causing everything to go awry. I'm sorry sir. I tried to get a fix before coming and alerting you."

"Thank you son... you did fine. Bradford, what o'clock is it?"

"Almost twenty-past-two in the morning, sir."

"I don't have a good feeling here, Lieutenant. There's no logic behind this. Round up all the men on board and prepare the arms. Bring the ship to."

The officers took off in all directions as he stood at the port side of his ship trying to make sense of what was happening. The captain was fully aware that many ships went missing ships from this area — he felt there was reason for alarm. He had taken the *Contender* out and investigated several of these cases, but he had been unable to turn up anything.

He looked over the side and watched as the fog, a minute ago stationary, slowly began to move. He saw a small break in it and followed it as it moved closer, looking to see the water below it.

"What the...?" said the captain, noticing lights beneath the water's surface.

"What's wrong, sir?" asked Bradford. He had returned, along with a loaded pistol and his sword.

"Orbs of light, under the water," said the captain. "Titus!" he yelled.

Titus didn't respond.

"Bradford, get me Titus!" The captain commanded, as he continued looking over the side of his ship.

"Sir, he's not there," replied Bradford.

"What do ye mean he's not there!" yelled the captain. He stood and looked for himself, scanning the ratlines and the crow's nest high above the deck of the ship for his look out. "Does anyone know where Titus is?"

The crew stood mumbling amongst themselves, unaware of the whereabouts of their shipmate.

"He was here only an hour ago," said Bradford, "when they changed watch."

"And now he's gone?" sneered the captain, his stress clearly showing. "Would someone please climb aloft and give me a report? I need to know what's going on here!"

Bradford grabbed on to the ratline and ascended high above the crew. The rest of the men were assembling on deck and the captain yelled to them. "Situate yourselves at all points of the ship! Cover the bow and cover the stern! Cover the starboard and cover the portside!" They arranged themselves on all sides while they waited for further command from their captain.

Bradford reached the top. "Sir, it's odd. The fog is only moving around us! It's about a hundred yards out in all directions!"

"Can ye see beyond the fog, Lieutenant?" the captain yelled back to him.

"No sir, it's dark — wait! I see a light, many lights —"

Suddenly an orb of light shot across the length of the ship towards the lieutenant, knocking him off the top of the look out post. He screamed as he fell straight from the top of the masts into the fog and the dark water below.

Silence fell over the entire ship. Captain Mather didn't know how to react. He had no idea what he was preparing to fight against. The air grew even colder, so quickly that the deck of the ship was becoming slippery with ice. The entire crew waited with their swords drawn and their pistols and arms loaded. Several stayed below deck and manned the cannons as they too watched through the gun ports, waiting for whatever they were about to combat.

"THERE, ABOVE US!!" one man yelled.

"NO, HERE IN THE FOG!" yelled another from the opposite side of the ship.

"THEY'RE EVERYWHERE!" yelled another.

All around the ship the orbs of light darted in and out. Some moved at tremendous speeds through the air above while others shot quickly through the fog surrounding the ship. The men continued watching them as they drew their weapons close.

One ball of light, about a foot in diameter, strayed from the rest and hovered about twenty feet directly above the deck. It discharged some sort of electrical static all around its outsides.

"What is it?" asked one of the men standing nearest to the captain. They watched as the hovering sphere slowly transformed into a thick, mist-like form and descended to the deck.

"My God..." said the captain. "It's an abomination." He stood there, stunned.

The mist moved towards the captain, transforming itself from a cloud-like form, to a human-like shape, and finally, a pirate. He walked slowly across the surface of the deck towards the captain.

He stopped about two feet away with his complete focus entirely on the captain. The captain's hand was on his cutlass, but he was too frightened to draw it — everything happened before he could even react.

"Are ye the one behind our erroneous ship disappearances?" the captain asked the pirate.

The pirate smiled underneath his large sopping-wet hat. His mouth appeared rotten to the captain and his breath smelled of death. "Yer boat is mine. Yer crew is mine," he commanded in a rough and garbled voice.

"Not tonight," said the captain, as calmly as possible.

BOOM!

They both turned to see Solomon, the navigator, standing close by. His musket was pointed at the pirate and a small stream of smoke flowed from the end of it. He just shot at the brute — and the lead ball passed right through him.

The pirate began laughing, gruffly. He turned to Solomon and frowned. He raised his arm and pointed at him, his demeanor changing to one of pure hatred.

As if under direct command of this pirate, three more orbs deviated from their path outside the ship and flew directly across the deck. They materialized just as he had and flanked the young navigator on all sides.

"Solomon!" the captain yelled.

Solomon looked to his captain. He tried reloading his musket, but as he lowered it, they penetrated him with their swords from all sides. Solomon's musket dropped and the captain watched in horror as the life drained from his navigator's face. His body fell to the ground in front of his crewmembers.

Immediately upon his body hitting the surface, something began moving around him. It was transparent and formed a thick, mist-like shape. It was his soul — and it rose from his corpse — right before their very eyes!

One of the pirates looked at the soul and then turned to the one in charge. He grabbed Solomon's soul and disappeared into the night air.

"FIRE!" screamed the captain.

A hurl of guns blasting and bullets whizzing followed as the entire crew went to battle with the pirate intruders. The *Contender's* upper deck was soon engulfed in a nebula of blinding smoke. The other orbs surrounding the ship began manifesting so quickly, the soldiers could not reload their weapons fast enough. None of the shots affected the pirates, so the soldiers began drawing their swords.

They went into sword-to-sword combat with the pirates, but realized quickly enough, that too put them at an extreme disadvantage. Each time they swung at them, the pirates quickly dematerialized into a cloud of vapor — and then manifested into a pirate again. Their efforts seemed futile as they swung through open air.

The captain clashed swords with two of them. His strikes were hopeless and he struggled to repel their evil swings as they came barreling towards him. All around him he watched as his crew was taken down one by one, and their souls too, until he was left alone on the upper deck. Sweat poured from his brow and he was growing weak.

Fifty pirates slowly surrounded him. He dropped his sword as they encompassed him completely. None said anything and he watched as they moved to one side, allowing the one in charge to come through. He looked up at the leader as he came to stand before him.

"Yer boat is mine. Yer crew is mine," said the pirate again, gruffly.

"Who are you?" asked the captain, weak and winded.

"Molodan." As the pirate began his grumbled laughing again, the captain felt the life draining from himself — just as it had from his young navigator. The remaining pirates manifested back into the orb form and began darting at tremendous speed over the surface and interior of the ship. They were searching for any survivors and, the captain now knew, souls. Molodan pulled his sword from the captain's chest as his body fell to the deck. His soul too was soon standing there in disbelief, and no sooner did he have time to understand his transition, than Molodan snatched him and disappeared off the bow of the ship.

On board the pirate vessel, Molodan and his crew began assembling. The pirate brute stood, poised on the quarterdeck with magnificent power, waiting for his crew to re-manifest. His clothes were wet and hung stiffly from his massive frame as he stroked his long, black, scraggly beard. He said nothing to them and none of them spoke as they looked up at him. Slowly, they parted and a single man walked up between them.

He was human, not of their kind, and was sickly and emaciated. In his hands he carried a chest and he moved towards Molodan with a weary limp. The chains bolted around his ankles clanked. His bare feet were scarred, scabbed and bleeding. He struggled to make it to Molodan.

Molodan watched him as he came closer, until he stopped at the base of the stairs that led up from the main deck. He curled his finger at the man, beckoning for the chest. The man struggled as he carried it up the stairs to him.

Molodan opened the chest. He took out three cloth-covered objects and unwound the string holding the fabric to them. They were of metallic origin and no larger than the hands of the colossus holding them. Carefully, he began fitting them together.

The first piece was longer than the other two and cylindrical. In its center sat a perfectly rounded stone, as blue as the ocean. The other two pieces were flat and round. One was larger than the other and Molodan placed these two in his left hand, the smaller one directly inside the larger. On the larger piece, the script *Patefacio Prodigium* was neatly engraved. There were holes on the top and bottom centers of both the circles so, when they were put together, they lined up perfectly. Molodan grabbed the cylindrical piece and slid it into the center, locking them all together. He held the completed object in front of his dark eyes, looking it over closely.

A pirate standing at the ship's wheel watched him intently. Molodan looked over to him. The one controlling the ship held his arm up, while glancing between the open water and a spinning compass placed next to him. He directed his sight towards Molodan, then to the compass, and then to the open water.

Molodan knew they were close for he changed his stance to face the front of the ship. Upon seeing the pirate at the wheel lower his arm, Molodan held the object in front of him by the end of the cylinder. He flicked the outer ring with his finger and it began spinning at a tremendous rate, causing the inner ring to begin spinning in the opposite direction. The round, blue stone in the object's center began to glow. He chanted, *"Patefacio Prodigium… Patefacio Prodigium… Patefacio Prodigium."* Once these words were uttered three times, an intense noise began ringing from the object. A shockwave of energy blasted from the object towards the front of the ship, and extended out far beyond the ship.

In the quiescent waters near the ship, a single barrel floated away. It had been on deck of the ship, but was knocked off during the battle. Wrapped around it were two arms, holding on tightly for dear life.

Bradford was momentarily knocked unconscious from his fall from the ship, but regained his awareness during the gun battle. He struggled to keep out of sight and kicked his legs lightly under the water to try and distance himself from the ship as much as possible. The fog shielding him began evaporating. When it was nearly clear again, he noticed the intruders' ship. It sat off in the distance about two hundred yards away from the *Contender*.

He recognized it as a Collier Brig. They were used for coal transport, and he figured that its current inhabitants had probably hijacked this one. Its wooden exterior appeared to be painted with some form of darkening substance, possibly tar, and even the sails seemed fashioned from some type of black canvas. He could see movement on its upper deck, but could not see what was going on. The remaining orbs flew back towards the black vessel and it began moving away.

Bradford struggled to stay with the barrel. There was nothing on it to easily grip and his arms were quickly becoming fatigued. His body hurt from the fall against the water and his exhausted legs dangled below him.

On top of the shock of watching his shipmates being murdered and their souls taken, he felt the air around him start vibrating with great intensity. It sent shockwaves across the surface of the water and the sound from the amulet grew louder by the second.

"My God," he said as he clutched his barrel tightly. It was unlike anything he had ever witnessed. His body was growing weaker by the minute as he clung to life just yards away from his own ship.

As the sound rang out over the dark water and the energy continued to drive forward from the ship, a large hole began emerging. It was so immense that the entire pirate ship could fit right through it, and it appeared that was their intent. A silvery doorway materialized with astonishing speed as the pirate ship moved closer to it. The ringing sound of the object diminished after the gateway opened, but it sent a pulsating tone across the air that could be heard for miles. The ship entered the hole slowly and just as the last of it passed through, the doorway dissolved quickly — as if it had never happened. The waters around the gateway were now silent.

Luckily for Bradford, they had not destroyed the *Contender*. He struggled with the last of his remaining energy and kicked his legs behind the barrel as he made his way to his ship. He grabbed hold of a rope hanging over its edge and began climbing back to safety. "Thank God," he panted. He had survived.

CHAPTER SEVEN

SALMAGUNDI & GLOGG

Jeremiah had not moved for days. He had hardly eaten — his skin was pale and his small frame was becoming gaunt. The cool November air blew across the water and whisked his fine, brown hair below his triangular hat. He watched the ocean horizon, transfixed. Day and night he had sat on pier number three, waiting for his father's return.

"Jeremiah," said Ebineezer. "We really ought to get ye away from here."

"Mr. Drake, I've told you… I'm not leaving here until he returns."

"But, son, it's been almost two weeks now."

"I'm not leaving, Mr. Drake."

"Boy, please, listen to reason. If ye father was to return, he'd have done so already."

"I'm not leaving," Jeremiah insisted.

Ebineezer took a deep breath. "He's feared dead, Jeremiah. The scouts have all returned… they turned up nothing after days of searching. Not even their boat was found. I'm afraid it's physically impossible at this point for ye father to be alive. Please come with me. He's not coming back."

Jeremiah looked down and started crying. Ebineezer kneeled beside him and put his arm around him. "I know, I know, let it out. Aye, it's good to cry sometimes."

"WHY HIM!" Jeremiah screamed, "WHY HIM!"

"Sometimes we never know the reason why. Could have been a storm… could have been anything."

"He was all I had," he said, sobbing.

"I know," said Ebineezer, looking helpless.

"Now I've lost both my parents!"

Ebineezer coached him into returning to the inn and they walked away from pier number three.

Jeremiah went straight to his room, closed the door and fell upon the bed. Tears streamed down his face. The emptiness inside him was too overwhelming and he closed his eyes, wishing he was dead also.

"I'm sorry about ye father," said a voice.

Jeremiah's head rose up. No one was in his room. "Daniels?" he asked.

"Yes." The shadowy figure emerged from a dark corner.

"How did you know?"

"We know everything on this side."

"Then please, tell me of my father's fate!"

"I'm sorry… I cannot do that."

"Why not?" cried Jeremiah.

"I can read ye thoughts, I can feel ye pain, but unfortunately me limits are within the walls of this structure right now," said the shadow as it moved slowly against the wall. "At least until I move on… and me time is nearing."

"Then what do I do?"

"Ye have a purpose. We all have a purpose. For whatever the reasons that caused these horrible things to happen — there is a reason. Ye must be strong. The answers will come to ye eventually."

"Is there any way you could find out about my father?"

"Not at the level I am on now… one day, aye. My time here is diminishing quickly, however. I must prepare to go."

"Please don't leave," Jeremiah pleaded.

"Me purpose here is served."

"And what is that?"

"Ye, boy. Ye. I have been waiting for ye arrival. And one day it will make sense to ye too. I must go, but please, do as I instructed before. I can't stress its importance enough." And as Daniels uttered those last words, he began disappearing.

A knock came on his door. "Jeremiah?" said Ebineezer.

"Yes, Mr. Drake?" He was sitting up now, tears still streaming down his face.

"Can we come in?" he coughed.

"We?"

"Aye, the captain and I." Ebineezer and Van Russel cracked his door and peered inside before entering.

Jeremiah nodded.

Van Russel said nothing as Ebineezer continued his hacking cough. He pulled a handkerchief from his pocket and covered his mouth as he tried easing the barking fit.

"Are you alright, Mr. Drake?" asked Jeremiah, his attention turning away from his own misery momentarily.

"I'll be fine," Ebineezer said, still coughing. "Comes and goes. The captain and I wanted to talk to ye." Van Russel looked at Ebineezer's handkerchief and rolled his eyes.

"What?" Jeremiah asked. He rose up and looked at the hand-kerchief. It was spattered with blood.

Jeremiah felt confused and overwhelmed again. "What else?" he asked as he wiped away his tears.

"Don't ye two worry 'bout this. It comes and it goes. When I start coughing badly, it gets a little bloody. Just from the violent coughs though — no worries... no worries."

Van Russel spoke up, "Jeremiah, ye know ye can't stay here in this old inn forever. We came by to see if ye'd be interested in being part of me crew."

"Father would never allow —" he stopped when he realized what he was saying.

"It'd be good for ye to get away from this here inn right now," encouraged Van Russel. "And of course, we'd always come back between trips."

"That's what my father said too."

Van Russel cleared his throat. "What happened to ye father was especially unfortunate, lad. But it would serve ye well to get away from this area for a while, even if it's only temporary. I'd let ye make that decision ye self. I have a position open aboard me ship and I'm offering it to ye for the time being."

"What type of position?" asked Jeremiah.

"You could be me cabin boy," answered Van Russel. "Kind of like me assistant. And of course, with any rightful plundering, ye'd get fair shares as the rest of the crew. For the rest of me crew it's like a home away from home, with payment."

Jeremiah's head started hurting from the stress he was under and he knew he didn't have an answer right away. He looked at Van Russel and his bird, keeping his expression empty.

"Why don't ye sleep on the captain's offer?" Ebineezer suggested. His cough was calming and he urged Van Russel to let Jeremiah be for the time being.

"That'd be fine," said Van Russel. "We'll be leaving again soon, so ye think about it. And come find me aboard the *Nante* if ye agree to me idea."

The following morning aboard the *Nante*, with Ebineezer by his side, Jeremiah knocked at Van Russel's door.

"Come in," said Van Russel. He was hunched over and feeling beneath his table. Blessie was poised on his shoulder and as the door opened, she leaned down and whispered in his ear. "Oh, so ye changed yer mind," he said, still searching below the table.

"Yes sir, I did," Jeremiah replied.

Van Russel looked up. "Sorry, lost me musket balls and I am having a time findin' 'em. They rolled all over me cabin."

Ebineezer chuckled.

"What's so funny, innkeeper?"

"Oh, nothing, nothing at all," said Ebineezer. "Jeremiah and I had a long talk this morning, and he's decided to give it a go."

"Blimey! That makes the captain overjoyed!" exclaimed Van Russel. "Ye couldn't have picked a better day to decide. All me hearties are aboard today preparing the ship… we'll need to make the announcement."

"Jeremiah, I will leave ye with the captain now," said Ebineezer. "All will be good, boy. And ye know where I'll be." Ebineezer exited Van Russel's cabin.

Van Russel gazed at Jeremiah with a wide smile. "Lad, let's go meet the crew."

Jeremiah had noticed some of them as he walked aboard the large brigantine with Ebineezer. His focus must have been more on his pending talk with Van Russel, for he hadn't noticed all the activity that he saw now. The size of Van Russel's crew seemed to grow by the second as he watched them from the quarterdeck. They were strung in the sails and all on the ratlines. They stood on the gaffs and they covered the decks. And each time he looked at the stairs leading to the galley, more seemed to climb above and disappear below the main deck.

Van Russel called out to his crew, "ME HEARTIES, THE CAPTAIN NEEDS YE ALL TO REPORT ABOVE DECK. HE'S NEEDING TO MAKE AN ANNOUNCEMENT!"

The crew dropped from lines and climbed down ropes. They climbed up ladders and over the sides of the ship. Jeremiah watched in amazement as the entire crew of seventy-three assembled before him and Van Russel on the ship's main deck.

Jeremiah gulped as he felt all their eyes upon him. An overwhelming feeling of loneliness chilled his soul as he stared back at the large group of strangers. How badly he wished he could turn around and go back home.

"Men, crew… me hearties," Van Russel smiled. "Focus all yer deadlights up here and meet me newest cabin boy, Jeremiah. He's been through a lot and recently has undergone some significant losses of his own. Make sure ye all give him a warm *Nante* greeting."

"AHOY!" the crew roared.

"And now, I need someone that's willing to show me new cabin boy around and expose him to some introductions."

The crew stood silent. Jeremiah thought, were it not for the pestering seagulls, he'd have been able to hear a pin drop.

"No volunteers to show our newest crew member around?" said Van Russel.

"I'll show him," said a faint voice, somewhere within the crowd of ragged men. Jeremiah heard some laughter amongst the crew.

Van Russel squinted. "Was that ye Augustus?"

"Yes, sir," replied the voice. The laughing men parted slightly, revealing a boy, not much older than Jeremiah, standing in their midst. His face was pale and freckled and his long, red hair was pulled back in a tie. He looked like a dwarf compared to the crew standing around him.

"Leave it to the swabbie! The swabbie does the introductions!" they laughed.

"ENOUGH!" yelled Van Russel. "Or anyone I hear utter another comment will be swabbing the main deck for a week straight! At least he was man enough to volunteer!"

"Everyone, back to work! Augustus, come up here with the captain!" he yelled.

The boy made his way across deck as the men returned to their tasks. When he was close to Van Russel, he fell at the base of the stairs. The quartermaster stood beside him, laughing, and didn't offer to help him up.

"Ranjit, did ye do that?" Van Russel asked angrily.

"No sir," sneered the quartermaster. He was a large, bald brute of Indian descent. He was shirtless and his muscular frame was covered in tattoos. Jeremiah watched him walk away after answering Van Russel, not seeming the slightest bit intimidated.

"Are ye all right?" Van Russel asked Augustus.

"Yes sir… I am fine," replied the swabbie, catching his breath and dusting off his breeches.

Jeremiah knew the ship's swabbie was the lowest ranking position on board. His primary job was swabbing, or cleaning, the decks of the ship.

"Why don't ye show our newest member around," urged Van Russel.

"I'd be happy too," he said. "Welcome aboard, Jeremiah."

"Thank you," Jeremiah replied, watching Van Russel retreat to his cabin. "Did that bloke trip you a moment ago?"

"Ah, don't mind him… I don't. He's usually evil, but I've learned to put up with it."

"You shouldn't have to," said Jeremiah as he glared at Ranjit. The quartermaster was staring back at him as well. Jeremiah took an instant dislike to him.

"Leave it alone," urged Augustus. "By the way, I'm sorry to hear of your father."

"You know?"

"Oh yes. Most of us do. Word has been thick around town about your father and the fate of their boat."

"Oh."

"A peculiar thing and a horrible loss… I am sorry."

"Thank you, Augustus." He felt sadness overcoming him again.

"Well, are you ready for the grand tour?" August laughed.

"Certainly," said Jeremiah with a hint of a smile, still watching the staring quartermaster. "I don't think Ranjit is pleased by me being here either."

"Don't mind him," said Augustus as he led Jeremiah below deck. "He's not worth it."

The two entered the ship's crew space.

"This is where you'll be sleeping," said Augustus as they walked through a small room full of hammocks. They were hung close together and directly above one another in very tight quarters. They were an old, dingy brown color and were stained all over. "Sometimes they use these as shields during battle," said Augustus.

"Shields?" Jeremiah asked, horrified.

"Oh, indeed. Sometimes, when the captain and the crew are following orders to plunder a ship, those being plundered will use countermeasures. Securing the hammocks around the edges of the ship won't repel musket balls, but they can help deflect the grenades and the stinkpots."

Jeremiah didn't ask — he didn't want to know any more.

They exited the small sleeping room and proceeded down a short, narrow corridor to another set of stairs.

"Follow me down to the ship's hold," said Augustus.

They climbed down another set of stairs and landed in the ship's hold. It was damp and the water splashed against the outer wall next to them. Jeremiah stared down another long corridor. To his left were several rooms, each spaced about ten feet apart. It was musty and dark down below and he heard strange moans, echoes and pops. The light from above barely filtered through the cracks in the boards. There was little visibility. They heard the footsteps of the crew above them. A large rodent ran down the corridor in front of them.

"Might as well get used to the rats," Augustus snickered. "We're infested with them down here."

"Wonderful," said Jeremiah. "They seem to be everywhere I go."

A tall man walked out of the adjacent room, alarming them. "Oops, didn't mean to scare ye," he said pleasantly.

"This is Midget," said Augustus. "He's our cooper... and he's on our team."

"Your team?" Jeremiah asked.

"Coconut," responded the tall, lanky man. "A game we play aboard the ship. You'll see soon enough," he said.

Jeremiah watched as he walked away. Midget seemed nice enough, but why he was given that name was beyond him. He was as lanky as a cornstalk and a midget he was most certainly not. But he was friendly, nonetheless. And Jeremiah's curiosity was peaked by this game called 'coconut'.

They continued down the corridor and entered the next room on the left. It was filled from floor to ceiling with a bundle of barrels. A narrow path lay between them.

"These barrels hold our water, ale, flour and salted meat. We keep some fruit in here for scurvy prevention, but it always seems to go bad quickly." He pointed to another set of smaller sized barrels.

"And those are the crew's treasure," he laughed. "Full of wine and brandy. They'd be lost without those."

"Couldn't imagine," Jeremiah replied sarcastically.

"This next room holds all of our gunpowder," Augustus said as they continued down the poorly lit hallway. "Make sure you never hold a light down in this area. We'd all surely go out with a bang," he snickered. "Below your feet is the ship's ballast. Down there we have the weight of the ship... extra cannons, stone and anything else that'll help keep us upright. Not many venture down in that part."

"How long have you been aboard the *Nante*?" Jeremiah asked.

"Two years now. My father sent me off for work."

"You didn't come aboard on your own accord?"

"Are you kidding?" he laughed. "I wanted to become a writer, but my father felt my ideas were ridiculous and sent me away. He was a friend of the Captain's and I didn't have much voice in the matter."

"Sorry to hear that."

"No, don't be. It's a way of life for me now. And everyone has been most accepting. Well, that is except for Ranjit... and Lothar."

"Lothar?"

"Yes... the gunner. A sniveling rat if you ask me. He likes to run to Ranjit and report on others... trying to earn himself a leg up with the quartermaster. He's on Ranjit's team in coconut. They're a difficult pair to beat, those two. But mind yourself around him — he'll be watching to rat on you too. He preys on new crew."

"Thanks for the warning," Jeremiah said as they walked down the narrow hallway. "This game of coconut... what is it?"

"A game some of us play to pass the time while on the water. Only a few of us do it; the others watch and egg it on. It can be dangerous."

"Who plays?" His curiosity was getting the better of him.

"Four per team. On our team it is me, Midget, Belcher the cook, and Orville the helmsman. On theirs is Ranjit, Lothar, and a variety of others — whoever they can sucker to team with them from the crew," he continued. "It typically doesn't matter who else they have though. Ranjit and Lothar together make strong competition. I swear sometimes their nastiness is what makes them so good. We never have beaten them, but we love to play, so we continue to do so when given the chance. Breaks the monotony of everyday life on the water."

"Well, who might this be?" asked a short man as he approached from the last room on the right. "I heard you two talking down the hallway and was a wondering who was down here with me."

"Belcher, this is Jeremiah," said Augustus. "He's the captain's new cabin boy."

"Nice to meet you, Jeremiah," said Belcher as he looked up to Jeremiah. "I'm the cook." He let out a terrible, offensive-smelling burp.

"I see where you get the name," Jeremiah giggled.

"Sorry. I have a difficult time controlling it sometimes," Belcher said, embarrassed.

"Nasty as always, Cook," Augustus laughed.

"Well, must retreat to the kitchen, but it was nice meeting you Jeremiah. Need to finish cooking the crew's dinner."

"He turned away to finish in the kitchen, but bumped into a wall of a man standing behind him.

"Oh, sorry Ranjit... didn't see you standing there," said Belcher. He shuffled around the quartermaster to return to the kitchen. It seemed to Jeremiah that he wanted to avoid conflict.

"What's going on down here?" Ranjit asked. Lothar was right at his side.

Augustus spoke up. "I am showing the new cabin boy around. The captain is fully aware."

"Are ye now?" he scoffed. "Ye hurry and finish now... the deck is in need of a good swabbing."

"We'll be done shortly," Jeremiah said to him defensively.

"What did ye say, cabin boy?" he snarled. "Did ye just address me?"

Jeremiah didn't answer back and Ranjit grabbed him by the collar of his shirt. "Do we have a problem, cabin boy?"

Jeremiah looked at him square in the eyes. Ranjit let go of him and Jeremiah yanked away. As he followed Augustus back to the upper deck, Augustus turned and gave him a look of approval for his short, gutsy comeback.

"This game you all play," said Jeremiah.

"Yes?" Augustus asked.

"I think I just may be interested too," he said defiantly.

They walked across the deck and Augustus returned to his duties while Jeremiah stepped up to the bow of the ship.

He rested his hands upon the rails and gazed over the flat, barren ocean to the horizon. He prayed he would see *The Majestic* appear in the distant waters. He wondered what he had done in this life that caused him to endure the ill-laden fate of losing both his parents. Despite his present company, he felt alone, and his heart ached for his father. He had no idea who he was, where he was going, or what his future now held. He tasted the salty air and listened to the seagulls swarming above him as he closed his eyes and prayed.

"Did ye get introduced?" asked Van Russel, stepping up beside him.

"Yes, Captain... to several of the crew anyway."

"I can tell yer down. Would ye like to talk?" he asked in a fatherly way.

"What do you think became of my father, Captain?"

"I believe they probably got caught up in a storm. So unfortunate and I hate it for ye."

"Do you think *it* was quick?"

"Aye. I'm quite sure it was quick," he said. "Why don't ye rest tonight? Tomorrow we'll review ye duties as me cabin boy."

A bell rang loudly over the surface of the ship.

"It appears our meal is ready. Come and eat with the captain tonight," Van Russel said to him.

Jeremiah followed him to the great cabin where he shared the space with the crew for meals. Van Russel informed him that, due to the size of the crew, they'd break off in four groups — each consisting of about eighteen to twenty crewmembers. They'd rotate turns on who'd eat in the great cabin and tonight it was Van Russel, Jeremiah and several others from their group, including Augustus. Jeremiah pulled up a chair between him and Van Russel. The remaining crewmembers could eat on deck — or wait for their group's turn in the great cabin.

"And what might ye be gracing us with off the menu tonight?" Van Russel asked Belcher.

"Salmagundi and biscuits," he replied. "And I've concocted ye all a special drink tonight… glogg," he smiled. "We've got a new crew member on board tonight and I figured we'd break him in with our specialties." The crew in the cabin hooted joyously.

"Aye, a fine choice Belcher," agreed Van Russel.

"Salmagundi?" Jeremiah turned to Augustus.

"A mixture of things," he replied excitedly. "It's not often we get that. It's usually just biscuits and half-starving, not salmagundi and glogg."

"Glogg?"

"Just wait!" Augustus said to him giggling. "You'll see."

Van Russel whispered, "Jeremiah, salmagundi is a mix of meats: turtle, fish, chicken, pork. And Belcher throws in some fruit and vegetables when they haven't gone bad. Usually it's eggs, grapes, mangos, whatever he can find to throw in that thar pot," he snickered. "Then it's covered in salt and pepper and sprinkled with a bit of oil and wine, right before it's served up to ye, of course."

"And a right fine meal at that," piped in Midget, directly across the table. He appeared as excited as the rest of them.

Belcher brought their food to the table: a bowl full of biscuits, plates with servings of salmagundi, and a large bowl full of liquid. He carried it carefully to the table.

"Yer glogg is served," he said with a smile.

Jeremiah received his plate and took a bite of the salmagundi — he was starving. He started chewing it and noticed the crew watching him intensely. He felt unsure as he put it in his mouth but was surprised as he began chewing. He started coughing from the strength of it and the room roared with laughter.

"Ye'll get used to it... need to acquire a taste for it, apparently," laughed Van Russel.

"I did add some garlic and mustard seeds this time, but it should still be alright," said Belcher.

"Belcher, ye did great," said Van Russel. "He's just never eaten it."

The men passed the bowl of glogg around and drank heartily. They handed it to Jeremiah and he sipped just a drop from it. He let it sit on his tongue for a moment and noted the reactions of his crewmembers.

He thought it tasted incredible! He followed with a heavy swig and passed it to Augustus, who readily drank three times what he was able to swallow.

He grabbed a hard roll from the bowl, but just as he was about to bite into it, he noticed something moving on it. "What is that moving?" he blurted.

Augustus leaned over to see. "Oh, that's just a weevil maggot, a bug that gets in our bread."

Jeremiah was mortified. The room burst out in another roll of laughter as they watched him react.

"Just flick it off," said Augustus. He apparently wasn't fazed by the bugs in the bread, nor was anyone else.

Jeremiah looked closer. It was small and oblong with a black head and it wiggled and writhed in the indentation on his biscuit. He flicked it off, and it landed on the table in front of him. A knife came crashing down after it hit.

"There," said Van Russel. "I killed it. Now you can eat yer bread." He took a bite of the biscuit and chewed insistently.

"Pass me the bowl!" he ordered. His shipmates laughed hysterically. Jeremiah couldn't help but laugh with them as they finished the feast.

After dinner, Jeremiah fell exhausted into his hammock. His stomach was full from the feast and his lips still tasted of the sweet glogg. The room spun around him as he tried to relax to the sounds of his new shipmates playing a game of cards at a small, rickety table within the sleeping quarters. The booze was playing them better than they were playing the cards and they laughed and yelled as the night drew on.

Augustus was asleep below him. His larger dose of glogg had already completely worked its evil upon him — it had thrown him into a helpless state an hour earlier. His snores were loud and obnoxious, but unnoticed by his crewmates who were completely absorbed by their game.

Jeremiah closed his eyes and stretched in his hammock. As he drifted off to sleep, he reviewed the day's events in his mind and couldn't help but replay scenario after scenario of his father's fate: had it been quick, or one of slow, torturous misery?

CHAPTER EIGHT

The Secret Meeting

They had drifted far off course. Their target fishing location was a few hundred miles away and they were helpless. *The Majestic's* compass wasn't working and they used the moon and the constellations at night as their only navigation. It really made no difference though — the mainsail was ripped beyond repair and no one had thought to stock a replacement before they'd set out on this miserable trip. They had been drifting for weeks and the food supply on board was down to nearly nothing. There was only enough water for another day, possibly two, if they rationed it to the very last drop. The crew's mouths were parched and their stomachs cramped from hunger.

Father stood off the bow of the ship. He scanned the horizon for a hopeful glimpse of another ship that could save them.

He observed the dark, low-lying clouds quickly approaching them on the port side.

Wiley walked up beside him.

"I shouldn't have ever left him," he said sadly. "We should have been home weeks ago."

"You were trying to earn a living, Jonathon... no harm in that," said Wiley.

"He must be beside himself. I know my son," he said as he rubbed his head and struggled to think of a solution. "If only there was a way to let him know..."

The wind was picking up and the water moved roughly as it slapped against the side of the ship. The sinister clouds were swiftly approaching and Wiley called out to the men on board. "Looks like we're about to face a rough one, gents!"

The men scurried around on deck securing the rigging and the smaller sails that were still functional. Some of them tied ropes around their waists — anticipating what they knew was coming.

Father stayed at the front of the ship. He hardly seemed affected by the storm brewing around him.

Within minutes the waves were mounting. Some of the swells were topping fifteen to twenty feet and they tossed *The Majestic* around in the water like a twig in a small, brackish stream. Their undersized fishing boat rocked one moment and shifted backwards the next at the mercy of the thunderous storm. The rain poured down upon them and they struggled to stay standing on deck as one large wave after another came barreling over the ship's sides.

Father turned to find Wiley, but his friend was at the other end of the ship, tying himself to the mizzenmast. Father struggled to maintain his balance amidst the constant bucking of the ship in the water and he advanced slowly aft.

"Secure yourself! Tie a rope!" they screamed at him. But it was no use — his terror intensified as he progressed slowly across the deck. The crew watched in horror as a monstrous swell began growing off the starboard side. It must have been fifty feet high and it came rising out of the water directly towards them.

Father turned to see the annihilating wave when it was but seconds from crashing down upon them. It shifted the boat to a forty-five degree angle and he looked up at its crest curling over the top of them. "JEREMIAH!" he screamed.

"Father!" Jeremiah cried as he sat straight up in his hammock. He looked around — it was nothing but a horrible dream. His shipmates were still playing their game of cards and Augustus was still underneath him snoring magnificently.

Jeremiah sweated and his pulse bounded. His hands were as wet as his shirt and he flopped back on the hammock, sighing with relief.

He felt beside him for the cloth bag that held his belongings. He untied the linen case and he searched inside for the one item he needed — the leather journal. He could think of nothing else he wanted to do other than read it right now. It might help him take his mind away from the other.

The lighting in their sleeping quarters was poor, but with enough squinting and steady concentration, he would be able to read another of Daniels's chapters. He grabbed the worn journal and shifted himself in his bunk just enough to allow some light to better illuminate his reading. He opened the journal to the front and turned a couple pages to where he last left off. Soon he was immersed in Daniels's entry with no awareness of the others in the room with him...

October 4th, 1721
Tortuga

It was known as one of the most notorious pirate havens and buccaneer breeding grounds around. It was a place where men spoiled in their obnoxious affairs and where wickedness ran amuck. It was a boozing city where just about anything would go. It did provide defensible harbors from the military, however, and sailors as well as thieves would come here for refuge from the navy, the open ocean and the most wanted lists.

There were no pirate hangings, prisons, or gallows waiting for the criminals here. This was their home. Few here didn't have a nasty record or a bounty party searching for them, but here, they knew they were safe.

This night seemed no different from any other. It was loud and obnoxious and the coastline was crammed with every type of ship imaginable. Most had to moor far out and row into the grand pirate city.

Daniels hopped aboard a transporting vessel after he landed from his last naval stint aboard the *Contender*. Of course, he knew better than to don the clothes issued to him by the government, so he chose some garments that allowed him to arrive with more anonymity.

After the vessel anchored in the waters close to Tortuga, Daniels climbed into a dinghy with a crewmember from the transporting vessel and they rowed towards shore.

They landed at dock number eight and Daniels stepped out and flipped the other man a coin. He stood on the dock and tried to get his bearings. He had been here once before, but many years prior, and his memories did not match up to what he saw now. There had been some significant growth in Tortuga and he was a little unsure as to where the meeting would take place. The noise from the nearby streets filtered out to the water's edge.

He pulled a small piece of parchment from his pocket. It had been attached to the urgent letter he had received while on duty with the *Contender*. It wasn't very descriptive, but read:

MEETING:

SS OSIRON

OCTOBER 4TH

2200 HOURS

THE TAVERN

"They could have been a little more informative with their message," he mumbled to himself. He realized well enough that this meeting was important and probably even secret in nature, but a little more specification would have made things much easier. He hadn't a clue as to which tavern he was expected to be at — Tortuga was infested with many of them.

He just celebrated his fortieth birthday and was in the best shape of his life — the navy could hold credit for that. His brown hair was neatly combed and slicked back and he wore white calico trousers and a slightly oversized gray jacket. Around his waist a red silk sash was secured — the perfect attire for setting foot ashore here.

The ladies on Tortuga Lane seemed to find particular interest in him. They wooed and taunted him as he strolled by. They called to him from their balconies and they approached him from the roads. But little were they aware, this man's intent could not be faltered. He was here for one reason and one reason only. And he wasn't sure yet if coming here was a good idea at all. He looked carefully at all of the businesses, bars and havens lined up on the old, stone streets. Many a tavern existed here, but none specifically that really seemed to draw his attention. They were known by many different names, but none was called just 'The Tavern'.

One young, blonde lass leaned up against him as he approached a congested part of the street. Her face was hard, but she had a beautiful air about her.

"You look lost, honey. Do you need my help?" she slurred, the smell of ale upon her breath.

"Do ye know of a place that goes by the name, *The Tavern?*" he asked, skeptical that she would be of any real help to him.

"Oh yes," she said, "It's down through there." She pointed to a dark alley a short distance from the crowds of people. It appeared extremely uninviting and his gut told him it was a set up.

"Down there?" he asked. The noise around them was unbearable and he could hardly hear her responses.

"Yes," she giggled, pushing her bodice close to him.

"Ah, no thanks. I think I'll try finding it on me own." He pulled away from her and pushed his way through the crowd.

He walked up to another bar. *The Bar* was the only description on the sign in front of it. This was the closest thing he had found so far, but felt it really wasn't the place. He looked through the windows and the interior seemed no different than any other. Men and women sat around inside, boozing and enjoying the night's activities. Its patrons bore no particular interest with him and he knew he must continue searching.

As he pulled away he noticed a female watching him in the reflection of the window. She stood directly behind him and he turned to her. It was the same blonde lass that had offered him directions just a few minutes prior.

"You look lost, honey. Do you need my help?" she asked again. This time she stood with her hands on her hips and her voice was a little less slurred.

"Ma'am, I don't mean to be rude, but I've already told ye no. Thank ye anyway," he replied sternly.

However, as he watched her, the less intoxicated she seemed and she appeared to be waiting for his acknowledgement. She stayed in the same position, her hands still on her hips. He looked around. Was this a set up? Was she with someone else? Were they planning on dropping him in the dark, unwelcoming alley?

"I'm looking for a place known as *The Tavern*," he said again.

"Oh yes, it's down through there," she replied, pointing to the dark alley again. "Would you like my company?" she asked suggestively.

"Actually, that may not be a bad idea at all," he replied, figuring out that there was more to this, and her, than met the eye.

He held out his arm and she took hold of it. She played the part well he noticed — she immediately returned to a state of drunken stupor as they walked towards the dark, unwelcoming alley.

"Now play along," she whispered insistently. They were at the entrance of the alley and she threw herself upon him, grabbing him around the neck and giving him a close peck on the cheek. "Carry me in farther," she urged.

Daniels grabbed her around the waist and walked about ten steps into the darkness of the alley. They were now hidden from sight of the bustling activity just yards away from them and as far as the patrons were concerned, they were two young lovers amongst the many others on the streets.

"Didn't think I was going to be able to coax you into coming with me," she said, turning and walking away from him. "Follow me." She picked up her pace and moved quickly down the alley.

"So, who are ye?" he asked, trotting close behind her.

"The owner of *The Tavern*," she replied.

"But —"

"How did I know of you?" she asked. "Because I know of every meeting that takes place in my domain. I had a description of you and I knew the time that you would be arriving. It's not always that difficult to pick out those that don't seem to quite fit the mold here."

He thought he was fitting in nicely. "Did Osiron give ye this information?"

"Of course!" she smiled, looking back at him.

She stopped abruptly in front of a large, iron door. There was no handle on its exterior and she banged three times on the outside. A small, sliding partition opened and a pair of dark, beady eyes stared through it.

"It's me," she said firmly.

The door began opening and shrilled a terrible racket as it parted enough for the two to enter.

"Come on in," she instructed.

It appeared normal inside. The lighting was poor, however, and Daniels had difficulty discerning what lay in the dark corners of the mysterious room. There was a bar, many tables sitting empty about the room, and a bartender. He was who'd opened the door and he walked over to Daniels as he took a seat.

"What be yer poison tonight, sir?" he asked. His tone was deep, but welcoming.

"The strongest ale ye can muster," Daniels replied.

He watched the man walk away to serve up his brew and he noticed there were no windows on any of the walls. In fact, the only exit besides the huge iron door was a stairwell at the back of the bar.

"I know, the place is a little closed off," said the woman, carrying his glass of brown ale. "It has to be that way if the room is to continue being a secret meeting place for some."

"Of course," replied Daniels, marveling in the strength of the Tortugan beer. "And how did you get to be a part of this?" he asked her.

"One of the Society's members is a good acquaintance of mine. Other than that, I know nothing of its dealings... nor the dealings of any other meetings that take place here."

There was a loud knocking on the iron door and she hurried off to answer it. Three individuals entered — they were all wearing dark cloaks and their faces were hidden inside them. The owner spoke with them briefly before exiting down the stairwell behind the bar, along with the bartender.

The three turned towards Daniels. He was watching them too as he took hefty swigs from his glass. Each took a chair at his table.

"Are you Daniels?" asked one male voice.

"I am," he replied, looking around at each of them.

They wouldn't remove their cloaks and even with them so close, their faces were indiscernible in the poor light. No doubt it was intended to be that way. Each of them had something covering their mouths — probably a device to muffle or disguise their voices.

"I assume ye are the ones that sent me the letter requesting me attendance," he commented.

"Yes, we are the Society of Osiron and we have specially requested you to be here tonight," said the male voice. The other two sat quietly.

There was a long pause. "And ye need me for...?" Daniels asked, taking another swig from his glass.

"We have business of an extremely urgent nature that we need your assistance with," replied a female voice sitting next to him.

"Assistance?" he asked.

"Are you, by chance, aware of the many ships in these areas that have gone missing over the last year or two?" asked one of the men.

"I'm not meaning to be rude, but could ye show me yer faces or tell me yer names?" Daniels asked, aggravated. "Ye have requested me to come all this way and I am speaking with three individuals that I know nothing about, other than the fact that ye call yerselves the Society of Osiron. And what's up with the secretive garments?"

"I do apologize," said one of the men. "I should have entertained you with better introductions. You may refer to me as the Alchemist. The quiet gentleman sitting across the table from you is known as the Forger and the young lady to your right is the Candle Maker. We have another in our group — the Director — but he was unable to attend tonight."

Daniels laughed. "I'm sorry, but this is a bit much. Is this some idea of a joke?" he asked.

The man's voice deepened. "This is no joke."

Daniels felt the seriousness from the man speaking to him. "I apologize. I meant no insult by that. Please tell me what ye need from me."

"Do you not have a significant past that included thieving and the masterful yielding of a sword?" he asked.

"Ah, so that is it," he replied. "I figured this had nothing more to do than something associated with me past. I assure ye those days are behind me and I am now active in the Navy and the…"

"SILENCE!" the Alchemist yelled. "We are here on serious business and if you won't take the time to hear what we have to request, we will be on our way," he said firmly.

Daniels said nothing.

"Again, are you familiar with the disappearance of ships in these areas over the last year or two?" asked the Alchemist.

"Of course," Daniels said. "The Navy has investigated some of them but we have been unable to turn up anything."

"And you won't turn up anything," replied the Alchemist. "Let me explain to you what has been happening and why you have been requested here. As you know, we are the Society of Osiron, sometimes referred to as The Secret Society of Osiron. There are four of us and we operate underground — or in disguise, you might say, probing for information and distributing information in regards to the ship disappearances and the many bodies that have been found in the back alleys of Gordington Square. Not too long ago we were able to verify who was behind these murders and disappearances. Let me just say, it happens to be someone I am familiarly acquainted with."

"Alright, but I am a little confused as to why ye are seeking out me alone. Why didn't ye let the Navy know this before now and we'd have sent the entire naval fleet after them?" Daniels asked.

"Because the entire naval fleet would have been destroyed as well if we had requested them for such a futile task," interjected the Forger.

"And this job we are requesting of you can only be done by one," added the Candle Maker.

"By one?" Daniels asked, dumbfounded. "And the job would be?"

"To steal an amulet," said the Alchemist.

CHAPTER NINE

The Game
Revealed

B*ang!* The door to the sleeping quarters slammed closed.

"What was that?" Jeremiah rose quickly from his hammock, interrupted from his reading.

"Ranjit... pissed off," said a voice below him.

Jeremiah looked down over the side of his hammock. "Well, Augustus wakes from his eternal slumber finally," he laughed. "Why was Ranjit angry this time?" he asked, unsurprised.

"He lost in the game of cards," said Augustus. They both snickered.

"I take it our beloved quartermaster never loses?" said Jeremiah.

"Never," said Augustus. "Well, I am turning back in. Have a good night Jeremiah."

"You too." Jeremiah rolled over to his back and looked at the plank boards above him. The room was now dark. The crew just put out the candles for the night and he had no way to finish his reading — he was not sleepy. He tried carefully to climb from his hammock and not land on already sleeping Augustus. He crept out of the sleeping quarters and up the small ladder that led to the main deck.

The main deck was empty and silent. Everyone had turned in for the night — even the watch, for there really wasn't much of a need now while the ship was docked. Jeremiah moved over to the starboard side and peered down into the water. The night was cloudy, but the moon occasionally peeked out and Jeremiah watched its reflection show up in the rippled water below. The light breeze felt pleasant.

He could see light in the captain's cabin at the opposite end of the ship. Van Russel must still have been awake. He saw an occasional shadowing of the light, and then lightening — a sure sign that someone was moving around and in front of the lantern.

Life aboard the ship was very new for him. Unsure if he totally accepted it yet or not, it was what was dealt to him. If he'd had his druthers, he would have been in a totally different place around a totally different group of people — but he knew that wasn't an option now. At least everyone here seemed to accept him up to this point. Perhaps not the quartermaster, but he appeared to be that way with most.

He was happy he'd made a friend. Augustus, in some ways, was just as he was: quiet, lonely and scared. But he knew he was accepted by the swabbie and he accepted him in return.

Jeremiah gazed upon the ship. He anxiously awaited this game of coconut. He loved games, but was a little taken back by the comments of Ranjit and his leech, Lothar. Were they so difficult to beat because they were really so good? He wondered that maybe they just hadn't met their match yet. He had no idea what the game even entailed, so his curiosity was piqued even further.

He heard footsteps coming down the dock and he snuck across to take a peak. He couldn't tell who it was, but it was obvious he was headed to the *Nante*. Who would be coming aboard at this time of night?

The person walked to the ramp leading up from the dock and boarded the ship close to the captain's cabin. Jeremiah knew he couldn't be seen — it was dark where he was crouching and he was easily camouflaged against the ship. The man knocked on Van Russel's cabin door.

Van Russel was awake. He opened the door soon after and allowed the unknown visitor to enter. Jeremiah heard talking, but it was muffled. Nosiness quickly got the better of him and he scooted along the ship's railing until he was within earshot.

"And what is the urgent matter he is needing me for?" asked Van Russel.

The man replied, "He did not make me aware, Captain. The only information I received was that I was to come and find you and ensure that you arrived promptly at eight o'clock in his office in the morning."

"Eight o'clock, eh?"

"Yes sir, eight o'clock."

"That'll be fine. I'll be there," said Van Russel.

Jeremiah ducked behind the windlass as the door reopened. He heard the man's footsteps leaving. Van Russel exited his cabin, smoking on a pipe.

"Lad, ye can come out of hiding," Van Russel snickered.

Jeremiah rose from behind the windlass. "How did you know I was here?"

"A good captain always knows what's happening on his ship," he said. "Come over here and let's visit a bit. Yer obviously no sleepier on this night than I am."

They stepped in and Van Russel took a seat behind his desk. Jeremiah sat on a barrel to the right of it. Van Russel threw his feet up on top of it; leaning back and taking a long draw from his pipe.

"Ah… now this is a bit more like it, don't ye agree?" he asked.

Jeremiah smiled, his hands resting beside him on the barrel. "Absolutely, sir."

"One matter at hand I needed to discuss with ye is yer new duties on board me ship."

"Oh, yes." Jeremiah readily agreed. He wanted to work — he had been accustomed to it from a very young age.

"Well, a cabin boy's duties aren't that difficult really. Yer more or less me assistant, or me fetch-and-go."

"Fetch and go?" said Jeremiah, confused.

"Aye," Van Russel smiled, "I request and ye fetch and go."

Jeremiah laughed. "That doesn't sound terribly hard."

"Not at all."

Van Russel reached down to the chest beside him and opened the lid. He removed a bottle of brandy from his hidden stash. He uncorked the bottle and poured it in a small pewter cup sitting on his desk. "Ye?" he asked, holding up the bottle and offering Jeremiah some.

Jeremiah shook his head with disgust.

"Smart lad," he chuckled. He took a small drink and closed his eyes. A mischievous grin crossed his face. He swished it in his mouth and took a loud gulp afterwards.

Jeremiah snickered.

"Gotta love the brandy," he commented.

Jeremiah took notice of a shelf on the wall behind Van Russel. He hadn't paid it any special attention the first time he visited his cabin, but it took his interest now. Van Russel turned around.

"Oh, so yer interested in Coconut, eh?" he asked.

Jeremiah nodded excitedly. "Yes, I keep hearing about it. Are those the ones used in the game?"

"That they are."

"Will you tell me about the game, Captain?"

"So ye want to know about Coconut, eh?" he asked again, toying with Jeremiah. It was odd how no one really would talk about it, besides the fact that it was a game they played on board.

"Yes, yes!" he said excitedly. "Please tell me!"

"Oh, alright. It's nothing real spectacular, just a game we play on board when we're out at sea. Most just watch for the entertainment."

"I heard that only four play on each team," said Jeremiah.

"Correct," said Van Russel. "Now, the game has three parts. First, the betting; each team of four bets what they are going to play for. Sometimes it is their chores upon the ship, other times it is their wages that they'll make after they get off the ship. As ye can probably imagine, it's usually the chores," he continued. "Secondly, is the coconut dive. These eight coconuts sitting behind me are weighted. There are four different weights in the coconuts and there are two coconuts with each weight." He smiled widely. "Now, this is where it becomes really entertaining. Each team of four players goes to each side of me ship and lines up. Each of the team members has already agreed at this point which weight they will challenge. The four coconuts are lined up on both sides of the ship, in order of weight, and then they are released, simultaneously, into the water. As ye can imagine, those heavier coconuts sink faster and are more of a challenge for the person diving after them. The lighter coconuts are usually retrieved by those less capable swimmers."

Jeremiah interrupted, "They go after them?"

"Yes!" Van Russel laughed. "That's the fun of it, at least for the crew. After the coconuts are released, the entire crew counts out loud to ten. When ten is reached, all eight players dive in after the coconuts."

"So what is the purpose of the line attached to them?"

"So we can retrieve them if the player can't! The lines can be a bit dangerous too. Once, we almost had a sailor drown when he got caught up in it. So, we have a scorekeeper and he watches from up on the crow's nest and keeps track of who comes up with their coconut first. The first coconut to be returned to deck gets a score of eight. The second, seven... all the way down to the last coconut with a score of one."

"Sounds exciting enough," said Jeremiah.

"Ah, but it gets better, lad. The third, and final, part of the game is shooting the coconuts." He took another draw on his pipe.

"Shooting?" Jeremiah asked, enthralled with the concept. Van Russel had his cabin boy's undivided attention.

"Alright. The highest scorers from the coconut dive on each team are the ones designated to shoot the coconuts. Did you by chance see the catapult sitting below deck?"

Jeremiah nodded.

"Well not only do we use it during our battling with other ships, it is used for coconut. The player from each team is given four coconuts each. They are loaded one at a time and fired into the air off the side of the ship. It is the player's responsibility to shoot the coconut before it hits the water. One team gets a shot and then the next team gets a shot. We swap turns back and forth until all eight coconuts are either shot, or floating away in the water," he grinned mischievously.

"And how many points do you get for shooting each coconut?" Jeremiah asked, amazed at Van Russel's game summary.

"One point per coconut that ye shoot successfully. After all eight have been catapulted, the scorekeeper tallies up the total points for each team and announces the winning team from the crow's nest high above."

"Are the pistols or the muskets given to the players shooting the coconut?" asked Jeremiah.

"Nope. Only pistols are used and ye use yer own."

Jeremiah was fascinated already and he couldn't wait to watch his first game of coconut. Maybe he could play if someone would be willing to allow him the chance. He would love to be on Belcher and Augustus's team, but would adamantly refuse if approached by Ranjit. He knew the quartermaster probably wouldn't want him anyway.

"Sound interesting to ye?" Van Russel asked.

"Sounds positively brilliant."

"Well, I'm gonna have ye run along now. The captain has a meeting he must be in attendance at in the morning and I'm gonna get meself a quick wink or two."

"Goodnight sir," Jeremiah replied, and headed back to his own hammock to turn in for the night.

CHAPTER TEN

THE
MISSION

A wooden clock mounted to the governor's wall chimed on the eight o'clock hour and Van Russel, being persistently punctual, walked in the door.

The governor slammed his fists upon the desk. "THIS IS AN OUTRAGE! AND THIS HAS CARRIED ON FOR ENTIRELY TOO LONG! I was contacted by the Admiral yesterday to commission you and your men to capture them, kill them — whatever you have to do."

"Er... aye sir. I understand sir," replied Van Russel. He played with his mustache, twisting the ends nervously while the round, dumpy governor carried on.

"Do you, Captain? Do you have any idea of what we are dealing with here? An entire navy crew was killed aboard the *Contender* a couple of days ago and the claims of what happened to them after they were killed are preposterous! And do you have any idea how many other ships have been missing, from this very port even?"

"Are ye sure these claims here are accurate… sir?" Van Russel asked, skeptical that the governor was overreacting again to some rumor he had misunderstood.

The governor rose from his chair. "Accurate? Are you kidding me, Captain? A lieutenant from the *Contender* was picked up yesterday. He was on his ship, alone, with the bodies of all his naval shipmates and his poor ole captain! Those corpses had fatal wounds from swords. Swords issues by the navy couldn't cause the destruction those did. Doc Hazleton has spent the entire night examining some of these bodies and he can't come up with anything logical."

Van Russel's eyes widened, "Doc Hazleton, eh? I see. Well, ye know the town doctor isn't exactly fruitful in his knowledge of things medical anyway, Governor," he suggested.

The governor glared at him.

"Never mind," he said. He knew the doctor was the governor's close friend.

"All of the lieutenant's accounts we believe to be true, "As preposterous as they may seem, and it would explain the disappearance of so many ships from these areas. This one was the first and only ship to be found. Why they didn't sink it or destroy it is anyone's guess. In fact, I suspect these scoundrels are behind the disappearance of a ship from here two weeks ago. *The Majestic,* I think it was called… are you familiar with it?"

"Um…aye… intimately, sir." Van Russel scratched his head, coming to the realization that this wasn't just another of the governor's typical nonsensical missions.

"Well, there'll be no delays, Captain. You and your crew are to head after these murderers — immediately. Capture them, kill them, I don't care! Bring them back to me, dead or alive."

Blessie perched nervously on Van Russel's shoulder. "Not a good idea," she squawked as she shuffled on her spot.

The governor had turned his back momentarily but whipped around at the bird's comment. "Shut that stupid bird up, Captain!" he roared furiously.

"Aye, Governor… sorry. Blessie, hold yer tongue." The parrot hushed, but continued a low mumbling back in Van Russel's ear. "Do we have any idea on their current whereabouts?"

"Their whereabouts? YOU IDIOT!" the governor screamed. "We have no idea who or *what* they even are! How on God's green earth would we know where they moor their ship?"

Van Russel lowered his voice to a near whisper. "Pardon me for asking, sir, but if a full naval crew couldn't defeat these obvious brutal assailants, how would ye expect me crew to successfully take them all down?"

"Well, I guess that is what you will figure out when you find them… Captain," he sneered. "Isn't that what you do best?"

"I mean no disrespect when I say this, sir, but I don't think that would be a good idea."

The governor leaned over his desk. "Well, how about this offer then, Captain. If you choose to go against the wishes of the Admiral and myself, I will be forced to pull your papers. We will redeem the *Nante's* Letter of Marque and will indict all of your crew for illegal piracy," he said evilly. "So if it's the pirates you fear, Captain, you can face the gallows instead."

"Aye, sir… understood," Van Russel grumbled.

He turned and left the office of the governor. Blessie was insistent on getting her word out too, but held back at the command of her captain. Van Russel knew Governor Addison had no idea what he was forcing the crew of the *Nante* up against. It was irrational decision-making such as this that had cost many other ill-fated seamen their lives over the course of the town's history. The governor licensed Van Russel and his crew to plunder other ships legally and he was the one that benefited the most from their plundering, as far as he knew anyway. By all accounts he was a pirate himself — forcing others to do his raiding and pillaging while he sat back in his cozy office chair reaping the rewards.

Van Russel stomped away from the governor's office and threw his arms about flamboyantly as he mocked the governor. "Called me bird stupid and he called me an idiot," he protested. "We'll show that wig-wearing twit who's stupid."

Van Russel had faith in his sailors, but this was one fight he knew they had no chance of winning. Knowing the governor, however, he would have his personal spies scouting in their secret dinghies watching him to ensure he was following through with his orders. The backstabbing governor would love to find a reason to try and convict Van Russel and his men, despite all they had done for him. Van Russel prayed that there would be no encounters with these heathens.

"Blessie doesn't like it," remarked the bird.

He looked up in her direction. "Aye, girl. The captain concurs."

Back on the *Nante*, Van Russel called his entire crew to the deck. They filtered up from every nook and cranny of the ship and assembled in front of their well-dressed and purported fearless leader.

"Me hearties!" Van Russel addressed the crew with a smile. "This morning we've been ordered on a mission…"

"A mission?" asked Ranjit, standing nearest to the captain. He shook his head.

"Aye, a mission…" Van Russel paused. "Here recently a naval ship was taken down, the entire crew, by pirates. They left only one soul alive and brutally killed all the others. We were ordered by the governor this morning to hunt them down and do whatever we have to do to bring them to justice."

"And who are these pirates?" one sailor asked amidst the crowd of men.

"That we are uncertain of," replied Van Russel.

"How many of them are there?" yelled another.

"That we are uncertain of as well."

"Do ye know their whereabouts?" asked another.

"That too… we are uncertain of," the captain answered. He raised his hand to his forehead and rubbed intensely, embarrassed in front of his crew.

Jeremiah and Augustus had just arrived to the rear of the crowd and sat side by side on the ship's rails trying to get a clear view of Van Russel and his address to the men. They strained their necks to see and hear what was happening.

"What's going on?" asked Jeremiah.

"Yer guess is as good as mine. Looks like we're headed for the open water again," Augustus replied.

Ranjit leaned over to Van Russel, "Captain, just what about this mission are ye certain of?"

"None of it," Van Russel returned in a whisper.

Ranjit motioned to him and Van Russel leaned close to his quartermaster. "Sir, what are ye doing? Do ye think we could have discussed this before presenting it to the entire crew?"

Van Russel muttered back to him as the gathering crowd of sailors watched. "We haven't been given a choice here. It's either leave port now for these killers or have us all face trial and the gallows."

Ranjit growled, "The governor and his threats again."

Distracted, Van Russel turned back to his crew. "Where was I?"

"Ye were saying something about a mission to catch pirates," one of the crewmen yelled. There was an immediate discussion and talking amongst the crew.

"I'm sorry, me hearties. The captain's afraid that he knows little more than ye at this point, but we must make sail immediately."

"Do what? What did he just say?" they yelled. Van Russel knew the *Nante's* crew wasn't any more prepared for this than he was and had planned on at least a day or two more of leisure in Gordington.

"Me apologies, men. The captain will try and make it up to ye at another time. But for now, we must sail. Drop the sails and hoist the anchor. We've got some pirates we're needing to bounty," he ordered.

With respect for their captain, the men rushed around on deck initiating their assigned duties. They hoisted the anchor and rolled down the sails. Some of the crew waved to their female friends walking daintily on the docks while others went below deck to air their frustrations privately regarding their orders. Most of the crew aboard the *Nante* knew they were at the mercy of the governor and his orders, despite how ridiculous they typically seemed.

The bell outside the captain's cabin rang, letting the crew and the nearby patrons know that the *Nante* was headed for the water again.

Jeremiah stood on the bow next to Van Russel. He waved to Ebineezer as the *Nante* slowly started moving from the dock.

"Don't leave! Where are ye going?" Ebineezer cried.

"We're on a mission!" The captain yelled back. "Ye can thank the wonderful governor for that!"

"The governor?" Ebineezer fumed. He glared towards the governor's building.

His window could easily be seen from the docks and he, too, had a clear view of everything coming and going. His dumpy figure silhouetted the office window. As soon as the *Nante* was on her way, his shadow vanished from sight.

"We'll be back soon, Mr. Drake," Jeremiah yelled, waving.

They were a couple of hours into their obligatory voyage and had no idea where they were headed. The governor had given Van Russel a slip of paper with the coordinates of the *Contender's* position when it had been savagely attacked. Van Russel pulled the parchment from his pocket and yelled to Jeremiah.

"Yes, Captain?"

"Lad, take these coordinates up to the wheel and give them to Orville."

"Yes, sir." Jeremiah hurried off to the other end of the ship and Van Russel turned and stared out over the water, sighing.

He was risking his crew against an unbeatable foe and had been forced to leave port before they could adequately stock additional food and water rations. His crew, in general, were angry and borderline defiant. "Probably setting meself up for a mutiny," he muttered, "and I couldn't say that I'd blame them."

"I disagree, sir. Your crew thinks better of you," said Jeremiah, who had returned to his side, unnoticed.

"Ah, thanks lad," said Van Russel. "Come take a stroll with me on the deck."

"The crew seem upset, sir, but I don't think it's necessarily with you," said Jeremiah as they walked.

"Aye, but they're unstable at this point... we all are for that matter," said Van Russel.

"Maybe you ought to offer them something to lift their spirits."

"And what might ye suggest?" asked Van Russel.

They stopped as Belcher walked in front of them holding a wooden crate on his way to the kitchen. He greeted them as he passed, but tripped clumsily on a deck board. The crate went flying out of his arms, burst open on the deck, and its coconut contents went rolling in all directions. One landed at Van Russel's feet and he picked it up, grinning widely at Jeremiah. Jeremiah looked back with fire in his eyes.

"Lad, ready for some coconut?"

"Never been more ready!" said Jeremiah.

"Well, do the captain a favor then. Run up there to me cabin and ring me bell, loudly."

"Certainly," said Jeremiah and he rushed off to the quarterdeck.

CHAPTER ELEVEN

COCONUT

Ding! Ding! Ding! Ding! Ding! In moments the bell penetrated every section of the ship, from the crow's nest to the bottom of the hold. The men all stopped what they were doing and reassembled on deck.

"Me hearties, we meet again," Van Russel addressed them, attempting to be coy. "Being as it is that we are out here on the water searching for God-knows-what, with no idea where it is that we are to be looking other than some ridiculous coordinates, yer captain figured it was time to take a break."

The men stood silently as Van Russel reached into his coat pocket and withdrew a coconut. He held it high above his head. "So, what does me crew think about a game of coconut?"

The crew roared intensely following their captain's suggestion. They stomped their feet on the deck, hooted and shouted, and began the betting for which they were notorious. After all, this gave them an opportunity to place their wagers too.

Jeremiah watched Ranjit on the upper deck. He had a look about him, devious and cunning. This was just another day he'd relish the demise of his mates, as he'd give up some chores or make a few coins by being victorious.

Van Russel raised his hand. "Now, we must assemble the teams. Would the four players from each side please come up front?"

Ranjit and Lothar assembled their pack to the right of Van Russel. This time they'd be taking Patch and Collins, two of the sail men, as their two additional players.

To Van Russel's left assembled Belcher and Augustus. Orville was still at the wheel ensuring the ship had completely stopped before coming down. They all looked around for Midget.

"Has anyone seen Midget?" asked Van Russel.

"Maybe he's repairing the ship," said one of the sailors.

"Bularkey, there's nothing needing repaired on me ship now," Van Russel quipped.

"He's ill, sir," said another of the crew, walking up to Van Russel.

"Ill?" Van Russel asked.

"Yes, fever, chills and sweating profusely, Captain," he replied. "He's pale in color and bleeding from the gums too."

"Nasty scurvy," said Van Russel. "Someone go tend to our cooper and ensure he gets plenty of the freshest fruit we have on board." He turned to Belcher and his group. "Well, gentlemen, it appears you are down a player. Care to recruit another?"

"Don't think we've much of a say in it," replied Belcher. He turned to the crew. "Is there anyone here willing to commit to our team today?"

A small hand rose near the back. Van Russel motioned for the crew to part so its owner could be seen. "And who might be taking the place of Midget today?" he pondered loudly.

It was Jeremiah. He looked silly and small next to the towering sailors, especially since he was volunteering to endure a game of coconut with Ranjit and his mates.

"Lad, are ye sure?" asked Van Russel cautiously.

"Absolutely," said Jeremiah. Some of the crew laughed and others roared with excitement.

Van Russel walked back out to the center. "Now teams, it must be decided what ye are willing to bet in today's game. Will it be chores or will it be coin?"

The excitement from the crew was deafening. Both teams conversed among themselves and returned their answer to Van Russel in a whisper. Van Russel whispered back to them and they continued these back and forth efforts until he nodded in agreement.

"So it has been decided," said Van Russel. "Both teams have agreed to relinquish two days worth of chores to the opposing side. The losing team will still be expected to finish their assigned duties on ship as well the new duties they will have picked up after today's game."

The crew went wild. They taunted the teams and stomped their feet on deck. They sang their shanties and shouted and cheered at each other. Ranjit and his team stood with arrogant confidence, their arms crossed and a look of glorious victory already on their smug faces. Augustus, Jeremiah, Belcher and Orville looked at one another. Worry that they had just destined themselves to two days worth of hard labor aboard the *Nante* showed on their faces. The appearance of their opponents and their unforgivable attitude was quite intimidating to them all.

Jeremiah addressed his side, "Well, should we lose today, I wanted to let you know that I appreciate you letting me be a part of your team. After all, it's just a game, right?"

They all stared at him, but no one answered.

Van Russel took the center again. "Now, we must address the assignments of coconut weights." He turned to Augustus. "Swabbie, didn't Midget always take yer heaviest weight?"

"Yes, sir… he did," Augustus replied. He turned around to his team. "What are we going to do? None of us have ever tried challenging Midget's coconut," he whispered frantically.

"That's right," said Orville. "The other weights we are used to are difficult enough… there's no way."

"Let me do it," Jeremiah whispered. "I can swim very well."

"It's not an issue of swimming," added Belcher. "How deep have you ever dived, Jeremiah? The first coconut drops fast and by the time they count to ten, you've got a long way to go to reach it."

"And then you've got the issue of carrying it back to the surface," whispered Augustus.

"You'll never beat them with attitude like that. Give me a chance… what's the worst that could happen?" Jeremiah shot back.

"Jeremiah will take coconut number one," Augustus announced, looking over at his friend.

Van Russel gazed at Jeremiah with a look of desperation. "So ye wanted to play… looks like you'll get yer chance," he commented, barely above a whisper. Jeremiah smiled back at him.

The *Nante's* crew roared. Although it was questionable how the new cabin boy would handle coconut number one, the excitement and anticipation of watching was more than they could bear.

Amidst the noise and commotion, the two teams lined up on the ship rails opposite one another. Next to each rail stood four crewmembers. Each held a coconut and trailing behind them, wound neatly on the deck, were long ropes. Should the teams fail to capture the coconuts, they could be retrieved by pulling in the ropes to which they were secured.

The teams removed their shirts. Unlike the coconuts, they had no safety harnesses or assurance ropes. If they did not return from their dives, it was utter hopelessness for them. Retrieving a sinking body was a hundred times more challenging than retrieving coconut number one.

The crew of the *Nante* placed their bets and yelled their wagers. They looked at the two assembled teams and concocted side wagers on the team members' proven abilities. The physiques of

Ranjit and his crew would engender the faith of even the dumbest betting man. In comparison, Jeremiah and his team looked pitiful.

Jeremiah looked around at the chanting, yelling crew. They climbed on the ratlines and they looked from the crow's nests. They positioned themselves from the upper deck and peered over the rails. He listened to the wagers being made. They collected their coin and made their bets. They wagered their chores and bet their belongings. Whatever they had available, this was the time that they'd gamble it all. He peered down at the water below him. It was a mystical blue and he could see deep down below to the reef, glistening from the light of the midday sun.

Ranjit glared at Jeremiah from the opposite side. An air of evil was again upon the quartermaster's face.

"Are we ready?" asked Van Russel.

"Not yet!" yelled Ranjit in his deep, hateful tone. "I'd like to make a side wager with your cabin boy."

Van Russel rolled his eyes. "And what side bet would ye be asking?" he said. Jeremiah watched with exasperation as he waited. He knew he had nothing to offer.

"I want his leather hat," Ranjit said with a nasty confidence.

"My hat?" Jeremiah asked in horror. He couldn't part with it — it was a gift from Mr. Dobbit back home.

"And what are ye willing to offer, Ranjit?" Van Russel asked.

"A silver piece of eight," he laughed.

The crew's excitement grew even stronger. Ranjit had his eyes on the hat ever since Jeremiah first boarded the *Nante*. Jeremiah

noticed Ranjit's arrogant pose as he waited for him to make his decision. "Do it, do it, do it!" the crew chanted and yelled.

Jeremiah nodded, giving in to the pressure from his new
peers.

"So it is done," said Van Russel, disheartened. "A side wager
of a coin and hat will be placed between Jeremiah and Ranjit. Scorekeeper, make sure ye add the bet."

The two teams stood on the rails waiting for the signal. The
bell soon rang and all at once the eight coconuts were dropped in to
the water. The entire crew started counting, "One… two… three…
four… five… six… seven… eight… nine… TEN!" All eight players
dove in to the water.

Jeremiah felt the cool ocean water encompass his face as he
entered. Never before had he tried swimming in salty water and as
he opened his eyes, they burned badly. He followed the rope trailing
from the coconut and swam straight down after it. He could hear
odd noises in the water around him, maybe the noise from the ship
above or just the phenomena of the ocean itself. Bubbles streamed
past his face as he dove deeper. The pressure increased quickly in
his head and chest. It was nearly unbearable. He squinted his eyes
tightly and could see the coconut dropping below him with great
speed. He kicked with all his might and pushed his arms in such a
way that he moved even faster towards it, until he was able to grip
it with both hands.

He turned to move in the other direction and shot his view
across the underside the ship. The water was so clear that he could

view the team on the other side of the boat diving after their coconuts. He could see Ranjit directly across from him, about thirty
yards away. He too had just retrieved his coconut and was looking in
Jeremiah's direction. When he noticed the boy had also captured his,
he quickly darted towards the surface.

Jeremiah did the same. He tucked the coconut under his
left arm and was careful to move away from the trailing rope so
he wouldn't become tangled. He kicked with all his remaining energy back towards the water's surface. The pressure in his chest was
increasing and his body strained to take a breath of air. Bubbles
streamed from the corners of his mouth as he struggled to reach the
surface. He could see the glossy under reflection of the surface and
he made one final bound, exploding through the surface of the water, gasping. He heard the crew scream "Seven!" He had reached the
surface immediately after Ranjit and was the second to reappear.

Jeremiah panted as he worked to catch his breath and settle
himself from the adrenaline pumping through his veins. He looked
around; none of his team had resurfaced yet either. He couldn't
see the team on the other side but heard the crew as they cheered
Lothar, coming in at number six. He looked around at the trailing
ropes leading to his friends' coconuts. A stream of bubbles surfaced
in the water next to him and Belcher came barreling up out of the
water with coconut in hand. He was gasping, but laughing.

"Five!" the crew yelled.

Orville popped up right behind him and was given number
four. He and Belcher swam over to Jeremiah congratulating him on

his glorious coconut retrieval. Though he could not see what was occurring on the other side, Jeremiah heard the crew roar as Patch and Collins resurfaced, capturing the scores of three and two. They were only waiting on Augustus.

"Where is he?" asked Jeremiah, worried.

"He's never taken this long," said Orville.

They began to dive after him, but noticed another drizzle of bubbles surfacing in the water near them.

"Here he comes!" the crew yelled. "We see him!"

Augustus surfaced, coughing and pleading for air. His right arm was empty as he rolled onto his back and floated momentarily, thankful to be alive.

The crew looking down on them had silenced, waiting to see if the swabbie had retrieved the last coconut.

Augustus reached down and lifted the coconut out of the water with his left arm and threw it on his chest.

"One!" the crew screamed in excitement.

Augustus's teammates breathed a sigh of relief knowing that he was safe and that he had retrieved the last coconut — even if it was for only one point.

Everyone waited anxiously for the scorekeeper to tally the scores before moving on to third and final phase of the game. If one team was more than four points behind, they would have to forfeit — for the most points they could accumulate in the final part would be four. All attention turned to the scorekeeper high up in the crow's nest.

His arm moved out to the direction of Ranjit and his team. "For this side… nineteen points!" he yelled. The crew stood silent as he added the others' scores. All bets were relying on these points. He gestured towards Jeremiah's team. "For this side… seventeen points!"

The crew roared with excitement. Musketoons fired and pistols blazed, sure signs as to what was to come next.

"Excellent job, gentlemen," said Orville. "And Jeremiah, you're beginning to amaze me. Have you ever fired a pistol?"

Jeremiah grinned mischievously.

Orville slapped him on the back. "Knock `em dead," he said proudly.

Jeremiah looked up at Van Russel. He was watching the game from the upper deck. He nodded in approval of what he had just witnessed.

A rope ladder dropped over the side of the ship and Jeremiah and his team climbed aboard to prepare for the final part of the game.

Four of the crew carried the heavy catapult across deck to the starboard side. Another carried a crate of coconuts and sat them beside the catapult.

"Now for the final phase of the game," Van Russel announced. "Jeremiah and Ranjit were the first from each of team to surface and they'll be the ones participating in the coconut shoot."

"This is extremely difficult, Jeremiah. Pistols aren't accurate and the coconuts aren't airborne for very long," Augustus said to him.

"It'll be fine, my friend," Jeremiah said confidently, loading his pistol.

"Ranjit was the first to surface and therefore will have the first shot in today's game," Van Russel announced.

The quartermaster walked up to the ship's edge and watched as the crew loaded the catapult with the first coconut. Lothar and the others grinned as they waited for their declaration of victory.

"Are you ready?" asked the one manning the catapult. Ranjit nodded and the crew grew silent. He held his pistol over the side of the ship waiting for the coconut to be expelled.

Thump!

The catapult fired the coconut into the open air. It arched about fifty feet above the water's surface and Ranjit lined it up in his sights. *BOOM!* He fired his pistol and Jeremiah and the others watched in amazement as his coconut shattered just feet above the water.

The crew hollered excitedly and exchanged wagers. Ranjit turned to Jeremiah, a look of masterful victory across his proud face.

Jeremiah's team huddled together. "You'll now have to hit every one of the coconuts, Jeremiah. No one has ever done that," said Augustus. Jeremiah nodded and walked to the rail.

"Are you ready?" asked the man. Jeremiah nodded.

Thump!

Jeremiah watched as the coconut climbed higher and higher, until it reached its peak and began to drop. He held his pistol in front of him and… *BOOM!* He blew the coconut into oblivion high above the water.

The crew was becoming uncontrollable. Never before had coconut caused this level of excitement on the ship.

"The scorekeeper yelled down, "Ranjit… twenty. Jeremiah… eighteen."

Ranjit appeared furious that the new cabin boy had hit his first coconut. He positioned himself again and waited for his next.

"Are you ready?"

"Just fire the stupid thing!" yelled Ranjit.

Thump! His coconut rocketed out and he lined it up in his sights. *BOOM!* His pistol fired and his musket ball went blasting towards the mid-air coconut. It missed and the coconut splashed into the water yards away from the ship.

The echoing jeers and laughter from the ship infuriated him and he stormed off as Jeremiah took his stance.

Jeremiah looked down at his pistol and ensured everything had been reloaded just the way he had been taught. He looked up to the man controlling the catapult.

"Are you ready?"

Jeremiah smiled.

Thump! His coconut took a different turn, arching over towards the front of the ship. Jeremiah wasted no time. He lined it up in his sights, held his breath, and squeezed the trigger. *BOOM!* The coconut was blown into small pieces and showered the men standing nearest the rails. The ship sounded with unrivaled excitement.

"Ranjit... twenty! Jeremiah... nineteen!"

Ranjit was beside himself. Lothar and the others watched nervously as Ranjit again took the firing stance.

"Are you ready?"

Ranjit glared with hatred towards the catapult.

Thump!

Ranjit watched it in his sights as the coconut shot straight out in front of him. Just when he knew it was in the perfect position, he pulled back the trigger. *BOOM!* All watched as the coconut dropped into the water again, unscathed. Ranjit howled as the jeering continued.

Jeremiah walked quietly up to the front.

"Are you ready?"

Jeremiah nodded again.

Thump! BOOM! No sooner had he released his finger from the trigger than the coconut again blasted apart in the air, to the amazement of everyone on board.

"Jer-e-mi-ah, Jer-e-mi-ah!" chanted the crew.

Ranjit was completely beside himself. "BLASTED FOOLS! SHUT UP!" he screamed. They roared back with laughter.

"The scorekeeper called down again, "Ranjit... twenty. Jeremiah... twenty."

Van Russel walked up. "Well, well, well... it appears this day has been a bit more eventful than any of us anticipated, eh? Young Jeremiah, ye have displayed a masterful use of a pistol today." He paused. "There's one more shot in today's game!" he screamed, purposely roiling up the crew again. "Ye two decide. Since we are now at a tie, we can do this one of two ways. Ye can either fire at two coconuts at the same time or do as ye have until now and fire ye shots, one at a time."

Ranjit thought for a moment. "I say we shoot them together," he replied with urgency.

"And ye?" Van Russel asked Jeremiah.

Jeremiah looked at Ranjit. The quartermaster could hardly look back at him. "I guess that will be fine," he replied.

Van Russel turned to the man loading the catapult. "Load up two of them." The crew was screaming, nervous about their wagers. Jeremiah's team watched him and gave him the thumbs-up sign of approval as he took a stance just a couple feet away from Ranjit. The Indian's towering frame was enormous next to him. They both stood at the edge, their pistols in hand and ready for the last and final coconuts to be fired. Everyone grew silent.

"Ready?"

They both nodded.

Thump! Thump! The coconuts fired high into the sky above the ship, but while everyone was watching the coconuts, Ranjit kicked Jeremiah in the center of his knee. Jeremiah fell to the deck.

"Get up!" the crew screamed at him, unaware.

Jeremiah struggled as Ranjit lined up his coconut up in his sights and squeezed the trigger once more.

BOOM!

Jeremiah's heart sank when he heard the quartermaster fire his final shot. But one coconut splashed on the water's surface and the other barreled down immediately behind it. Jeremiah held his pistol over the edge of the rail, watched through a gun port and squeezed off his final round. His musket ball went barraging towards the coconut and just as it was about to hit the water, it exploded. A hundred coconut pieces dispersed in every direction and landed on the water.

The scorekeeper yelled down, "Ranjit... twenty..." He paused. "Oh never mind! JEREMIAH AND HIS TEAM WIN!"

The crew exploded and Jeremiah's team ran to him, lifting him up into the air.

"Atta lad," Van Russel called from the upper deck. "I do believe there's a lot more to ye than meets the eye!" He smiled and clapped with the rest of the crew.

Ranjit's team tried to console him, but he pushed away from them, storming into the hold below.

Van Russel looked off in the distance and turned back to Orville, who was standing near him.

"Let's get underway. A storm is approaching and there's still some pirates we have to catch."

"Aye, sir." Orville replied. He began yelling orders on deck to wrap up the game and get the ship back underway. After all, someone must do it. And it seemed that Ranjit was still having a conniption in the ship's lower hold.

CHAPTER TWELVE

THE VICIOUS VORTEX

A nasty blanket of clouds enshrouded the sky behind Van
Russel as he made his way across the deck. He looked at
them with concern, but his primary intent was to talk to the boy that
had done so well at coconut.

"Yer beginning to amaze me," he said as he walked up to Jeremiah, who was gazing off the bow of the ship. He held his hand
out. "I think this is yers." He opened his hand to Jeremiah, revealing
a silver coin.

"Ranjit's piece-of-eight?"

"Aye," said Van Russel. "Ye probably wouldn't have ever seen
it if I hadn't intercepted it. Ranjit is much too proud to bring it to
ye himself."

"Thank you, Captain." He looked at the stamped piece of oblong silver glistening in his hand. He had never held a piece of pure silver before, much less ever owned one. "Ranjit still looks pretty angry."

The both of them gazed over to the quartermaster and his teammates, who were now swabbing the decks in the place of Augustus. The ship's swabbie sat on one of the masts above the four, looking down at them. They glared up at him, but dared not say anything. They had lost fair and square — despite the fact that it was killing them all. This was the first time anyone had ever defeated Ranjit and his pack of coconut brutes.

"Don't worry about the quartermaster," Van Russel commented. "He's never had to deal with losing and it's a new experience for him. He'll be alright… just stay clear of him for a while."

"Yes, sir… I had planned on it," Jeremiah smiled.

The sky behind Jeremiah lit up. Dark, billowing clouds started forming and the lightning streaked down from within them. The clouds were moving upon them fast, swirling in the sky.

"I think we ought to prepare the crew for a bad one," he commented, holding onto his hat as the wind blew briskly past them. Blessie flapped her wings, but clutched Van Russel's shoulders with all her might. The crew took notice of the approaching storm as the ship began rocking in the surging waves. The sails flapped and popped against the increasing winds that constantly kept changing direction in the fast approaching storm.

"MEN!" Van Russel yelled. "Secure the rigging… we've got a nasty storm a coming!"

"Captain, what do you need me to do?" Jeremiah asked, grabbing hold of the rail to maintain his balance. The surrounding water was increasingly turbulent by the minute and the afternoon sky was quickly turning as dark as night.

"COME WITH ME!" Van Russel yelled. They hurried down from the upper deck towards the captain's cabin. The crew atop were yelling commands and securing the rigging as the *Nante* steered amidst the huge waves.

Orville struggled to keep control of the wheel. He yelled to Van Russel as he and Jeremiah began entering the main cabin. "Captain, the compass is screwy! It's spinning in circles and I have no idea of our heading. What do you suggest?" he screamed.

"Yer guess is as good as mine! Look around us… the beast is everywhere now!" Van Russel screamed back to him in the howling winds.

Waves splashed over the sides of the *Nante* and washed across the deck, knocking some of the crew off their feet and nearly washing some of them overboard. The hurling winds grew colder and thunder exploded around them as they were tossed about and tried to maintain their balance in the relentless and toppling waves.

Jeremiah looked out the windows of the captain's cabin at the enormous waves all around them. He felt his stomach coming up in his throat as they climbed to the top of one mountainous wave and down the backside of another. He lay down on the bed in Van Russel's cabin as nausea began overpowering him.

Van Russel poked his head in. "Stay in here! The captain's gonna go out and help the crew!" He slammed the door shut and Jeremiah cringed as he battled one wave of nausea after another. He struggled to keep from vomiting as he clutched the bed. He squinted his eyes and looked beyond the windows as the ship climbed the top of each oncoming wave. As he looked though, he thought he could see something against the darkening sky, approaching the *Nante* from the rear. But each time he caught a glimpse, the ship barreled down the wave, completely eliminating everything but the frightening ocean swells from sight. He struggled to his feet and moved towards the window. As the *Nante* climbed the next unrelenting wave, he scanned the waters behind the ship.

There it was again — another ship! And even though it was quickly becoming dark, the ship approaching appeared even darker. The ship was as black as night, even its sails. It was still a great distance behind them but it seemed to be moving quicker than the *Nante*. Jeremiah had a sickening feeling, even beyond his nausea, that the other ship was trying to catch up to them.

"I must alert the captain," he said. He stumbled through the cabin, clutching his stomach, trying to maintain balance in the constant shifting room. The violent winds fought with him and nearly ripped the door from its hinges as he opened it. He could see Van Russel assisting Ranjit as he secured some rigging to the yardarm.

"CAPTAIN!" he screamed.

Van Russel turned to him. "WHAT?" he yelled back. Blessie took flight from his shoulder and struggled through the air to the cabin and safety.

Jeremiah pointed behind them. "BEHIND US! ANOTHER SHIP!"

Ranjit and Van Russel saw nothing, but they were at the bottom of the unforgiving swells. The *Nante* climbed the next wave and they clutched the nearby windlass and scanned the waters behind them. As they reached the next wave's peak, they too could see it.

"He's right, Captain! There is another ship back there!" Ranjit yelled.

A look of despair came across Van Russel's face.

"What is it?" Ranjit asked him.

"Exactly what I was afraid of!" yelled Van Russel. "Get the remaining crew in the ship!"

Van Russel, Ranjit and the crew remaining on deck, including Jeremiah, struggled to the ship's hold. They all appeared exhausted and sickened.

Van Russel addressed them, "Me crew, we have something terrible approaching us from the aft." The ship moaned and creaked as he spoke.

"What's approaching us?" asked one of the crew, struggling to catch his breath.

"The pirates we were sent after," he replied, despairingly. "The captain needs ye all to gather your arms and man the cannons. I fear we've got a terrible fight upon us."

"Captain, how can ye be sure that ship is the pirates'?" asked Ranjit.

Van Russel turned to his quartermaster. "Because I get nothing but a feeling of death from that floating, black abomination trying to catch up to us."

Ranjit turned to the crew. "You heard the captain — gather the arms and man the cannons!"

The crew dispersed to their respective positions.

"Jeremiah, stay with me!" Van Russel ordered.

But Jeremiah, fearing he would lose his possessions, had already taken off on foot across the deck for his sleeping quarters. A gigantic wave came crashing down and knocked him sideways, dragging him across deck. His entire body was flushed straight through an open gun port, but he was able to grab a hold of its edges just as he was about to be devoured by the relentless ocean. He struggled to pull his body back in, made it to his feet, and hurried off to the sleeping quarters.

Once inside, he ran quickly towards his swaying hammock and grabbed the cloth sack that held his belongings. There wasn't much for him to try and salvage but he grabbed his dearest possession, the leather journal, and stuffed it into the back of his breeches. He grabbed the stone Ozron had given him and the candle from Madam Karla and stuffed them down into his pockets. He threw down his bag with his remaining possessions as he hurried back towards the door to find Van Russel.

Aboard the pirate ship, Molodan stood at the helm with his entire dastardly crew waiting below him. A misty fog surrounded the floating pirate citadel and the air was as cold as ice. A smell of death engulfed the entire ship, despite the blowing winds. Undaunted by the rocking waves or the intensity of the storm, the pirates stood perfectly still as their ship rode up one wave and back down another. They did not manifest into the spherical shapes, but stood with sword in hand, awaiting Molodan's signal to attack the *Nante*.

They saw it slowly approaching them amidst the gigantic waves. Molodan turned towards one of his crew and the fierce brute nodded back at him. Within seconds, the pirate ship was blasting one cannonball after another at the *Nante* from its open gun ports. The cannon balls hurled past the *Nante*, whizzing close to it and splashing in the violent waters. The pirate ship drew ever closer to the ship its crew was intent on destroying.

"THEY'RE FIRING AT US!" Ranjit yelled.

"I CAN SEE THAT!" Van Russel screamed back at him. "Go below deck and ensure that all cannons on the starboard and portside are primed and loaded! I'm afraid there's not going to be much of a window for us to fire back!"

Orville tried with all his strength to commandeer the ship away from the cannon rounds, but they were dropping and blasting on both sides. He took the wheel and spun it sharply to the left, causing the ship to jerk and shift sideways in the violent waves. The monsoon gales soon picked up the sails, filling them completely.

The *Nante* took a different course, with the pirates now to the rear starboard side. They continued firing upon them, but missed as the endless swells tossed the *Nante* up and down.

Ranjit barked orders to the crew. "Prime the cannons! Load the gunpowder and the iron! Prepare the fuses and open the gun ports! Pull the cannons within firing range! PULL MEN, PULL!" The crew tugged on the ropes against the pulleys, sending the ends of the cannons beyond the gun port openings. Water splashed in through the open ports, drenching the struggling men. The cannons shifted as the *Nante* rode each wave and one cannon rocked onto its side, pinning one of Belcher's legs underneath it. He screamed in agony as the others struggled to move the massive iron gun.

Jeremiah stood at the door of the sleeping quarters. Rain sprayed his face and water flushed past his ankles as he braced himself in the doorframe. He watched as Van Russel held on the windlass for dear life.

"CAPTAIN!" he screamed. "I'M COMING FOR YOU!"

"NO!" Van Russel yelled. "Ye stay put — captain's orders!" Van Russel looked helpless and terrified as he embraced the windlass. The waves came barreling over on him and his long, wet hair was tangled and matted on his face. His hat was nowhere to be seen and his clothes stuck to him as he tried to maintain hold.

Jeremiah looked to the helmsman. Orville's attention was on the biggest swell yet growing in front of him. Jeremiah noticed it, too. It was bigger than anything he had ever seen. The *Nante*, no larger than a speck in comparison, slowly began to climb it. Orville's hands clutched the wheel tightly and he closed his eyes as the ship moved in an almost vertical direction. He wrapped his arms around the wheel. "DEAR GOD," he pleaded, "HELP US!"

Just as the *Nante* reached the wave's summit and began to level out, Orville struggled back to his feet and opened his eyes.

"What is it?" Jeremiah yelled to him as he tried to maintain his hold.

Orville pointed out in front of them.

Jeremiah gulped as he saw the ferocious, swirling water funnel churning the sky and sucking up the ocean's water. He could see Van Russel still struggling to hold on.

"HANG ON, CAPTAIN!" Jeremiah screamed as the *Nante* moved towards the circling funnel.

Orville struggled to maintain control of the wheel, but they had been sucked straight towards the deadly vacuum and there was no turning back. The *Nante* began circling it at its bottom. The water funnel created a sickening inertia beyond anything else they had ever encountered — even the unrelenting waves they'd just experienced were nothing in comparison.

"It's gonna take us straight to Davy Jones's locker!" Van Russel hollered.

Jeremiah looked in horror at the funnel of water that seemed to go straight up beyond the black, swirling clouds. He thought it to be half a nautical mile in diameter. And the noise it was creating was even more horrifying than the sight itself. He braced his small frame within the doorway and held on tightly as the ship shifted to a sickening angle. Jeremiah felt the *Nante* lifting from the ocean's surface as the intense power of the vortex started rotating them towards the dark clouds above. The intense winds pulled at the sails, ripping some of them from the rigging and sucked them straight up in the funnel.

He thought they were out of the range of fire from the pirates, but he could see they were still following them and they too were being sucked straight up in the vortex along with the *Nante*. The pirates immediately started opening fire upon them again. A cannonball ripped through the last remaining sail and the yardarm holding it came crashing down. Orville dove out of the way, and it just missed him as it smashed against the upper deck of the *Nante*. It broke the gigantic wheel of the *Nante* and the wheel went rolling down the stairs towards Van Russel, where it stopped on deck.

"BLASTED PIRATES!" Van Russel screamed, as he clutched the windlass tightly.

"Hang on, Captain! I'll help you shortly!" Jeremiah hollered to him.

"Ye stay where yer at! Don't ye try coming out here!" he screamed again in the howling winds.

Below, Ranjit yelled to the men. "Get `em in your sights and fire!" The crew began lighting the fuses but they did nothing but smolder. The crashing waves had doused all of them beyond use and Ranjit struggled through the hold to find the extra boxes of fuses.

"Here they are!" he yelled as he threw them to the crew. "Make em count!" As the crew swapped the soaked fuses with the newer, dry ones, he prayed that the gunpowder in the cannons hadn't been destroyed too. Midget grabbed a torch attached to the hold's wall and lit the first fuse when the pirates were within range.

The fuse ignited and burned down quickly until it disappeared from sight within the cannon. The crew held their ears and waited. There was a long pause, but finally… *BOOM!* The cannonball went barreling from the *Nante* towards the pirates at a tremendous speed.

Molodan watched it coming across the length of the vortex when… *CRASH!* It burst through the hull of his ship. It made no difference. They still spun upwards around the vortex with the same velocity.

Molodan, unaffected by the movement of his ship, peered over the side. The hole was significant, but did nothing to affect the fate of their ship. Enraged that they had fired back upon him, he pointed his finger out towards the *Nante.* The pirates fired back, sending a barrage of cannonballs hurling towards Van Russel's ship. Most of them missed, but two more of them managed to strike the *Nante.* One blasted through the sails, ripping a gigantic hole and the other tore through the port side.

Jeremiah watched the wheel slowly sliding across the deck. He knew Van Russel was helpless and no one else could save him. The *Nante* violently hit a piece of debris flying in the funnel and the wheel slid the remaining length of the deck, pinning Van Russel's arm against the windlass. He screamed out in agonizing pain.

Jeremiah couldn't bear the sight before him. He released his hold from the door's frame and shot across the deck, soon falling straight on his stomach. He slid across the wet, slippery deck and was sucked up in the air from the vicious vortex.

Just before he was sucked overboard, he managed to grip a rope from a ripped sail. He crashed onto the deck and the wind was knocked completely from his lungs. He regained his breath and struggled back towards Van Russel with his chest aching from the crashing blow.

"FOOLISH BOY!" Van Russel screamed. "GET BACK TO WHERE YE WHERE!"

"NOT TILL I GET YOU OUT, SIR!" Jeremiah yelled. He gripped the massive wheel with both hands and tugged with all his strength to pull it free from Van Russel.

The pirates were firing upon them again and just as Jeremiah helped Van Russel free his arm, another cannonball came barreling across the deck. It struck the mizzenmast square in its center, causing it to split completely. It gave a horrendous moan as it tumbled down towards the deck. One of the massive poles slid across the complete length of the *Nante's* deck and bumped the large wooden wheel. This, in turn, struck Jeremiah in the chest and knocked him flying into the air and off the back of the ship.

"JEREMIAH!" Van Russel screamed in horror. Jeremiah reached to him as he was sucked into the vortex's edge and swirled around the outside of the massive funnel.

Jeremiah had been knocked a tremendous distance from the *Nante* into the icy, turbulent winds. Barely conscious, he struggled to keep his wits as he continued flying around the funnel's exterior. The winds and debris felt like knives against his body. He looked below him and watched in terror as the hull of the gruesome, black monstrosity approached him. Just as it seemed to completely run atop his body, he lost consciousness and his body fell limp as he continued swirling far below the *Nante*.

Molodan watched the entire incident as he chased the *Nante* in continual circles around the funnel. As the pirates approached the lifeless boy, the ship moved slightly and a large, deadly hand reached into the rushing winds. With little effort, it grabbed Jeremiah by the arm, pulling him from the water funnel, and threw him on the deck. Jeremiah lay at the feet of Molodan and his entire crew.

Van Russel moaned for Jeremiah as he looked over the side. "What have I done?" he cried. "He was only a boy! A cabin boy!" Desperation and hopelessness flooded his veins as he watched the top of the vortex coming closer. He looked down at the pirates who were circling below them. To his amazement, they started moving farther downwards and out of the vortex entirely. "MURDERERS!"

he screamed. "Come back and fight this captain! Time to face yer death too!"

The *Nante* was now spinning at an incredible velocity as it moved towards the top of the vortex. Van Russel closed his eyes and held on for dear life as he prepared to be thrown into oblivion.

A long pause ensued.

SPLASH! The ship was taken from the mouth of the terrifying funnel and ended up in a complacent sea waiting below. Their broken ship floated motionless in calm waters and Van Russel lay on his back, his body partly wrapped around the ship's railing.

He dared not open his eyes. He feared what would be waiting for him on the other side of death. However, it seemed like light was trying to penetrate his tightly closed eyelids. He remembered one of his dying shipmates years before talking of a bright light just before death — maybe this was it and everything was okay — maybe he was in that other place.

But the aching of his arms and back soon set in. "Yer not supposed to feel pain after death," he mumbled. As much as he hated to, he squinted one eye open. Light! He opened the other eye. More light! Wait — he wasn't dead! In fact he was more alive than ever. He looked up to the tranquil blue skies all around him. "What in the…" he said, looking around.

The *Nante*'s crew slowly began surfacing. Ranjit led the pack, taking a defensive stance as he assessed what was going on above deck. He ran to Van Russel. "Captain, are ye alright?" he asked, helping him up.

"Jeremiah!" Van Russel moaned again, rushing to the side of the deck. He scanned the waters, but the boy was not there. "Where did we end up? Where did the funnel go?"

"I'm sorry, Captain," Ranjit said. He pointed away from the ship. "That bit of land over there. Looks like Abrador Island. I think we're just a half a day away from Gordington."

Van Russel dropped to his knees, clutching the rail and looking out over the water. He had tried to make life better for the boy, but now he had lost him.

CHAPTER THIRTEEN

A Deadly Ship

Ranjit, Van Russel and the crew walked around the mangled and broken *Nante*. They were alive, but a feeling of loss overwhelmed them all, not for the ordeal they had just gone through, but for the loss of Jeremiah.

Van Russel walked from one side of the ship to the other, hoping that maybe Jeremiah had been spat from the mouth of the funnel before it disappeared.

"Sorry, Captain — I know he meant a great deal to ye," said Ranjit. "What in the name of God was that thing we came through?"

"No idea," Van Russel sniffled. "Must have been a gateway or something — never in me years on the water have experienced a phenomenon like that. Plenty of unexplainables, but nothing like what me crew went through today." He struggled on his feet, worn and beaten. His tangled hair and crimson coat dripped water onto the deck.

"Well, sir, I'll go make a damage assessment of her," said Ranjit, looking at the broken masts and sails scattered about the deck. "Looks like we may be floating here for a while."

"Me friend, the innkeeper, will never forgive me," said Van Russel.

"Sir, surely ye aren't suggesting this is your fault," said Ranjit.

"He was just a boy... just a young, innocent cabin boy. And he was trying to save me."

Ranjit shook his head. "I'll be below, Captain — we've got a hurt sailor down there."

Belcher was hardly responding. He was cold and clammy and his skin was an ashen gray. He had entered a state of shock shortly after the incident. The crew had wrapped his leg in some spare cloths, but the bandages were dirty. Ranjit feared they would lead to nothing more than an awful infection on top of the horrendous wound Belcher had already endured. Ranjit knew what must be done, and he left to alert Van Russel.

Aboard the pirate ship, Jeremiah was slowly coming to. He opened his eyes and looked around, but it was pitch black and he could barely see his hands in front of his face. His body shuddered from the intense cold and the foul stench of the room was overwhelmingly nauseating.

He felt walls enclosing him, each only a couple of arm's length in each direction. The walls were cold and slick. The surface on which he had woken was hard and appeared wooden, very much like the plank flooring of the *Nante*.

Jeremiah tried to stand but the top of the tiny room was only about four or five feet high and his head bumped the ceiling. It inhibited him from standing and stretching completely.

"Where am I?" he asked as he continued feeling around him.

He had no idea where he was. If he had died, was this death? His chest ached horribly from the blow of the ship's wheel and his clothes were soaking wet.

"Help," he whispered.

He heard nothing but pops, echoes and moans; typical sounds heard deep within a ship. "Am I the on the pirate ship?" he asked. How could that have happened? He knew he wasn't on the *Nante*. He remembered nothing more than trying to help Van Russel during the storm. "Hello?" he whispered again.

"Shhh," came another voice.

"Hello? Who is that?" he whispered.

A tiny sliding door on the wall behind him opened. "Stop that, before you call them back down here again," said the voice through the hole.

Jeremiah scooted closer to it. He could see a pair of eyes on the other side, and light coming from a room on the other side of the wall. "Who are you?" he whispered.

The door closed abruptly, but Jeremiah wanted to know where he was. He knocked lightly on the door.

"What!" the voice whispered back.

"Where am I?" Jeremiah whispered.

"Aboard Molodan's ship," said the voice.

"Who's Molodan?"

"Pirates!"

Jeremiah's eyes widened with fear. How had he ended up here? "Who are you?" he asked nervously.

"I'm a slave aboard this ship. Please, be quiet," pleaded the voice. "You're going to call them down here if you keep it up."

Jeremiah's concerns were too great. "How long have you been here?"

There was a pause, then, "Longer than I can remember. Now that's enough! Please, don't talk to me!" Heavy footsteps echoed from the floor above them. "Now you've done it! They're coming!" He slammed the small door shut.

Jeremiah listened to the footsteps cross the floor above him, and then he heard them coming back and it sounded as if they were now on the same floor as he was. He could feel the vibrations of the steps through the floor. And when they were very near, they stopped.

The door to his cell opened and a long, dark arm reached in and grabbed him by the shoulder. It yanked him up and out of the cell. The brute was bigger than any man he had ever laid eyes upon and the stench coming from him made Jeremiah gag. The colossus pulled him by the arm to the waiting crew above.

Van Russel shook his head. "Are ye sure there's no other options?" he asked Ranjit.

"Sir, come see it for ye self. It's pretty bad and he's hardly even responsive."

"We have no doctor aboard. What are we to do?" Van Russel asked. "We'll have to use Midget. Has anyone checked on him since we landed here?"

"Yes, sir," replied Ranjit. "He's doing better from the scurvy. He actually came up from the hold just a short time ago. He's at Belcher's side."

"Thank ye, Quartermaster. Fetch him for me — would ye? I need to talk to him before we do this."

"Aye, sir." Ranjit left to retrieve the ship's cooper and his tools. Midget had been ill from a nasty case of scurvy, but the fresh fruits they had forced upon him over the last day had made him a little more viable. Though the conditions presented to them were quite unsanitary and dangerous to say the least, if the operation wasn't performed, Belcher would undoubtedly continue to lose blood, become septic from the infection of his wound, and surely die.

Van Russel propped himself against the rail of the ship. How could life be so wrong on such a beautiful day? Why was this happening to them? In all his years of being a captain, never before had times been so trying. At times like this he didn't want to be a captain at all. Even the job as the ship's swabbie seemed like a better alternative: no stress, just a simple job to be done and no other harsh decisions to be made concerning the lives of so many others.

Around him, the remaining crew from the hold began filtering onto the deck. They all looked at the ship in disbelief. Never before had they seen it in such a state. They began lifting the mast and the sails that littered it.

The tall and lanky cooper emerged from the hold and walked up to Van Russel. "Sir, were you looking for me?" Midget asked.

"Aye, I was. How are ye feeling Midget?"

"A little better, sir. I've definitely seen better days."

"We all have. I haven't seen Belcher yet, but I've heard he's not doing well," said Van Russel.

"No sir… he's not. I just left him. He's close to death right now, he is."

"I believe ye know what we must do."

"Amputation?" Midget asked hesitantly.

"Aye… afraid so. Do we have a viable medicine chest?"

"Negative, sir. We have a medicine chest, but nothing that'll help us with this. We have no opium on board."

"Then what do ye suggest?"

"Wine and brandy," said Midget.

"Oh me," said Van Russel. "Is there nothing else?"

"Afraid not, sir."

"What will ye need?"

Midget thought for a moment. "I've got the tourniquet and we'll have to use one of me saws. I'll need some men to hold him down."

"Is that all?"

"Umm… well, I'll need the cleanest place we've got on board to do the surgery, probably the kitchen and," he thought again, "his stitches — well, we'll have to use the needles and heavy thread we use on the sails."

Just the thought of what they had to do sickened Van Russel and he worried if Belcher would even survive it. Many times amputations performed in these types of conditions proved unsuccessful.

"Are ye alright, Captain?" Midget asked. "Ye look a little green around the gills."

"Um… aye. I'll be fine. Go ahead and prep the kitchen. I'll go get our cook some brandy."

The brute threw Jeremiah down on the deck of the pirate ship. He landed on his stomach and moaned from the pain when his sore chest hit the surface. He looked around him. He was completely surrounded by the pirate crew. He shivered violently from the cold and the stench was more than he could bear. He had no idea what they could possibly want from him and his heart pounded through his chest, fearful that they were preparing to kill him. He looked at the swords in their hands. They were much different than the swords the crew of the *Nante* possessed. These were silver, the blades fat and wide.

None of the pirates uttered a word, not even the brute, which was obviously their leader. They hovered over him as if they were waiting on something. But for what?

One of the other pirates walked up through the waiting crowd. In one hand he had some rusty iron chains and in the other he carried a rope. He leaned down and pinned Jeremiah on his back.

"NO!" screamed Jeremiah as he fought and kicked at them helplessly. "Please!"

There wasn't any sense in trying to scream or plead for help. These heartless pirates had only one intent — and that was to hurt him. He felt he was about to get the treatment that many other souls had probably endured prior to him.

Jeremiah kicked and fought and screamed at them, but they exhibited no emotion. Tears streamed down his face as they shackled the chains to his ankles. Secured to the end of them was a large, rusty iron ball. Around his chest they secured a rope and they tied it in a way that it would be impossible to break free. They lifted him up and carried him to the front of the ship.

Jeremiah feared for his life. He knew this would be the end of his existence. He cried for his mother and father, but there was no one there to help him in this time of desperation. He looked out over the water. The sky around them was as dark as night and the water below seemed cold and endless.

They were preparing to keelhaul him. The pirates carrying the chains and ball behind him threw them over the edge first and the pirate holding Jeremiah threw him in immediately afterwards. He screamed as he plunged into the water.

At first he tried treading the water, but the chains made it virtually impossible and he struggled to keep his head above the surface. The weight of the ball and chains yanked him under the water, causing him to breathe it in. He was drowning.

But just as he started to lose consciousness, the pirates pulled on the rope secured to his chest, forcing him back above the water's surface. He came up coughing and vomited water from his nose and his mouth. They pulled the rope even tighter, forcing his body up against the front of the ship. He tried to swim away, but it was useless. He had no control over what they were doing to him.

They pulled him from the portside to the starboard side of the ship, scraping his body on the barnacles growing on the ship's hull, ripping his shirt open and the flesh from his back. Jeremiah screamed in agony as he bled into the ocean.

Jeremiah moaned with despair — the saltwater entering his open wounds burned terribly. The water around him tinged with red. He tried to catch his breath, still choking from the initial fall in the water. He tried to turn around and maintain a hold on the ship, but they pulled him across the hull again. Exposed to the barnacles again, he screamed.

"Why are you doing this to me?" he wailed. But they did not answer. Again he was dragged to the other side and exposed to the rigorous torture. His body was quickly growing weak and soon he ceased to fight, and simply dangled from the end of the rope.

Upon the lead marauder's command, Jeremiah was lifted from the water. He dangled from the rope like a piece of bait and just as his feet left the water, sharks began circling the front of the ship drawn by the fresh blood. Another minute in the water and he would have been completely devoured. But maybe, he thought, a short, terribly painful stint with the sharks would be better for him than the grueling, drawn out torture the pirates planned for him.

They dropped him back on the deck of their ship and crowded around him. They watched his gaping, bleeding back paint their deck a shade of red as it spilled out quickly from his wounds. His body felt numb from the pain and the cold and he half closed his eyes, nearly passing out from the shock of it.

He felt another pirate walk over, unfasten the shackles from his ankles and untie his rope. He lifted Jeremiah's lifeless body and carried him down to the hold. He was thrown back into his cell to await the next round of punishment.

The surgical team had assembled in the kitchen on the *Nante*. Belcher was laid out on the main table and Midget, Ranjit and Van Russel were the only ones present. No one else had any desire to help with the removal of his comrade's leg. Most couldn't even stomach such a sight, but these three were there for him.

Belcher was barely conscious. He did have enough awareness to know that they were preparing to remove his leg. Van Russel stood next to his head, pouring brandy in his mouth and coaching him to drink it. Belcher was unable to swallow properly and most of the brandy rolled from the corners of his lips.

"Are we ready?" Van Russel asked Midget.

"Just about, sir," he replied. He took the cutting saw, poured more brandy over the teeth of it and then placed it into the kitchen stove's fire, attempting to sterilize it. "Never used this saw for cutting off legs," he said. "I guess we'll find out."

Ranjit grabbed a thick piece of leather and placed it in Belcher's teeth. "Bite down on this, Cook. We don't want ye swallowing yer tongue." Although he was hardly conscious, Belcher nodded.

"Alright," said Midget, "I need one of you to move to his head and hold him down by the shoulders and I need the other to come over here and help hold down this leg."

Ranjit moved to Belcher's shoulders and pinned them in place with his large hands. Van Russel moved below Belcher's knee and held pressure on the lower part of his leg. Midget grabbed the tourniquet and placed it on Belcher's upper thigh. It had two leather straps on the lower end of it and Midget secured them around his leg, buckling them off on the other side. He placed his hand on the metal handle at the top and began twisting it tightly, minimizing the blood flow to his leg.

Belcher moaned from the tightening tourniquet.

"I know friend… it hurts," said Midget.

"Bite down on that leather," Ranjit instructed again.

Midget assessed at which point he should remove the leg to give Belcher a fighting chance. "I think above the knee is best." He pointed to it. "Captain, pour some more brandy over this spot where I'll be cutting."

Van Russel grabbed the bottle of brandy and poured the remaining liquid onto Belcher's leg. Only a few drops were left and landed on Belcher's skin next to where the bone was protruding. "Need me to get another bottle?" he asked.

"No — there's not time. Hold him down." Midget grabbed the saw from the stove's fire and placed it just inches above the skin. "May God be with you," he said.

"Are we finished?" said Van Russel, some time later.

"Just about Captain. We need some leeches to place on these wounds. You know — to help with fighting any infection. I do think we have some of those in our medicine chest."

"I'll go get them," Ranjit replied. "Do ye need me to keep holding him down?"

"No, putting the last stitch in now — he's actually done quite well with this part."

Ranjit left and returned quickly with a small glass jar. He unscrewed the lid and pulled out its four inhabitants — large, slippery black leeches. They curled and writhed in his hand and he placed them directly upon the site of the stitches.

"Let's leave these here for a couple of days. After our friends have done their work, we'll cover the site with flour and a cloth dressing. That's all I know to do," said Midget.

"I'm quite impressed, Midget," said Van Russel, "sickened, but impressed."

"Aye, thank you Captain, though only time will tell if he'll survive."

They lifted the feeble cook and carried him off to his hammock.

Van Russel knew he must send word about what happened to them and alert Ebineezer of Jeremiah's demise. Van Russel had no idea of their current whereabouts, but he knew his one trusted friend could do it. Blessie had proved a valuable messenger in the past and he knew she would come through for him again this time.

He went to his cabin and she was sitting on the back of his chair waiting for him.

"'Bout time ye showed up," she cawed.

Van Russel smiled at her. "That's me girl. Ye know the captain has been very busy today."

"I believe it," she squawked again, shuffling on her perch.

"Blessie, yer captain has an urgent mission for ye. I need ye to take a message back to the innkeeper. Think ye can do that for me?"

"Of course," she replied. "Need an apple."

Van Russel sat down at his desk and Blessie jumped onto his shoulder. She nuzzled her beak into the side of his cheek. "Yer captain

has missed that," he said lovingly. On a small piece of parchment, he
wrote:

> Ebineezer—
> We encountered the pirates. Jeremiah
> was lost at sea. Some of me crew is hurt
> and the ship is in terrible shape. We'll
> begin repairs immediately and will
> return to Gordington soon. Please send
> immediate word to the governor.
> Respectfully,
> Van Russel

He rolled it up neatly, placed it in a small metal cylinder and
fastened it to Blessie's leg.

"Now take this to the innkeeper, girl. Ye know what to do."
He kissed her on top of her beak and carried her to the door of his
cabin.

Blessie took flight and flapped away from the *Nante*, soon soaring in circles high above it. Van Russel watched her as she circled
high atop their ship. It wasn't long before she found her direction
and flew out towards Gordington.

"Good luck, girl," said Van Russel as he watched her fly away.
"I know ye'll find him."

Hours later, at the Brubaker Inn, Ebineezer was preparing for bed.
Business had been slow on this night and he only had a couple of

quiet guests staying with him. He had not given them room number one — it was sitting vacant for Jeremiah's return.

He hadn't been feeling well. His coughing episodes were acting up again and his blood-hacking spats had completely drained him. The brandy was kicking in, working its slumber-inducing spell upon him. He yawned and stumbled to the front door, preparing to close up for the night.

He peered outside. No one was on Banyard Street and even the Wharf seemed unusually quiet. He shut the front doors and proceeded to the small bar. As he leaned down and blew out the tiny candle, he heard a knocking up against the front window. He walked over to the door and immediately recognized Blessie flapping on the other side.

"Blessie? What are ye doing here?" he asked, opening the door for her.

"Message from the captain," she cawed, flying over to the bar.

"A message? Oh my… the captain never sends his bird unless there's bad news to share." He removed the parchment, reading it quickly.

"NOOOO!" he cried, throwing himself on the bar with the bird. "Jeremiah, oh noooo."

Blessie sat quietly, watching Ebineezer's reaction.

"How could they lose him at sea? Him of all people!" he sobbed.

"We found the pirates," she cawed back at him.

"Pirates… those despicable pirates," Ebineezer moaned. "Jeremiah was like me son… and I was the one that sent him off with that crew." He lifted Blessie and carried her over to the door. "Thank you Blessie. Now go find yer captain and tell him I got the message."

CHAPTER FOURTEEN

THE COLORED CANDLE

"Help me," Jeremiah pleaded as he became conscious.

"I'm here," said the slave in the cell next to his, "but I can't help you. Please, talk to me in a whisper."

"I need to get out of here," Jeremiah begged. "They dragged me underneath their ship."

"Detestable pirates," said the slave. "I'm sorry boy. I know how bad it is. My scars are evidence enough of what these killers are capable of. They've keelhauled me many times too. If only someone would one day put an end to them."

"Is there a way?" Jeremiah shivered; his body wracked with pain.

"There is, but there's not a man alive that would ever dare to try."

Jeremiah struggled to lean closer to the small, open door. "How?"

"Are you serious, boy? Who do you think is going to try? You?" the slave snickered sarcastically.

"Just tell me," Jeremiah insisted.

"Well, alright. If you want to kill them all you have to kill the one in charge... Molodan. They feed off his energy."

Jeremiah panted, his back stabbing with pain, "What are you talking about?"

He heard the slave lean closer. "I'm sure you've figured out by now that these pirates are already dead. They transform into balls of light or they can manifest into the shape of a pirate — that which they used to be. They typically prefer the pirate shape."

"Balls of light?"

"Oh yes. Obviously you haven't seen that yet. It's quite horrifying if you're on the receiving end of it. I saw it the first time when they attacked my ship long ago. They killed every one of my mates but me. Why they decided to keep me alive I'll never know. Well," he paused, "actually, they probably left me alive to have someone to torture regularly... and to have someone to help with the ritual."

"Ritual... what ritual?"

"When we go back to Abaddon, the place they come from, they have to open a door of sorts to get back. That's when the ritual is performed. I bring the chest with the amulet to Molodan and he opens the gateway."

"So if someone was to take his amulet, they wouldn't be able to return... correct?"

"Precisely. One tried and was almost successful, but they caught up to him and killed him. Never did get the chap's name, but he was a brave one. I wouldn't recommend trying, or you'll end up with the same fate he did. Can't imagine it being any worse than what they've done to me though. Most times I wish I was dead," he said sadly.

"So what does this amulet do?" Jeremiah asked.

"Not sure how it works exactly, but Molodan is the only one that uses it. Oh yeah, this is what I was getting at a minute ago. He uses all of his energy in addition to the energy from the amulet. His energy is consumed with the gateway and therefore, there's a very short window of time when he's defenseless."

"But if he's already dead, how can you kill him?" Jeremiah persisted.

"Straight through the heart. He's only half dead. His platoon of pirates comes straight from the gates of the netherworld. Legend has it that he made a deal with the devil which gave him his unlimited power. His energy is undefeatable. And that's how these other heathen's function — straight from him. He has ultimate control over all of them."

"His pirates come from Abaddon also?"

"His pirates are former slaves. Back in Abaddon, the realm of the dead, there are hundreds of them — sailors that he took back for that specific purpose. The ones he decided not to kill are kept there.

But he's got plenty of dead souls waiting too… no telling what he's thinking. In fact, many of them have been taken back in the very cell he's holding you in now. I don't know why he has so many… he must be planning on creating an even larger army of them. Right now, many of them are there starving, waiting, and unsure what fate lays waiting for them — it's a horrible thing, it is."

Jeremiah shuddered.

"Are you alright, boy?"

"I'm hurting and I'm freezing. It's so dark over here," Jeremiah said.

"I've got a torch over here, but it's too big to pass through this opening. I'm sorry." He paused for a moment. "Do you have anything over in that cell that will light? Maybe you can feel a quick flash of warmth. Do you have anything dry?"

"No," said Jeremiah, but then he remembered something he had in his possession. "Actually, I just may have something." He felt down in his pockets. Yes, it was still there, although the wick was wet. He could feel the stone from Ozron nestled down in his pocket too. And amazingly, the journal was still in the back of his breeches. It was soaked and the pages were all stuck together, but somehow it had survived the fall from the *Nante* and being keelhauled on the pirate ship. He handed the candle to the slave through the tiny window.

He knew the slave was holding the candle near his torch in an attempt to dry the wick out. "This one of the oddest candles I have ever seen. Where did you obtain this?"

"Back in Gordington. From a candle maker."

"Gordington. My, I haven't heard that name in a long time," said the slave sadly. "Brings back many a good memory. Ah, it's lighting now."

Jeremiah could hear thunderous footsteps above them again.

"Alright, here it is," said the slave as he passed the candle back to Jeremiah through the small opening. "They may come again soon. We need to stop talking before they drag the two of us back out there again. If you hear them coming, blow out the candle."

"I will," said Jeremiah. "I didn't get your name."

"McKinley."

"Thank you, McKinley."

McKinley slid the small door closed and Jeremiah sat the small, burning candle on the floor next to him. Though it was just a little candle, it did a marvelous job at lighting up the small cell. It had a strange odor unlike anything he had ever smelled before. But it definitely improved the stench of his confines. The flame was different from any other ordinary flame — it had a tinge of green to it. Maybe this is what Madam Karla meant when she said it was a special candle. Even though it was just a miniscule flame, it provided a hint of warmth. It was better than nothing.

Jeremiah looked around at his confines. The walls were wooden and smooth, not wet as he'd originally thought, but slick with a black soot of some sort. There were scrape marks on all the walls. Jeremiah shuddered at the thought of who might have made them and wondered if they were still alive somewhere. The door had a modest, square window in the middle of it — large enough for an arm to reach through and grab him. There was a holder on the wall behind him. He wondered if it might have held a torch at one time, but it seemed unlikely as the ceiling was so low.

Jeremiah removed his brown vest and his wet, ripped shirt and clumped them into a small ball. He laid it down upon the floor to give him something to rest his head on. Though he was shaking and nearly frozen, removing the wet shirt actually proved a little more comfortable than keeping it on his body. He lay on his side, aching terribly from the wounds that stretched around to his stomach and arms. He nestled as close to the small candle as he could.

The journal was completely soaked. He fingered through the pages, pulling them apart delicately, until he came to where he had last read. The candle provided only a smidgen of light for reading, but it was enough. As he lay there, breathing in the mysterious fumes from the candle and feeling a sense of unusual dizziness, he picked back up where he left off.

October 15th, 1721
I have done as the Society of Osiron requested. I was able to find these pirates with relative ease, but getting aboard their ship was a challenge in itself. Last week I watched in horror as they brutally attacked and killed another crew and sunk their ship. I snuck aboard their ship through an open

gun port and have been waiting for some time now.

I am also still unable to find a convenient time and place to remove the amulet from their possession. It is being held in a small chest, but the chest is in another room a floor above me and is under constant watch by these pirates. I will have to wait until such time that they attack another ship, but I am fearful that the small amount of food and water I have will not last me.

Should that happen, I will try and figure out something else to make it off of this ship alive. I am deep in the hold right now. I can hear them moving about in all parts of it and I had a close call yesterday when I thought a slave they are keeping in a cell a floor above spotted me. I tried to make it up there, but realized soon enough that it would have been impossible...

Jeremiah looked up from his reading. "Slave?" he asked himself. "He must have been talking about McKinley in the cell next to me! He was right here and McKinley didn't even know he had been hiding just a floor below him."

I tried to make it up there, but realized soon enough that it would have been impossible to obtain it at this time. I am able to see through a small hole on the side of their ship.

I have spent the last week mapping out their route to the Miridian Mountains where this brute has an amazing treasure trove. My map also contains specific directions as to where the exact landing spot is at the mountains. I stayed behind when they visited this deadly place in hopes of being able to steal the amulet. However, some of them stayed behind as well and made it impossible for me at this time.

I was quite impressed with their maneuvering ability in the Miridian Mountains. In all of my years on these waters, few souls have ever dared challenging those treacherous waters and those that did always died. We however, made it ashore with no difficulty. The map contained in the back of this journal will show you where the pathway begins to the treasure *hidden at this location. I was able to steal two doubloons from their treasure chest prior to them taking it into the Miridian Mountains. Though I was unable to see the full treasure, from this chest alone I believe it to be more than one man could ever imagine.*

"Map?" whispered Jeremiah. He thumbed to the back of the wet leather journal and carefully pulled the pages apart. There was no map — just blank pages. It must have fallen out at some point prior to him finding the journal. However, as his fingers held the back cover open, he noticed a small indentation on the upper back corner. He ran his fingers across the inside of the back cover, feeling something underneath it.

It was small, round and hard. He moved his fingers closer to the binding. It appeared to have been opened and then resealed with some sort of sticky substance. He worked his fingers on it, scraping away until it peeled apart just a tiny bit. He squeezed his finger in and pried it apart carefully.

There was something there. He pulled it apart, revealing a gold coin and a map. The map too was slightly wet, but had been somewhat protected in its secret place. The parchment it was drawn on was folded up in a neat, little square, but he was able to pull it apart rather easily, revealing the details of the Miridian Mountains and the route to the pirates' treasure. He had no idea what the coin was or how Daniels had obtained it, but it most definitely had the appearance of gold. He held it close to the flame and examined it closely before stuffing it down in his pocket next to Ozron's stone.

He was feeling different than usual: tired, but also woozy. Maybe it was just the combination of his recent ordeals and his lack of sleep. He wanted to close his eyes, but was afraid the pirates would come back and get him again. He also wanted to read more of the journal.

Jeremiah carefully placed the folded map in his pocket. He picked up the journal and shuffled around for a brief moment, trying to find the most comfortable position with his wounds. He was unsure where he had left off and the wet pages of the journal stuck together like molasses. When he tried pulling them apart again, the pages began ripping and most of the print was left missing or illegible. "Oh no," he said, worried that the important entries were now destroyed. He continued working at them page by page, until he found one that was readable. It appeared to be the last of Daniels's entries:

November 19th, 1721

I feel that I am reaching the end. I feel him getting closer. Over the next few days I will take what I have obtained and see if I can locate the Director. Though I wasn't able to meet him in my initial meeting with the Secret Society of Osiron, I think he is *here somewhere in Gordington Square. I know Molodan is close on my trail and I have gone through tremendous, tiring efforts to hide from him. He has an uncanny way of honing in on this amulet and I know that if I don't relinquish it to the Society soon, I will be next on his list of victims.*

The innkeeper I met tonight seems he may know much about these parts. I will check with him to see if he has any knowledge of this Secret Society of Osiron. At first I thought he may be the one I am seeking, but after closer examination... well, he's probably not. I was told the Director was a business owner, but I have no other knowledge of his identity. I will check with this innkeeper in the morning at either rate...

The rest of the page was blank, but Jeremiah could see what appeared to be blood spatter across the page and over the words. He wondered what the spatter was from and if it was in fact blood… was it from Daniels?

He sat the journal down, but wondered what he had missed in the ruined pages. He did realize the significance of what the ghost was trying to emphasize to him and why it was so important that the information be shared. His guess was that Daniels knew some of the same information as McKinley regarding the destruction of Molodan. He hoped that was all he missed from the pages that had been destroyed.

His body was beginning to feel inconceivably odd. It was much more than sleepiness or pain. He felt a strange fuzziness radiating on his skin, but in some places, especially his head, it went all the way through his body. "What's happening to me?" he whispered.

Jeremiah closed his eyes as he felt the freakish sensations overcoming him. It was overpoweringly unnatural to him, although it wasn't an alarming feeling. "Is it the —" he said as he looked over to the candle.

He rolled onto his back as the effect worked upon him, not noticing the pain from his wounds. His entire body felt as if it were vibrating on the floor. He heard strange clicks and pops and his entire environment began reverberating as if a heard of cattle were running upon the surface. His heart began pounding so intensely that it felt as if it would beat straight out of his chest.

And then, the most amazing thing happened. Although his eyes were closed, he could see perfectly clear. "How could this be happening?" He tried to remain relaxed as best he could and sit back up. The more effort he put into it, the louder the whirring and buzzing in his entire mind and soul became. He rolled to his side, as if on instinct, and then the separation occurred.

This was the most phenomenal thing he had ever encountered! He struggled to his feet, although it felt much different than normal. Amazingly, his head wasn't touching the ceiling in his cell any longer. He looked down where his body still lay sleeping.

He was now completely comfortable: the chilled air of the ship no longer affected him, he could no longer feel the pain in his flesh, and he stood there wondering if he had just died.

But he couldn't have. He could see the rise and fall of his chest and hear himself breathing. He looked around. The environment was similar, but now had a strange, transparent look about it. He could see McKinley sleeping in the cell right next to him, along with his torch. "Amazing."

He could also see through the floors above him. In fact, he could see everything happening through the filmy surfaces all over the entire pirate ship. Molodan was on the upper deck and the pirate crew was dispersed through the ship. Most of them were in the physical, pirate-looking form; however, he could see some radiating balls of light darting around the ship on all levels.

He held out his hands directly in front of his face. He stared at them with great intensity and the more he looked at them, they began dissolving right before his very eyes. "This is brilliant! Madam Karla knew exactly what she was talking about when she told me this candle was special!"

He reached for the door, wondering if he was still confined in his current state, but his hand went right through it. He laughed as he tried it again. As his hand penetrated the filmy door it felt like it was passing through water.

He built up his nerve and decided he was going to attempt walking straight through the door to the other side. He took a deep breath, though he really didn't have lungs to breathe, and made a quick, small leap straight in the direction of the door in front of him. Amazing! It felt as if he had just skipped through a light flowing waterfall, and he realized immediately that he was on the other side of his cell.

Jeremiah didn't know where to go from here. His body was still in the cell, and he knew he couldn't leave it behind. He could easily see everyone else moving about the ship and he began to worry if they could, in turn, see him too. Walking was strangely different, and in this new environment, he could hear strange noises and thought his name was being called.

"Hello?" he whispered, but realized that his voice came out garbled, for he had no vocal cords to speak from. "Is anyone there?" he tried again, with a little more clarity this time.

From the opposite corner of the room, a strange and brilliant light emerged. "They've found me!" he whispered and froze. He didn't know where to go or how to get back in his body. There was no use trying to go anywhere else — there were pirates in every other part of the ship. The light continued growing in size.

Jeremiah noticed this light was different from the spherical balls darting all over the ship above him. This light had glowing warmth to it. He began to feel calmer and he knew that this wasn't something to be feared. After all, Nefron came to him in a similar form and was nothing but playful.

This light was the most comforting, warming light he had ever laid eyes on. Although its brightness grew in intensity by the second, he could look directly at it without it blinding him. Maybe it was just because he was without body… or maybe this was just a dream.

"This can't be a dream," he commented. He had an ultimate awareness of his surroundings, much more so than when he was in his physical body. Dreams were surreal in comparison to what he was experiencing. All of his senses were completely alive.

The radiance continued to intensify and Jeremiah could see something forming within it. It obviously wasn't Nefron or one of the pirates. It was much larger and he could see a face forming within, becoming more familiar with every moment.

CHAPTER FIFTEEN

THE AMAZING ESCAPE

C ould it be? It was!

"Mother?" Jeremiah cried.

"Yes," she said, her voice echoing warmly. She was more beautiful than he ever remembered. She was not emotional, but rather calm, peaceful, and smiled at her son.

"How?" he asked, barely able to speak. He lunged for her and their souls reunited. They connected and Jeremiah shook within her light. Even in the spiritual form, they were able to embrace as they had so long ago in the flesh.

"You are now in the astral," she said, her arms still around him. "You have projected beyond your physical body."

"I can't —" he choked, "I can't believe you're here." Streams of joyful tears ran down his astral face.

"I've always been here. As quick as a thought, I am right here. Whenever you have needed me, I have always been close," she said.

"Can you stay with me?" he pleaded, desperate to hang on to her.

She pulled away from him. "Not now, Jeremiah. And you haven't much time. You must get off of this ship," she said lovingly, but sternly.

"There's no way!" he cried.

His mother pointed to the wall on their right. "Yes, there is," she insisted. "Take the keys to your cell. Hide them. When the time is right, you must get off this ship."

Footsteps thundered immediately above them. They both looked up. One of the pirates was making his way across the floor overhead towards the stairway that led to Jeremiah's holding cell.

"I must go, they're coming! Hurry Jeremiah!"

"No! Please don't leave me!" Jeremiah cried. "I need to know about —" But before he could ask her about his father's fate, she vanished. The pirate was almost to the stairwell and Jeremiah rushed over to the keys hanging on the wall. He tried reaching for them, but his hand moved straight through them. How was he supposed to do this? He tried again, but still couldn't grasp them. "Concentrate," he said as he extended his hand again.

The pirate was climbing down the stairs. Jeremiah focused all of his energy upon the keys in front of him and heard a small clink as he grasped the ring. Quickly, he moved across the floor and pushed them through the window in his cell door. He moved back through his door as the pirate turned the corner. Jeremiah concentrated on his body and, as quick as a flash, he was back in it.

He pretended that he was still asleep and unconscious. He need not worry about the candle — it had already burned down and was nothing more than a warm puddle of green wax on his cell floor. He could hear the heavy breathing of the brute as he peered inside his cell, checking to see if he was still there. The pirate stood there momentarily, and then left. He didn't notice the missing keys.

When Jeremiah thought the pirate had left, he breathed a tremendous sigh of relief. However, the realization that he was back in his body set in quickly. Pain surged throughout his extremities. He tried to remain still, for the more he moved, the greater the pain.

He heard a cell door open, but it wasn't his cell this time. His breathing became faint and shallow as he listened to the pirate waking McKinley and removing him from his cell.

"How did they unlock his cell? Did they notice they keys were missing? No, they must be using another set," he whispered frantically. He cracked one eye open. McKinley's cell door was still open and the torch inside it illuminated the room momentarily — enough for Jeremiah to see the pirate's frightening face looking in on him. Jeremiah closed his eyes until he knew for sure that they were gone.

A short time had passed when Jeremiah realized some other unnatural phenomenon was taking place aboard the pirate ship. A brilliant light was advancing from the deck of the ship and it was visible through the tiny cracks of the ship's exterior. Immediately afterwards, the entire ship began vibrating and humming. Jeremiah remembered what McKinley had told him about the gateway. He couldn't help but believe that was what was now taking place. This must have been why his mother had been so intent on him getting off. If he was to go to Abaddon aboard this ship, his fate would be sealed. He couldn't allow that to happen.

Jeremiah struggled to his feet and grabbed the keys. He knew time was running out. He would have to risk being seen. He carefully placed his arm though the open window and felt for the keyhole. Once he had found it, he inserted the key and freed himself. "Exit. I must find an exit."

He rushed to the opposite side of the ship and found the hole from the *Nante's* cannon blast. It was the dead of night but whatever was happening above him illuminated the entire night sky and surrounding ocean. Jeremiah suspected that Molodan was using the amulet.

"I must get off this ship immediately," he said as he peered through the gaping hole. Going up wasn't an option and moving lower in the ship would not work. Even his small frame couldn't fit through the current size of the breach. If only the hole was a little larger. He began kicking the boards closest to the hole. The vibrations were intensifying and the ship slowly moved forward.

One of the boards began to come free, but he couldn't get it to open any wider. Out of desperation, he tried pushing with his hands. He knew his time was almost out. "Come on you stupid thing!" he yelled as he pushed with his last remaining energy. The board broke loose and he fell into the water, right behind it.

He went in headfirst after the board, but just in time. When he resurfaced, he could see the silvery and gigantic gateway opening above the water's surface. He was nearly touching it himself and he kicked violently away from it. He watched the filmy surface of the portal as the pirate ship moved further into it. Suddenly it vanished from sight, as did the gateway itself.

Jeremiah was left alone in the water, hurt, and clutching the board. His body was exhausted and the cold saltwater caused his wounds to burn terribly. He knew he wouldn't last long. He placed his arms over the top of the board and propped himself up on his elbows as he scanned the surrounding waters. There was no land in sight from what he could tell and the night was dark and empty. He feared that something would come up from the bottomless abyss below his feet and devour him. There was nothing he could do. He watched the area where the portal had closed. He wondered if it would reopen, and if Molodan and his crew would search for the one that had escaped their confines.

A couple of hours later Jeremiah was struggling to stay afloat on the board which continually bobbed up and down under his weight. He was becoming increasingly tired by the minute and he spread his upper body across the board the best he could as his eyes began to close from exhaustion.

As a hint of morning drew near, a small flittering light darted over the waters. It zigzagged with tremendous speed and seemingly with intent towards Jeremiah, clinging to life in the lonely, barren ocean.

Jeremiah was nearly unconscious from fatigue and his head occasionally bobbed underneath the water. "Help," he said as he choked on the water. The light arrived and hovered momentarily over Jeremiah's head. Jeremiah could see it watching him, almost as if it were assessing how best to help him. He knew it was Nefron. His head bobbed beneath the water's surface and Nefron grabbed a clump of his hair and pulled.

Jeremiah felt the tugging and heard the nisse emit a shrill scream. Jeremiah was too exhausted to react but the noise rang out for miles across the water and through the air.

A short time later Jeremiah became vaguely aware of claws on his arm. He forced his eyelids open to see Blessie perched there with Nefron.

"We thought he drowned!" Blessie said to Nefron.

Nefron didn't speak, but he mimed what needed to be done. He moved his arms and fluttered in a fashion that told Blessie the boy didn't have long.

"I'll get help!" cawed Blessie. She immediately took back to the sky.

Jeremiah faded in and out of consciousness. When he came to, Nefron was still holding onto his hair, but his vibrations were weakening and his bright glowing light was slowly starting to dim.

He would share the boy's fate if Blessie didn't come through for them soon.

Jeremiah grinned tiredly when he saw the silhouette of a ship on the horizon. He opened his eyes wider to see the *Nante* moving with slow precision. It now only had one working sail, and it struggled with the wind to move them to their destination. Blessie flew around the ship, swooping near the water, directing her captain and his crew to Jeremiah.

As they came close, Jeremiah looked up to them and could see Van Russel standing at the ship's fore as he pointed to him. The red feather on his new gargantuan hat blew about in the wind. Tears streamed down his face as he approached.

"How could it be true!" Van Russel exclaimed as he bent over the side. "Men, get him out of that thar water now!"

Three crewmen jumped over the side of the ship into the water next to Jeremiah. They grabbed him and supported him above the water as they struggled to get him back to the ship.

Within hours, Jeremiah awoke on a bunk in the captain's cabin, surrounded by his friends. Van Russel had taken a nap and had his feet propped upon his desk, his head back, snoring obnoxiously. Ranjit was there. He stood up against the wall, rolling his eyes at Van Russel, waiting for the boy to come to. Augustus sat at his side and motioned to Ranjit as Jeremiah looked around.

"Captain!" Ranjit yelled, upon the signal from Augustus.

"What? Huh?" he snorted. "He's awake?"

They all rushed over to him.

"Captain?" Jeremiah asked, with a slight smile.

"Yes, lad… we found ye, but we can't take all the credit." He pointed back over to his desk where Blessie was perched. Nefron was buzzing at her side. They too had their eyes upon him. Nefron flew over to him and walked up the length of his stomach and chest, stopping directly in front of his face.

"I think someone has taken a special liking to ye, boy," Van Russel commented.

Nefron bowed to Jeremiah, jumped up and hovered over his chest, and returned to the table where Blessie was perched, waiting.

Van Russel walked about the room with silly steps. "Aye boy, all the credit must be given to Blessie and Nefron. Without the two of them, we'd have never found ye." He rushed over to Jeremiah and hugged him. "Ye scared the captain… and he's happy ye are back." He placed Jeremiah's hat back on his head. "We found this amidst all the rubble on the deck. I can't believe it didn't get sucked away too." A single tear welled up in his eye.

"Aye, Jeremiah, it's good to have ye back on board," Ranjit said to him.

Jeremiah looked up to him. *That must have been difficult to say,* he thought. "Thank you, Ranjit… it's good to be back," he said. Jeremiah looked over to his friend. Augustus was all smiles, but looked like he still couldn't believe that Jeremiah was back with them. He too reached over and gave Jeremiah a hug. He still didn't say anything, but there was no need to — Jeremiah knew his friend had missed him.

He rose quickly from the bunk and sat up on the side, excitedly. "Captain, the Secret Society of Osiron — we must have them meet."

Van Russel looked surprisingly confused. "Lad, how on earth do ye know of that?"

"From the journal," said Jeremiah. He felt about himself. "Oh no! I left it on their ship."

"What journal? I have only recently learned of this Society myself."

"Daniels's journal. We must meet with these people! I now know how to destroy the pirate Molodan and his crew," he said.

"Alright, alright, lad… I know the Society," Van Russel replied, quite surprised. "Let me send word back. We need to head back to Gordington anyway. We'll have the Society meet when we get there." He rushed over to his desk and pulled out another piece of parchment. As he had before, he ripped off only a small piece before dipping his pen and writing the urgent message:

> Ebineezer —
> Jeremiah is alive. Please assemble the
> Society upon our return. We plan to be
> in Gordington Friday night. Please be
> ready.
>
> Urgently Requested,
> Captain Van Russel

He rolled it up and looked at his bird.

"I know! I know!" Blessie cawed as she moved across the desk to him.

"Blessie, take this to the innkeeper. He'll know what to do," Van Russel instructed. He placed the message in the container still attached to her leg and the parrot took off, darting out of the door towards Gordington.

Ranjit turned to Van Russel. "What if they come looking for the boy?"

"We must get out of here now. Give command to set sail for Gordington immediately. When they notice he has escaped, they could very well come back right here. Since our wheel is gone, the crew will have to assist Orville in manually manipulating the rudder."

"Aye, Captain." Ranjit gave the orders to the crew and they steered the *Nante* back towards Gordington where Van Russel and Jeremiah would meet with the Secret Society of Osiron.

THE
SECRET SOCIETY

Ebineezer filled his old pewter tankard to the rim. He held it up and chugged it, before slamming it back down on the tiny bar. Although usually his time with his brandy was typically one of slow enjoyment, this was not such a time. His hands shook nervously as he anticipated their arrival. He looked at his clock, then back to the door and up at the clock again before pacing the floor of the inn.

Where were they? What held them up? "This is doing nothing for me health," he muttered. "Maybe that ole fool Doc Hazleton has a remedy for this too."

Thunder suddenly roared as lightning streaked the night sky. Large gusts of sweeping rain followed, quickly drenching everything. He eyed the front door. "Of course, I reckon the weather has to be perfect every time," he said sarcastically.

The Director had people waiting and he was waiting too. Nothing could move forward without them, so they must hurry themselves and be there as they said they would be. The letter brought by the bird said this was the night. If in fact it was, then why hadn't they shown up before now? He grabbed his nearly empty bottle of brandy. As he removed the bottle's plug, he heard the front door opening behind him. He turned, "Oh, could it be? Thank God!" he yelled. He hurried to embrace Jeremiah. Jeremiah moaned slightly from the innkeeper embracing his sore back, but Ebineezer did not notice. He was too overjoyed to have Jeremiah in his presence again.

"It's good to see you again, Mr. Drake," Jeremiah beamed.

"Oh, and it's great to see ye again boy."

"Are ye gonna hug me too?" asked Van Russel, entering the inn.

"Would ye like a hug from the innkeeper, Captain?" asked Ebineezer.

"I want a hug," Blessie cawed. They all laughed.

Ebineezer removed Jeremiah's hat. "They didn't hurt ye too badly, did ye boy?" He moved his head around, inspecting his face as a mother would.

"He wouldn't let them," said Van Russel, before giving Jeremiah an opportunity to respond. "He showed them… yes he did!"

"So, Mr. Drake, you are the Director, aren't you? You were the one Daniels was coming to meet?" Jeremiah asked.

Ebineezer's demeanor immediately changed. "Who did ye just say, boy?"

"Daniels," said Jeremiah.

Ebineezer turned to Van Russel.

"I haven't said a word, Innkeeper," Van Russel assured him.

Ebineezer needed another drink. He emptied his brandy into his tankard and took a long swig. "My Lord, how do ye know that name?" he asked.

"I've met him. Here. His ghost," said Jeremiah.

Ebineezer blew the brandy out of his mouth. "What!" he gasped.

"Yes," said Jeremiah. "Before I left here I spoke with him. In fact, the night you and the captain came to my room to speak with me, he had just left."

"Jeremiah," said Van Russel cautiously, "ye mean to tell me that ye weren't talking to yeself before we entered yer room? There was a dead man's ghost in the room?"

"Yes, of course," said Jeremiah, matter-of-factly.

"Oh God, I need another bottle of brandy," panicked Ebineezer.

"Poor me one too, Innkeeper," added Van Russel.

"We came here to meet, not drink," Jeremiah said, frustrated.

"Ok, ok, the lad is right," said Van Russel. "Is everyone here?"

"Yes, downstairs waiting," said Ebineezer.

"There's a downstairs?" asked Jeremiah.

"Oh yes," laughed Ebineezer. "We still have a few surprises left for ye, boy. Now, go grab that candle off the bar and ye two follow me to the room in the back."

Jeremiah and Van Russel followed Ebineezer to the cigar room in the rear of the inn. Jeremiah knew which one it was as he had seen some meetings there before, though he wasn't included then. Van Russel shut the door behind them.

"Jeremiah, come over here with the candle," Ebineezer instructed. He removed a picture from the wall and slid a small table away from the wall's edge. "Ok, now come a little closer." Jeremiah held the candle close to the wall as Ebineezer felt around the wallboards. He knocked on them lightly with his knuckles until he found the right one. "Alright, here we go." He pushed in on the top edge of the plank and the wall shifted slightly, making a resounding noise. A cloud of dust resulted and an area of the wall just large enough for them to pass through sank in slightly and slid sideways.

"Ready?" Ebineezer asked.

Jeremiah nodded.

"Stay close to the sides," whispered Van Russel.

They walked in; Ebineezer first, and then Jeremiah, and Van Russel last.

"Stand here," Ebineezer blurted firmly, immediately upon entering the dark room.

They stood on a stone platform as Ebineezer felt for a handle on the other side of the wall. Jeremiah held the candle close.

"Aye, here it is." He pulled down on the lever and the wall closed perfectly, as if there really wasn't a door there at all. This area was quite musty, even more so than the old inn itself. They could see only as far as the short range of the candle, allowing a few feet in any direction.

"Stay close to the sides," Van Russel instructed again.

Jeremiah looked down. Descending from the platform on which they were standing was a winding stone staircase. He kicked a small rock that was sitting next to his foot. He listened; there was a long delay before he heard it hit bottom. He knew it would be certain death if he were to fall off these steps.

"Aye, it's long way down."

They began their slow descent.

"What is this?" asked Jeremiah.

"The entrance to the Secret Society," replied Van Russel.

Jeremiah could feel his heart racing. He had no idea what to anticipate next, or who would be waiting for them at the bottom.

"I used to call it the stairway to Hades," chortled Van Russel.

"Van Russel, please," said Ebineezer. "Not now. Jeremiah, stay as close to the sides as possible."

"Arrgh, sorry Ebineezer."

"This used to be a well long ago, many years before the inn was constructed. We don't know who built the stairs into it, but it worked out nicely, especially since the inn was built around it. Must have been used for other secret purposes long ago too. The room at the bottom had already been dug out as well."

Their voices echoed slightly and the candle struggled to light their way as they descended further. Jeremiah strained to keep it still and the flame lit, holding his hand in front of it. He could only see the back of the innkeeper's head as they descended and he dared not look down. The steps were constructed equally and he timed the motion of his feet with each step. Ebineezer had no difficulty — he had obviously been through the routine many times.

"No one would ever find you down here or dare try," said Jeremiah.

"Aye," replied Van Russel. "Thus, the reason it makes a perfect meeting place for the Society.

As they came closer to the bottom of the stairwell, other noises indicated that they were not alone. Their pathway became lighter and the muffled, echoing noises became voices speaking. Jeremiah knew they were close. The voices were becoming much more pronounced to him now. In fact, he thought he recognized one of them.

"IDIOCY! PURE IDIOCY! The boy could have been killed with stunts like those!" the man yelled.

"It was Governor Addison's idea. He sent them on that mission," said another.

"That mindless governor has no business making any decisions! He's a blatant nincompoop!" The voice stopped when Jeremiah and his companions entered from the stairwell.

Jeremiah knew that voice.

"Hello young one," Ozron smiled, catching his breath from his outburst.

"Ozron! So great to see you again!" Jeremiah ran to the man he barely knew and hugged him. But it felt right and his presence there was more than comforting. It was strange — Ozron felt like a life-long friend.

"Come take a seat Jeremiah. We have much to discuss tonight," said Ozron. "And let's introduce you properly."

Jeremiah looked around the room. He knew everyone there. Madam Karla, the candle maker, sat on the table opposite him, smiling. "Hello Jeremiah," she said pleasantly. "Nice to be seeing you again. Have you used the candle yet?" Jeremiah began to respond but she quickly interjected. "Oh, never mind," she said with a huge smile. "I can tell from your expression that you already have." She winked at him, devilishly.

There was the blacksmith, Boswell. "Hello son, nice to see you again." He didn't have much to say, but Jeremiah could feel the sincerity in his voice.

"So this is it," said Ozron. "Welcome to the Secret Society, or Osiron as some of us frequently refer to it. Osiron is our code name for it."

Jeremiah spoke up. "Yes, it all makes sense now." He looked around the room. "Daniels wrote in his journal of the Director, the Forger and the Candle Maker." He pointed to Ebineezer, the blacksmith and Madam Karla in turn. "And he spoke of the Alchemist.

But... there is no alchemist." Everyone turned to Ozron. "You?" asked Jeremiah. "I thought you were a —"

"A peddler?" Ozron cut in, laughing. "I go by many things... and being a peddler is just one of them. It is not necessary for most to know anything more."

"Of course," said Jeremiah. The pieces slowly started to fit together in his head. He turned around to Captain Van Russel. "But come to think of it, he didn't speak of any captain."

"Van Russel has just been recently inducted to the Society," said Ozron. "He knew nothing of our commissioning of Daniels. Nor did the innkeeper... Ebineezer knew we had commissioned a man, but knew not his name or who he was, initially. Those meetings were conducted in Tortuga before we started meeting down here. But as I said a minute ago, we have much to discuss with you. Everyone please come and sit down."

Jeremiah examined their meeting room. Even though it was all stone and far below the surface of the ground, it was pleasant and inviting. A large fire roared in the far corner, venting through a small shaft to the surface above. Their meeting table was a huge, solid piece of hickory, rounded and smoothed to the perfect dimensions. Around the room, scrolls and books lay stacked. Jeremiah wondered if they were used as references for this secret society.

"Being that there is so much to cover, I will start at the beginning and will include as much detail as I can remember," Ozron said.

Everyone sat around the table and waited for the old man to begin. Madam Karla spoke up. "Go ahead, Ozron. We're ready."

"In the year fifteen hundred and twenty three, I was but a young lad. I was in my early thirties, and so was my closest of friends, Rousseau. It was during this time that both Rousseau and I began dabbling in the areas of alchemy and he and I together created a key… a gateway of sorts… an amulet. We found some ancient scrolls that instructed us on the process, though they were eventually lost. We had the ingenious idea that this amulet we created would open up doors to other worlds for us to explore, to experience… to conquer. At first, it didn't work. But, we came across another old, Latin scroll that had the missing ingredient we were looking for." He looked about the room and pointed to one of the old, dusty scrolls. "It was in that last remaining scroll there that we found the words that would activate the gateway. *Patefacio Prodigium*."

"*Patefacio Prodigium*? What does that mean?" asked Jeremiah.

"*Open the Portal*. Yes, we were but young and stupid, and most unaware of what opening these doors would bring."

"It was in this year that he and I were working on a coal-transporting ship. Late one night while everyone slept, we decided we would give the amulet a try. It was three o'clock in the morning when we assembled the amulet. And it was at this time that our lives would change forever.

"Unbeknown to us at the time, this time of the morning is the exact time when the veil between their world — those of the dead — and ours, is at its thinnest. I suspect that is the time that he whom we now call Molodan opens and closes the portal. We opened the gateway and sitting on the other side was Molodan — an evil, cunning, and ruthless soul. He was waiting to be set free and we gave him the opportunity, right then and there. He came at us with full force, manifesting into different shapes, forms against which we were defenseless. He killed the entire crew, took our ship as his own, and stole our amulet. He now had a key to come and go between both worlds as he pleased. Only two survived his attack that night. Rousseau and I escaped off the side of the ship. All the other innocents on board died."

"Rousseau and I made a pact never to give up until we put an end to what we had begun. We attempted to kill the fiend, only once, and as a result of our further stupidity, Rousseau was killed. But not before he was able to tell me something.

As he lie there dying and gasping for his last breath, he told me he would return, sometime within the next two hundred years, to defeat Molodan. He said I would know when he returned. And I did know when I saw him again. In fact, it was recently when I saw the fire in one young boy's eyes, I realized that Rousseau had returned."

"I'm a bit confused Ozron. If this started two centuries ago and ye were here when it started, when did ye die?" asked Van Russel, looking befuddled.

"He didn't," answered Jeremiah.

There was a long silence.

"Oh me!" yelled the captain, "Shiver me timbers now!"

"Good boy," said Ozron. "I think you're catching on. Now, for two centuries this evil fiend would kill sporadically, but nothing like what it has been the last few years. He's been taking ships and killing the patrons of Gordington Square regularly. I believe this behemoth from the abyss is fully aware of Rousseau's return and feels threatened. He's now killing at every opportunity and he's taking souls back to where he came from. God only knows why."

"He's using them as slaves," said Jeremiah. "The slave aboard the pirate ship told me all about it. He's planning on building up his own army of pirates or something."

"Then it is what I feared," said Ozron, "This situation is becoming dire."

Jeremiah watched as the Society sat quietly and none seemed shocked to hear what Ozron had to share. Ebineezer sat back in his chair, sipping on his remaining brandy, a look of exhaustion and dizziness crossed his face. Madam Karla sat with the perfect posture in her chair, her arms crossed, nodding. Boswell had both arms propped upon the table, supporting his chin as he listened with open eyes. But Van Russel seemed to be hearing most of this for the first time. He looked confused as he helped himself to a bowl of dates sitting on the table.

He fed some to Blessie and he smacked his lips as he chewed. Even Blessie made a loud chewing noise as the captain fed her. Van Russel eventually looked up from his private meal to see the room silent, and staring at him. "Oh, er, sorry," he said.

Ozron rolled his eyes. "Where was I?"

"You were telling us that you feared the situation that is now coming to pass," answered Madam Karla.

"Oh, yes. Anyhow, Jeremiah, this Society, the people you see before you, was organized by me in hopes of recreating the key, or the doorway, that Rousseau and I created so long ago. Everyone has their purpose here in ensuring the secret is maintained, and some of us have put our skills to use in order to attempt to recreate this doorway. Up until now we have been unsuccessful."

"And where does Daniels come in all of this?" asked Jeremiah, scratching his head as he tried to take it all in.

"Daniels was commissioned by our group last year to try and steal back the amulet. He had been known for his abilities of petty thieving and he was remarkable with a sword. We figured him perfect for the job, eh, if you want to call it that."

"And he was successful," added Jeremiah, "at least until he was killed, here in the inn."

"Yes, we had come very close," said Ozron, "but our lack of communication with the innkeeper cost Daniels his life, and cost us the amulet." He shook his head sadly and looked up at Jeremiah. "How do you come here already knowing so much of this man, young one?"

"I've spoken to him and I've read his journal," said Jeremiah.

Ozron's attention turned to the innkeeper.

Ebineezer cut in, "Oh aye, he just told me too. He's spoken to his ghost, right here in me inn on more than one occasion. And me dead guest shared his journal with him too. If ye want to know what I thought of it, well, I found it a bit…unsettling."

"But how has Jeremiah been able to converse with the ghost of our client when the innkeeper had no knowledge of him being right here in the inn?" asked Boswell.

"Maybe with assistance of a special stone Jeremiah had in his possession," Ozron hinted as he looked at Jeremiah, smiling.

"The stone… of course!" exclaimed Jeremiah.

"Stone? What stone?" the other members asked.

"Never mind that now," said Ozron, "Jeremiah, this journal you speak of — where is it?

"It was lost, Ozron, when I escaped."

"Oh bother, every time we come close, it's something else," said the old man, shaking his head and pacing about the room.

"But I do —" Jeremiah tried to speak, but was cut off by Van Russel.

"Regarding the ghost, aye, I found out that I almost walked in on him too. And it 'bout threw me stomach in a fisherman's knot when he told me." He began chewing on his dates again.

Ozron looked at Van Russel, disgusted. Van Russel obviously hadn't been paying attention. "At this point, everything has failed. I am unsure of what to do now." He sat down in a chair away from the rest of the group, exhausted.

"Well, we must obtain the amulet," said Boswell.

"And how do you suppose we do that, Blacksmith?" asked Madam Karla.

"Umm, dunno, maybe lure him?"

"What do you mean, lure him?" asked Madam Karla.

"The way I see it, the amulet is our only option at this point. We have tried recreating it, unsuccessfully. We have tried stealing it and came close," said Boswell.

"Lure him with what?" exclaimed Madam Karla. "We have nothing, other than our souls that he would want!"

"What if we take his treasure?" asked Jeremiah. "He would certainly come after that if he knew it had been disturbed."

"Oh boy, that's pure hockey pock! Nonsensical, nonsense!" yelled Ebineezer.

"Aye, been hearing stories of missing treasures on the waters for years. `Fraid it's nothin' but a story," added Van Russel.

"No, it's true!" yelled Jeremiah. "I can —"

Everyone, except Ozron, burst out in anxious laughter. Jeremiah tried to talk, but was subdued by the others' laughter and claims of false tales.

"Let the boy speak!" Ozron yelled. The room turned silent. "Jeremiah, go ahead. Tell me what you know of this treasure."

"In the Miridian Mountains… it's there."

"What exactly is there?" asked Ozron.

"Molodan's treasure. Everything he has ever looted. More than one man could ever imagine, as Daniels put it."

"So, ye didn't exactly see this treasure then, lad?" asked Van Russel.

"No."

"The Miridian Mountains are some of the most treacherous waters ships have ever dared to enter. Davy Jones's locker is flooded with the hulls of hundreds there. I believe this treasure to be nothing more than a myth," sighed Van Russel.

"It's not, though!" exclaimed Jeremiah.

"We have no proof of it," said Madam Karla.

"Pure hockey pock, if you ask me," said Ebineezer.

"Much too risky for something that might not be there," added Boswell.

The room broke out in argument. Ozron covered his face and shook his head out of frustration. No one would give Jeremiah the time to explain what he knew and why he knew it.

"HERE!" Jeremiah screamed, slamming his hand upon the table. "YOU WANT PROOF? HERE IT IS!" He pulled his hand away, revealing a gold coin and a map.

Ebineezer's mouth dropped. "Bring those over to me, Jeremiah." He looked at them carefully. "Um, oh my, I believe the boy might be telling the truth. That's just like the coin Daniels gave me before he died."

Ozron came close to Jeremiah and kneeled beside him. "Jeremiah, tell me, where did you get these?" he whispered.

"From the back of Daniels's leather journal. They had been glued into the back cover. I removed them prior to losing the journal."

Ozron smiled widely. "Attaboy," he whispered. "Now, does anyone in this room have anything else to dispute with the Society's newest member?" he asked, raising his voice again. Jeremiah looked up at him and he winked back. The room was silent, but all eyes were upon him and they looked with confidence and approval.

"Now we're getting somewhere," said Boswell.

"So, what do ye suggest, Master Bloom?" smiled Ebineezer.

"Take his treasure, and lure him to us," said Jeremiah.

"I agree with the boy," said Ozron. "The fiend is a selfish one, as he is with his souls. No doubt if we disturb what he has taken, he'll come a hauling. But we must plan first and be fully prepared; this will be no easy feat."

"Yes, reminds me," said Jeremiah, his tone lowering, "keel-hauling, it's time for payback."

"What are you talking about?" asked Ozron.

Jeremiah stood and turned. He raised his vest and shirt and the members gasped.

"This was their way of showing me," said Jeremiah with quiet rage.

"Oh me," said Ebineezer. "I didn't think they hurt ye."

"Oh aye, meant to tell ye about that," Van Russel commented, embarrassed.

"Just my back," said Jeremiah. "Not my pride."

"And those were the words of Rousseau, many years ago, when he received the same punishment," said Ozron. "It's good to have you back." He patted Jeremiah on the shoulder.

"I bet this Rousseau was good with a pistol, wasn't he," said Van Russel.

"The best," said Ozron.

Van Russel nodded as he munched on his date. "Aye, the captain can believe the story now."

It made sense to the rest of the Society's members also. Jeremiah was Rousseau, reincarnated. Although Jeremiah had no recollection of his life before this one, his purpose began to make sense to him... just as the ghost of Daniels had once told him. He knew now that all the events in his life had led up to this and the drive inside him was in full gear now. It was strange, however; the fear that seemed to overcome him in all aspects of his life was diminishing. And even though he knew of the dangers ahead, he did not fear them. He was pumped for the action, ready for justice and sought revenge for what the pirates had done to him and so many others.

He relaxed back in his chair and stared at the other members and they stared back at him. A new sense of strength fell over the room. Everyone knew what must be done.

"We'll head out tomorrow," said Van Russel. "There's no time to spare."

"I agree," said Ozron. "But first we must meet with your crew and plan how this will be done."

"And when we have lured him, then what shall we do?" asked Boswell.

"There's the issue of taking him down," said Jeremiah.

"That's correct, young one. We must find a way to eliminate him," said Ozron.

"Is there a way?" asked Madam Karla.

"Yes," said Jeremiah. "When Molodan has the gate —"

But as Jeremiah began explaining the method of Molodan's demise, the room rattled. Ozron held up his finger for silence. They all looked around; everything appeared to be fine. Then it happened again. Like a small, fast earthquake, the room shook lightly. The members felt the quick vibration and watched as the scrolls moved slightly. The logs on the fire fell, throwing up a small shower of embers.

"What is that?" asked Madam Karla.

The men in the room gazed at each other. Undeniably, they felt they knew what it was.

"Everyone stay here!" Ozron instructed. "I am going to the surface. Shut the door to this room and do not open it until I come back!"

"Oh no, me inn! I'm coming with ye, Ozron!" yelled Ebineezer.

Ozron and Ebineezer hurried from the room and began ascending the staircase to the surface. Boswell followed them to the entrance and pulled another lever within the meeting room. A huge stone door emerged from the side and closed up the room of Osiron, the Secret Society, shutting Jeremiah and the others inside.

CHAPTER SEVENTEEN

PIRATES' REVENGE

W hat was that?" asked one of the patrons, looking confused amidst the blustering song and music in the Wharf.

"What?" challenged the bartender. "I hear only the cries of yet another loss," he boasted as he walked away from the table of yet another muddled victim.

"Please, not my boat!" cried an intoxicated elderly gentleman upon the floor. He grabbed the leg of the bartender, but the bartender kicked him away.

"Yer loss, my —" Suddenly a thunderous boom rattled the bar. This time it grabbed everyone's attention and the music stopped abruptly.

There was silence in the room.

The bartender started again, but as he opened his mouth a cannon ball thundered through the wall of the Wharf, hitting him square in the chest, sending him through the other side of the bar. The elderly man dodged it by only a few inches. He looked up for the bartender, confused.

"We're under attack!" yelled a patron, looking out through the exploded hole and seeing the pirate ship firing from the bay. Everyone scurried, half drunk and stumbling.

Indeed, the town of Gordington Square was under barrage. Molodan and his crew were in the bay and all sixteen of their cannons fired sequentially upon the buildings and the other ships docked near. The demon in charge of them was searching for the boy who had escaped his evil, floating fortress. He was determined to get him back and he brought along a full crew and arsenal to do so. Gordington was not prepared, nor had they ever been forced to defend themselves. Arming themselves against these villains was futile and the townspeople ran for their lives, scurrying in all directions, screaming and confused. The men grabbed their muskets and positioned themselves in strategic areas close to the bay.

Molodan was still aboard his ship. He frowned towards the town as his cannons fired below him. Smoke engulfed his ship of death. His men waited for the word to go ashore. The pinging of musket fire from the men of Gordington could be heard against the ship. Despite the efforts of the townspeople though, their defenses were hardly noticeable to the pirates.

One lucky shot hit Molodan in the arm and he looked down at the fresh hole in his coat. He pointed his finger at the town. His crew took this as a sign to attack and transformed into orbs. They moved with tremendous speed towards the Square.

Ozron and Ebineezer reached the top of the staircase. Ebineezer peeked through a small hole in the wall and could see the orbs darting through his cigar room.

"What are they?" he whispered, turning towards Ozron standing next to him.

Ozron looked. "Death, my friend. Those would be Molodan's. Wait until they exit before you go out there. You will be defenseless against them."

Ebineezer gasped loudly as he watched one of the spherical shapes manifest into a full-blown pirate walking through his inn. The pirate heard his gasp on the other side of the wall and walked over to inspect the source of the noise. Ozron and Ebineezer ducked behind the wall. They could hear the beast on the other side, breathing heavily as he peered through the cracks of the wall. They listened as his monstrous steps walked away.

Ozron turned to the innkeeper. "Idiot! You could get us killed like that," he hissed.

"Sorry, Ozron. Never in all me years have I ever seen anything like that." Ebineezer sat down and pushed his back against the wall as he heard them searching his inn, creating a terrible racket as they tore it apart. "Me inn!" he cried. "They're destroying it."

"Mind you not that now, innkeeper. The inn can be repaired easily enough. That's the least of your worries."

"What if they find Jeremiah?"

"The boy is safe," Ozron assured him.

Ebineezer shook his head. "These pirates are really beginning to grate on me nerves," he said as he listened to the cannon fire blasting through his inn.

"It's not just your inn," said Ozron. "They're destroying the whole town out there. I must get to my cart at the other end of town." He looked for a means of escape.

Aboard the *Nante*, Van Russel's crew awoke to the loud blasts. They jumped from their bunks as the barrage of cannon fire engulfed the town and the already broken *Nante*.

"Men, get up!" Ranjit roared. "They've come looking for the boy!"

It was what everyone had feared. The pirates were back to get him.

Ranjit and the rest of the crew assembled their muskets and grabbed their swords. Some ran to the upper deck and some stayed below, manning and arming the cannons. The *Nante* hadn't been positioned in the water for a cannon fight and there wasn't time now to try and maneuver it. They did the best they could and began priming their cannons for action.

Ranjit and the others were ready. The cannons within range of Molodan's ship began firing, striking it twice on the port side. The pirate ship rocked in the water from the monstrous explosions.

"What in the...?" Ranjit asked in horror as he watched the glowing orbs rocketing towards them.

"IT'S THE PIRATES!" yelled another of the crew.

"MEN, PREPARE TO FIGHT!" Ranjit roared.

The glowing orbs flew to the *Nante* and hovered over the main deck. The crew watched in disbelief as they manifested first into a mist and then into pirates. They came at the crew with swords swinging, but luckily the *Nante*'s crew was also adept at sword fighting.

Ozron saw no more pirates moving about the cigar room, nor did he hear them. They might have been in the orb-form flying quietly, but he felt confident that they had realized the boy wasn't there and moved on to some other place. Just as he began to move the lever to open the wall for escape, he heard another set of footsteps moving up the stone staircase.

"Do ye hear that?" asked Ebineezer. "Something is coming up me stairwell."

"Yes, I hear it too," said Ozron. "Don't say a word. It may just be a pirate that snuck in. I've seen them go through walls before in the orb form."

"Oh, me! What will we do?" whispered Ebineezer frantically.

"Stay calm, Ebineezer," Ozron said. "Wait and listen."

They watched the darkness of the stairwell as the footsteps became more pronounced. The rest of the Society had been instructed to stay locked in the bottom, so all it could be was a pirate that had somehow managed to make his way in. They could see a silhouette coming into view. Neither Ozron nor Ebineezer had anything to fight with; they both held their breath during the final moments as the shape moved into the light.

"Good grief, Boswell! Did I not instruct you to stay with the boy?" Ozron scolded.

"The boy is fine, Ozron," said Boswell. "He's in safe keeping with the captain and Madam Karla. I figured you needed more help than they did, so I decided to come on my own accord."

Ozron thought for a moment. "Alright, Blacksmith... thank you for coming." Ozron felt that now was as good a time as ever to make a run for it. He didn't know how he would make it to other end of town, even on his horse. Arien was safely tied up behind the inn, for protection from the storm. But the downpour had passed shortly after Van Russel and Jeremiah arrived and there was now just an occasional sprinkle or two.

Ebineezer pulled the lever and the wall opened. Ozron stuck his head out and looked around. "All appears safe," he said. He and Boswell exited and Ebineezer promptly pulled the lever again, closing his self inside.

"I'm going to get on my horse and ride to the other end of town," Ozron said hurriedly. "I have my peddler's cart hidden there in the stables and I may just have something to fend off these pirates."

"I'll watch your back, old man," Boswell assured him. They snuck quietly through the inn and escaped unnoticed through the back entrance.

Ozron climbed onto Arien. She was neighing and blowing and hitting her hooves upon the ground. "Yes lady, I know," Ozron said to her. "We're going now. Boswell, good luck."

"Thank you Ozron. I'm going to stay here and —"

As Boswell was giving Ozron his assurance, a pirate walked around the corner of the inn. Boswell looked frantically for something to use as a weapon. There was an old board propped up against the building and he quickly grabbed it.

Ozron didn't know how to help him.

"Go, old man! I will take care of this!" Boswell shouted to him.

Ozron took off in the other direction, but stopped as he reached the opposite side of the building. He watched as Boswell swung the board, but it had no effect on the pirate. The brute raised his sword and struck Boswell in the middle of his chest. Boswell dropped to the ground and the pirate turned towards Ozron. Ozron knew that he could do nothing for his friend. On Arien, he fled down a back alley, hoping to find a concealed path to his cart. The pirate took off after him, but soon lost interest when he came upon a couple of potential victims.

Ranjit and the crew were in sword-to-sword combat. They were adept at defending themselves against the swinging swords coming barreling at them, but it was quickly wearing them down. They knew they couldn't do much, except to try and keep defending themselves and their ship. The crew below still manned the cannons, firing upon Molodan's ship. They had successfully hit it three or four times now, but it really wasn't turning the pirates away. If anything, it made them come with additional force.

Ozron rode Arien as fast as the wind. The horse took valiant strides as she worked to get her master to his cart. There were screams all around them and one crashing boom after another as the pirates were slowly blasting the buildings on every corner. They weaved in and out of alleys and through the running patrons. Many people were lying dead upon the streets and Ozron knew that time was quickly running out.

He saw his cart just ahead and he swung his legs over to the left. As soon as they reached the stables, he slid off, ran to the cart, and swung the back door open. He fumbled through the vials, concoctions, and goods that he peddled from town to town. He grabbed a long, crooked staff from its hiding place, along with a few glass jars. Frantically, he unscrewed their lids, mixing and shaking their contents, causing them to change and bubble. Just when he thought they were right, he grabbed the staff and held it up straight.

On the end of the staff was a large, round, glass bulb. Ozron removed the glass sphere, poured the mixture into it and then reattached it to the staff. He scanned the village for the best place to use it.

One of the alleys close by led to a hill that overlooked Gordington. Figuring this would be the best location, he jumped onto Arien and rode quickly towards the hill.

Molodan was watching the entire fight from the upper deck of his ship. His eyes constantly scanned for anything unusual, threatening, or the boy. It wasn't long before he noticed Ozron and Arien riding high up past the town. Arien was a startling sight, even for him, for he could see her for exactly what she was. A glistening white horse with a silver horn protruding from her head contrasted nicely against the smoking town engulfed in flames.

Molodan knew there was something threatening about the sight. Up until now he had remained in the same spot as he directed the fight around him. But now he quickly dematerialized and shot, in orb form, away from the ship. He flew with lightning speed over the top of the water, the piers and all the commotion in the town. He stopped for nothing.

Ozron kicked Arien's sides lightly with his feet as she galloped up the hill. Over his shoulder, he watched the fire and smoke blowing up from the top of the town. Suddenly, he saw another startling sight — a giant glowing orb.

Ozron knew this orb looked different from all the others. It had a bluish appearance and was much larger than all the others soaring around the town. And this one was coming right for him.

He yelled to Arien, "Run girl! Run fast for Ozron!" He whipped her reins as they struggled to reach the top of the hill. He could see it right in front of them, but feared Molodan would reach them first. He knew they'd leave no soul alive. Arien moved with great speed, taking long, silent strides over the wet ground, almost as if she were floating.

As Arien made it to the spot, Ozron began to slip off of her. Before he reached the ground though, Molodan arrived. The orb knocked Ozron away from the unicorn. He went flying in one direction and the staff flew in another.

Ozron quickly rose to his feet and watched as Molodan transformed himself back into his pirate shape. Molodan came with heavy steps towards Ozron, pulling his cutlass from his side. Ozron knew he was defenseless and thought quickly for a solution — but there was none. Molodan reared his sword back and Ozron held up his hands to try and deflect as much of the blow as possible. As the sword came swinging through the air, Molodan was struck in the back of the head with Ozron's staff. He wasn't the slightest bit hurt by the blow, but was distracted enough to stop his sword.

Both Molodan and Ozron looked to see Johan Burdett holding the staff. Behind him were Ivan Flick and Jeremiah. Molodan displayed an atrocious look of wickedness when he saw Jeremiah. He headed directly for him.

"Jeremiah, No!" Ozron screamed.

Molodan was in near reach of the boy, but as his arms extended to take him, Arien came tromping through the fiend, knocking him into the mist form again.

"THROW ME THE STAFF!" Ozron yelled to the butcher.

Johan threw the staff through the air and Ozron caught it, just as Molodan reformed as a pirate. Ozron grabbed the center of the staff with both hands and raised it into the air. He brought it down with extreme force, causing it to strike the ground violently.

Molodan had Jeremiah in his grasp and was about to remove his soul from his body. But just as he began his abhorrent technique on the boy, the bulb at the end of the staff discharged some of the brightest, blasting light they had ever seen. Johan and Ivan covered their eyes from the intensity of the light that was now lighting up the entire sky, the bay, and the town.

Molodan's expression turned to one of extreme rage, but he quickly dematerialized and sped away from the light.

"Yes!" Ozron yelled, seeing his light did indeed work. He watched as the remaining pirates evaporated and the pirate ship fled with great speed away from Gordington.

One pulsating wave of light after another continued to blast from the staff, radiating out for miles. After several minutes, when Ozron knew the coast was clear, he lifted the staff and turned the bulb counter clockwise. The light diminished, returning the night to normal.

They could hear no cheers of happiness coming from the town, however. Those left alive were running for water to extinguish the flames and others sat in the roads and buildings moaning for those whom they had lost.

Ozron turned to Jeremiah, exhausted and frustrated. "Do you have any idea how dangerous it was to come up here? I told you to stay in the safety of the room!"

"I was called up here, Ozron. I came upon request!" Jeremiah hollered back defensively.

"Called up here? By whom?"

"By me," said a female voice. Ozron turned to Arien. "You?"

"Yes," the unicorn replied. "I was worried for you after Boswell was killed, so I sent the message for help only to the boy."

"Well, um…" Ozron was at a loss for words. "Arien, thank you, but we would have been alright."

"No, we wouldn't have," she said, "the extra time the butcher bought us made all the difference."

"Well, maybe you are right. To all of you… thank you," said Ozron.

"Boswell is dead," Johan reported.

"No!" gasped Jeremiah.

"I am aware… I saw the fiend do it to him," Ozron informed them, sadly. "Enough is enough. Gentleman…" he addressed Johan and Ivan, "if you would, run back into town and help the people. Jeremiah, come with me. We have a meeting that urgently awaits us."

Johan and Ivan ran back towards the Square as Ozron assisted Jeremiah onto Arien's back. He climbed up behind him and they rode with great speed back towards the Square.

It was time to finish what Molodan had started and they were all ready to do whatever was necessary. Molodan had killed their friends, stolen their souls, burnt their town, and now it was time for payback.

CHAPTER EIGHTEEN

The Miridian Mountains

J eremiah walked up pier number three with Van Russel, Ebineezer, and Ozron. Van Russel seemed half in shock and half furious. He yanked his oversized hat from his head when he laid eyes upon his barraged brigantine, now completely in ruins and barely floating. Blessie took off from his shoulder and flew to the broken ship.

"PIRATES! I'VE HAD ENOUGH OF THESE PIRATES! THEY'VE COMPLETELY DESTROYED ME SHIP NOW AND IT'S TIME TO PUT AN END TO THIS!" Van Russel screamed.

Jeremiah hadn't seen him so angry before now.

All around them the town was smoking, smoldering, and in places, still on fire. Cries came from all directions and the townsfolk still ran about with pails of water, trying to extinguish the inferno with water from the bay. Some had even used the horse trough sitting in front of the Brubaker, but it was quickly emptied. Many of the ships along the piers were in the same state as the *Nante* — broken, blasted and mangled.

Ebineezer turned to get another look at his inn. It too lay in ruins. The roof was partly caved in and there were huge holes scattered about its face from the many cannonballs that had pummeled through it. He looked nauseated at the sight of it. Jeremiah knew the inn was like Ebineezer's child and his sole source of income.

Ozron put his hand on Ebineezer's shoulder. "It can be repaired easily enough, my friend. As can the rest of the town… and the *Nante*."

Unlike Van Russel, Ebineezer simply looked at the inn sadly, shaking his head in disbelief. "Never thought I'd see her in such a state."

They climbed aboard the *Nante*, stumbling over the broken boards, masts, and pieces of sail that littered most of her.

Ranjit and Lothar walked up to them.

"The crew?" Van Russel asked.

"We all survived, Captain," Ranjit reported, still out of breath. "We've several that are hurt, but the pirates didn't take any of us down. A few more minutes though, and it would have been different."

"Very good, Quartermaster. I need the two of ye to come to me cabin with the rest of us."

The group of six entered his cabin as the remaining crew worked around them to salvage what they could. There wasn't much on the deck that had been left unscathed.

Van Russel addressed them all as he shut his door behind them. "It's time we put an end to this. It's time we get back what is ours and stop the killing and maiming by these blasted pirates. The captain has had enough!" he screamed.

No one said anything. Everyone was sitting around the cabin looking at one another, listening to his address as they decided in their own minds what ought to be done. Ozron was the only one standing, his arms crossed and his chin supported by one of his hands, thinking intently. Jeremiah and Ebineezer sat next to one another, bent over with their hands propped upon their knees, still trying to take it all in. Lothar sat next to Ranjit and both of them were looking at Van Russel.

"We'll need a new boat," Ozron spoke up, breaking the silence.

Everyone's attention turned to him.

"I would imagine it'll need to be something smaller than this brigantine, maybe a sloop, something that will maneuver better in the waters near the mountains," he added.

"Mountains? What mountains?" Ranjit asked.

"The Miridian Mountains," Van Russel answered.

"The Miridian Mountains? Captain, why on earth would we go there?" Ranjit asked, startled.

"To get the fiend's treasure. We're gonna lure him in… then try and kill him," he said through gritted teeth.

Ranjit and Lothar looked at one another with wide, open eyes. "Captain, I mean no disrespect, but we could hardly defend ourselves against him this time. And the Miridian Mountains? Have ye gone completely screwy? That place is cursed — haunted by the ancients!" said Ranjit, not believing what he was hearing.

"Few have ever survived taking their ship in there. And those that did were taken down by the very spirits that haunt those grounds. Captain, please," Lothar pleaded.

"It's already been decided, men," Van Russel said firmly. "At this point, I agree with Ozron — we must first decide which ship we're gonna use to get there."

Ranjit shook his head, in total disagreement, but spoke up again. "If it's a sloop you seek, use the one a couple of piers down. I saw them carrying Smith, its captain, away just before you arrived. I'm sure their crew will be more than willing since their captain was killed."

"Very good, Quartermaster," Van Russel replied. "Please go now and let them know we'll need to borrow it immediately. And hopefully with a little better planning, we'll be able to fight these heathens with a little more accord than we did tonight."

Ranjit left with Lothar at his side, leaving the rest of the group in the cabin staring at one another, blankly.

"You must go tonight," Ozron said to Van Russel. "There's no more time to spare. Leave Jeremiah here with the innkeeper and me. He's been through enough... and taking him to the mountains, I feel, would be a bad idea."

Jeremiah looked up to him, surprised. "Ozron, no. I want to go with the captain."

"Jeremiah, lad, Ozron is right. Listen to him. We almost lost ye once... we don't want to risk losing ye again. It's extremely dangerous where we're going," said Van Russel.

"Why are all of you deciding this for me? I want to go. I am going!" he shot back, defensively. "I found the map and I'm going to help steal the treasure!"

Jeremiah, Van Russel and Ozron gazed at one another and turned towards Ebineezer. He sighed, shrugged and shook his head before looking back down at the floor.

"Thank you, Ebineezer," Ozron commented facetiously. "Alright then, young one — you can go. You know the dangers ahead, but apparently there is no swaying you."

Van Russel shook his head nervously. "All right then, let's get prepared," he said to them. "Ebineezer, take me bird. She's not going with us on this one."

It was just before daybreak when the crew of the *Nante* set sail for the Miridian Mountains. However, there were only half of them now, for the sloop they were traveling on was much smaller than the brigantine. Those left behind were ordered to begin repairing the broken ship.

A sloop was much better for their intent. With its shape and size, it could maneuver much more easily in the treacherous waters that surrounded the mountains. The one they were on now only had one mast, compared to the *Nante*'s three. The crew that was needed to manage it would be much smaller than that of the *Nante*.

Jeremiah was pleased with the captain's decision about who to bring along. Midget was there, along with Augustus and Orville. They were three of his favorites and their presence settled his anxious nerves. Typically, Augustus wouldn't have been considered, but due to his size and his speedy ways, it was universally felt that this job may be a bit more fitting for the swabbie. He knew Van Russel also chose about eighteen others to assist them in the tasks ahead of them.

All of the new crewmembers were stretched out in the hammocks below deck. They were exhausted from the night's battle and they knew they would need the rest before this dangerous mission. Only Jeremiah was awake. Sleep was a constant struggle for him, especially with recent events in his life. He too lay on a hammock begging for much needed rest, but it just wouldn't come.

After an hour's worth of tossing and turning in the uncomfortable hammock, he crept quietly out of the room. He decided to return to the deck to see if the captain could use his assistance for anything more.

He walked up to the main cabin and knocked lightly on the door.

"Come in," said Van Russel.

Ranjit, Lothar and Van Russel were all hunched over a table, looking at the map Jeremiah had provided. It was strewn across the table and Ranjit was using the nautical ruler on it, mapping out the best path from Daniels's drawings. He looked frustrated as he worked, still shaking his head in disbelief that they were about to enter this treacherous area.

"Couldn't sleep?" said Van Russel.

Jeremiah shook his head.

"Come on in then. We're just trying to map out the appropriate course to the mountains."

Lothar said nothing, but glared at Jeremiah.

"I guess we'll go with the route this Daniels person has provided," Ranjit grouched. He threw the nautical ruler down on the other map they were using for comparison.

"Calm down, Quartermaster! This is the only option we've been left with!" Van Russel scolded.

"We've already lost enough, Captain. That place is cursed. The ancients haunt the soil we'll walk upon. We could lose everyone if we try going through with this."

"So what else do ye suggest, Ranjit?" Van Russel asked. "If ye have some better alternative to this dilemma, yer captain would love to hear it now." Van Russel waited for his answer.

Ranjit stormed out of the cabin and Lothar was right on his heels, as always.

Jeremiah didn't say anything, but felt this was partially his fault.

"Don't mind them. They're just scared, as we all are. They just show it differently."

"Captain, is there some other way than these mountains, do you think?" asked Jeremiah.

"No, it's the only way. For one, if there is a treasure, we could most certainly use it now, being that all has been destroyed. And, we need a way to bring him back to us. We'll be there by nightfall. I'd recommend ye try again and get some rest. Ye'll most certainly need it."

Jeremiah nodded and exited the cabin. He returned to his hammock where he lay for what seemed hours, before the idea of sleep seemed agreeable again. It was midday by the time he was finally able to close his eyes, but he was able to sleep, nonetheless. The Miridian Mountains were only hours away and he knew he must rest, if only a little, before they set foot ashore there.

"WAKE UP! WAKE UP!" the crewman screamed as he ran from the room. "We're there!"

Jeremiah awoke groggily from his sleep and looked about the room as the last couple of crewmembers went racing out the door. There was an awful moan and the sloop rocked violently in the waters. He jumped from his hammock and tried to maintain his balance as the room tilted back and forth in the darkness. The hammocks swayed and he could hear the few belongings on the floor rolling from one side of the room to the other.

He poked his head out of the sleeping quarters and looked down the hallway that led to the ladder and the upper deck. He watched as the legs of the last crewmember climbed up and disappeared. Water came splashing down though the exit and rushed through the corridor, surrounding his bare feet. It was night and no doubt they were again challenging ferocious winds and treacherous waters. Jeremiah splashed down the hallway, bumping into the walls of the narrow corridor before climbing to the surface.

All around him the small crew screamed to one another and Ranjit was barking orders to all of them. Orville struggled to keep the sloop upright and on path in the waters waiting to take them straight to Davy Jones's locker.

Lothar stood off the bow, tied securely to it with roping, and helped Orville direct the ship. They dodged one massive boulder after another and avoided the jagged reefs under the water's surface. Lothar was soaking wet, from one wave after another crashing onto him and the deck.

"Jeremiah, over here!" Captain Russel yelled from his cabin. He was standing in his doorway with arms extended, bracing himself. The sails popped and stretched just feet above Jeremiah's head as he struggled to make it to Van Russel.

"What do you need from me?" Jeremiah asked, half-winded, as he made it into the doorway.

"To stay in here! We don't want a repeat of last time!" Van Russel screamed amidst the howling winds that cursed them for attempting to come close.

Jeremiah braced himself in the doorway, watching with Van Russel.

They were but a couple thousand yards from one of the most-feared places any shipman ever dare go. Just feet below the hull were the littered remains of hundreds of ships from the previous centuries.

Rumor had it that these mountains were haunted by the ancients; evil, ruthless souls that lost their lands many centuries before. Few had ever survived entrance to the mountains and most of those that did were eventually taken down. The dead were said to come up out of the ground, quietly and swiftly, and would immediately drain the life from anyone with whom they came in contact. They were believed to be waiting up in the jungles and the massive hilltops that lined the cursed islands.

These rumors had been going around for centuries, and most believed them to be true. Governor Addison himself had ordered two parties to investigate the mountains over the years and both times, the crews did not return. No one knew if the legends were true, but some believed it could have been the dangerous waters that surrounded the mountains or Molodan's pirates that were the real culprits.

"Two large boulders straight ahead!" Lothar screamed to the helmsman.

Jeremiah watched as Orville struggled to steer the ship between them. The starboard side scraped violently against one, causing a terrible racket and knocked most of the crew off their feet.

Luckily the hole created by the collision was far enough above the water line that the ship could stay afloat. Just as they cleared the boulders, another gigantic wave came at them from the side, knocking the sloop sideways and nearly toppling it over. Again the crew were knocked off their feet and most slid across the deck although, miraculously, everyone stayed on the ship. Falling in these waters would prove deadly, for there was no way to turn around and save lives in these deadly seas.

But as everyone held on to whatever they could find, bracing themselves for the next major impact, the waters calmed.

Jeremiah and the others looked around at one another. Could that have been it? Was that all there was to the warning waters that were keeping them from entering? Granted, they were still quite atrocious and dangerous to say the least, but nothing compared to the spiraling, ocean funnel they had encountered just days before.

After they glided with ease for several minutes, the small crew began to cheer. They could see the mountains in the moonlight and knew they had done it — many of them felt that they had conquered what no other could. Although they had made it to the coast in one piece, Jeremiah could see the look upon Van Russel, Ranjit and some of the others. He knew they feared even more what lay waiting beyond the crests of the mountains.

"Excellent job, men!" said Van Russel. "Go ahead and drop anchor. We'll moor here tonight and go ashore in the morning."

The following morning, Jeremiah stretched in his hammock, yawn-
ing greatly.   He looked around the sleeping quarters — he was
the only one there. He could see daylight seeping through the tiny
cracks of the ship's exterior. He decided to go atop to see what was
going on and where the crew had gone. He could hear them walking above him and feared that if he didn't make his presence known
quickly, they would go ashore without him. After all, he knew the
captain feared for his safety and would probably leave him behind if
given the opportunity to do so.

As he walked on deck, he couldn't believe the sight in front
of him. The Miridian Mountains were some of the most spectacular things he had ever laid his eyes upon. The crew must have been
equally amazed, for they were all there too — staring out to the
glorious crests.

They appeared to be composed of two gigantic peaks, with
many hills and valleys scattered across their surfaces. They were like
a lush green blanket and they appeared to extend for many miles. On
the beach closest to the crew, the sands were as white as the sloop's
sails.

Just yards from the water's edge were the jungle perimeters.
Jeremiah saw wild birds swooping in and out of the massive, tangled
trees and vines.

The water was some of the clearest Jeremiah had ever seen.
He scanned the horizon for the ragged waters they had come in on,
but amazingly, it all seemed perfectly still and tranquil. The others
too seemed confused.

"Nothing here is as it seems, men," Ranjit said. "The treacherous waters are just beyond ye line of sight. It's trickery of the eyes."

"And that's what scares me," Van Russel said. He pointed to the dinghies on the deck. "Ranjit, we'll leave a few behind — everyone else goes ashore in these. Ye decide."

"Captain, what will we carry the treasure back in?" Jeremiah asked. "Won't we need our hands free in those steep jungles?"

"An excellent point. Does anyone have any idea how we can secure the treasure and bring it back easily?"

Augustus walked up. "Captain, there are many leather satchels in the hold below. They have straps and they'd work fine."

"Excellent, swabbie. Go and fetch those for us, would ye? Get as many as ye can carry. Midget, go below and help him," Van Russel instructed.

Van Russel looked towards the uninviting jungles that were but yards from where they were standing. There was a small path that led into them — just as Daniels had outlined in his map. Van Russel pulled Daniels's parchment from his pocket, took a half-hearted look at it, and refolded it before returning it to his pocket. Around him, the men were loading the dinghies with additional water, arms, and rope. Most of them had pistols strapped to their chests and swords attached to their sides.

"Are we ready?" asked Van Russel.

"Aye — as ready as we'll ever be," said Ranjit.

Van Russel climbed into the dinghy with Jeremiah, Orville, Augustus and Midget. Others were there too, and grabbed oars to help row them in to shore. In the second dinghy were Ranjit, Lothar, Patch, Collins and several others. In total, there were twenty in their group. No one spoke in either dinghy as they rowed towards the shore. It appeared as a tropical jungle paradise, but Jeremiah knew that was precisely why it was important to keep his guard up.

Once on shore, they pulled the dinghies far from the water's edge up near the jungle's entrance. Jeremiah looked up at the mouth of the trail in awe — it was about forty feet high but only several feet wide. Although the jungle looked lush and green from a distance, up close it was dark and foreboding. The trees were massive and heavy vines hung from the tops of them. Wild birds swooped low above their heads and the chirping and shrieking sounds coming from within were frightening.

"Captain, I'll ask ye one last time. Are ye sure ye want to do this?" Ranjit asked.

"Men, move ahead," Van Russel instructed, ignoring his question. Jeremiah watched Ranjit shake his head and move to the front. The large Indian pulled his sword from its sheath and walked into the mouth of the jungle with a fighting stance. The others fell close behind him, their swords also drawn.

They walked through the overgrown trail for several minutes before Ranjit stopped. He turned to the captain, who was near the back with Jeremiah.

"Captain, where to from here?" he yelled. The path seemed to split off, though in both directions the tropical vines that grew everywhere obstructed it.

Van Russel pulled the parchment from his pocket again and held it in front of his face. He turned it left, and tried it right. "Um…" he said.

"What's the problem, Captain?" Ranjit yelled.

Jeremiah sensed the tension of the crew.

"Well, it appears that Daniels didn't actually come ashore. His map only details where we were supposed to start," said Van Russel hesitantly.

"That's right. He didn't come ashore here. His map is only to the entrance," said Jeremiah.

The group mumbled uneasily. Ranjit glared at Van Russel, shaking his head. He too had seen the map, but had only been interested in the part that showed them how to get into the mountains. It was obvious to Jeremiah that both Ranjit and Van Russel figured there was more to the map when they initially mapped out their travel route on the water.

"So what do ye suggest we do now, Captain?" Ranjit sneered.

"I guess we'll keep moving ahead, Quartermaster," Van Russel retorted, with the same disrespect.

Ranjit whipped around and moved farther down the narrow, overgrown trail. He swung his sword, knocking down the vines that obstructed their path.

They had walked for another hour when Ranjit yelled that there was an opening ahead. He continued swinging his sword at the mammoth leaves and vines in his way, but stopped abruptly as he reached the clearing.

"Whoa!" he yelled loudly as he raised his arm straight in the air.

Everyone stopped. Jeremiah could see a few in the front looking down, but couldn't tell what it was they were looking at. He noticed they began backing up.

"What's going on up there?" Van Russel asked, pushing his way through his men. "Move aside. The captain will have a look." Van Russel walked to the front of the line next to Ranjit and the others and Jeremiah watched as he too backed up uneasily when he looked down.

CHAPTER NINETEEN

THE TREASURE TROVE

J eremiah knew there was no way they could go around it. He looked to the left and right of it and there wasn't a crossing anywhere.

A giant void extended about twenty feet across to the other side of the path. Even in the light of day, this emptiness that extended across the earth was black as night. It didn't appear to have a bottom to it — it dropped into nothing, literally.

"How do ye suppose we get across this?" Van Russel asked. "It's way too far to try and jump across."

Ranjit grabbed a rope tied to one of the trees on his other side. "This rope? It's tied to that branch up there," he said, pointing to a long, thick branch that extended out over the void. "We're all gonna have to try and swing across. I guess those that don't make it, don't come back," he said rudely.

"Well, I guess I'm not going to need this," Van Russel said, removing his hat. He looked at it for a moment and then looked down into the emptiness. "Ah, what the heck. Already lost another one," he blurted as he tossed his hat into the dark unknown. It flew out in front of them and dropped into the darkness, where it quickly disappeared.

Ranjit glared at him, horrified. "Why did ye just do that!" he screamed. "Ye probably just woke it up!"

"Nonsense," said Van Russel, clearly growing tired of Ranjit's defiance. He grabbed the rope, pulled it tightly as he backed up a few steps, and started running. He swung out over the void, but just as he neared the other side, Ranjit's suspicions proved correct.

Jeremiah and the others watched in utter terror as large, black, swirling phantoms flew up and out of the abyss. They swooped in and out of the black unknown, and they appeared just as the group had imagined them. They looked to be ancient, with large, extending hands and a trailing black mist that followed them.

Van Russel plopped down onto his rear end on the other side of the void. "See?" he yelled. "Easy and nothing to worry about!" He had his back to them, but promptly rose to his feet, dusted himself off and turned around. When he turned, he cringed and his eyes grew as large as coconuts.

The void was now flooded with many of the phantoms, shooting up and out of it and diving back in it.

"What do ye suggest now, Captain?" Ranjit screamed.

Van Russel shrugged.

Jeremiah knew they must do as Van Russel did and swing across the void. One by one they crossed, just missing the reach of the phantoms that glided through the air around them. Maybe they were just toying with them and appeared more frightful than they actually were.

Everyone had made it across, successfully, leaving Ranjit and Collins remaining. Ranjit looked to Collins. "Go ahead — I'll go last," he said. Jeremiah's heart beat rapidly as he watched Ranjit give Collins the go-ahead.

Collins grabbed hold of the rope, took a step back, and swung. But as he crossed, one of the phantoms rose through his feet and passed directly through him. Jeremiah watched in horror as it drained all the life from him — just as the age-old tales had described. His body completed the swing and dropped to the ground at their feet.

Most of them covered their mouths and turned their heads at the sight of their crewmate.

"No!" Patch screamed as he dropped to his knees in front of his close friend, but gagged when he was able to get a close-up look. His friend's body was shriveled like a dried grape and his eyes were glazed over with a milky haze. He appeared as if he had been dead for a long time. A couple of the crew helped Patch to his feet and walked him away briskly while the others screamed to Ranjit, "Come now! Time is running out!"

Jeremiah watched Ranjit grab hold of the rope, soaring with great speed across the void. Ranjit looked down at the space below his feet as he went across. One of the phantoms swooped upwards towards him, but, using the strength in his muscular arms, he was able to shift his body in mid-air and dodge the phantom. He hit the ground firmly with two feet and ran up through the middle of the group. "Follow me!" he ordered.

Everyone picked up the pace, including Van Russel, and followed Ranjit up the trail into the mountains. Behind them, the phantoms swooped back and forth across the path, diving in and out of the ground. No one dared look back. Jeremiah knew there was no way they could return the way they'd come. As badly as he and the others hated leaving their comrade behind, he knew there was nothing they could do for him now — not even his body. He knew they would share his fate if they dared try.

It wasn't long before they were all winded from the steady, uphill run. Not all of them were as fit as Ranjit and they knew they must take a break. Jeremiah watched as Ranjit started slowing his pace. Jeremiah and the others slowed and gathered together, but they were all cautious, looking around at all times. Jeremiah gazed down the trail behind them, but he could no longer see the phantoms that had taken their friend's life.

"Pass me the water," Van Russel said to one of the crew drinking from the water cask. "Haven't run like that in a long time," he said, struggling for breath. He took a heavy swig from the small, wooden cask and passed it around to the rest of the crew.

This area was in a moss-covered clearing. Midget pointed out the softness of the ground to everyone. Soon they were all kicking their feet upon it and feeling how it would strangely give in as they applied additional pressure to it.

Most of their group was centralized in a large circle in the clearing, but Jeremiah and Augustus sat several feet away from the others. They silently shared a cask and wiped the sweat from their faces as they enjoyed a quick break after the up-hill sprint.

"Do you hear that?" Augustus asked.

"Yes, I do… what is that? Captain!" Jeremiah yelled.

Van Russel and the others turned to him. "QUIET!" Van Russel yelled to the crew.

Everyone listened.

"I hear hissing," Lothar whispered.

"Hissing?" Ranjit asked, pulling his sword from its sheath.

Everyone slowly rose from the moss-covered ground looking around for the source of the hissing noise. They couldn't see anything — all appeared normal.

Patch wiped the tears from his face and dusted off his breeches as he stood. He felt something causing his chest to itch and raised his shirt, looking to see what was behind the irritation. Van Russel, who was closest to him, jumped back.

"Good night, man! What is that thing?" Van Russel screamed.

Crawling around on Patch's chest, were three black and red hissing cockroaches that were the length of three doubloons. Patch yelped with fear as he brushed the insects from his skin. As if on cue, some of the others did the same, realizing they too had the atrocious bugs moving within their clothes. They all jumped up and down, trying to quickly rid themselves of the cockroaches.

Jeremiah and Augustus stepped backwards. They hadn't been sitting in the same area as the rest of their mates and they wanted no part of the bugs. Jeremiah watched as the crew attempted to rid themselves of the cockroaches and smashed them under their feet. Jeremiah gasped as he saw another startling sight.

Although the crew was unaware, the soft, moss-covered ground was giving in as they jumped. Jeremiah and Augustus motioned to the captain and his crew, but they were so preoccupied with the bugs that the boys yelling from the sidelines were the least of their concerns.

POP! CRACK!

Two, large, branchy trap doors opened below their feet, dropping all seventeen men. They screamed as they fell. Jeremiah and Augustus ran over and peered, horrified, over the edge of the gigantic pit. The crew was about fifteen feet down, but none of them were hurt yet. Cushioning their fall were millions of hissing cockroaches. They had squashed many as they fell, but soon started sinking quickly down in them.

"THROW US A ROPE! GET US A ROPE!" screamed the crew, neck deep. Even Ranjit was yelling as the enormous insects climbed all over his bald, shiny head and the front of his face.

Jeremiah and Augustus ran nervously. Many of the ropes had fallen in with the crew but Augustus had luckily thrown one set over his shoulder when they'd unloaded from the dinghies. Jeremiah looked quickly for a place for Augustus to secure it.

"OVER THERE!" Jeremiah yelled amidst the screams of the crew. He pointed to a large tree just a few feet away from the opposite side of the pit.

Augustus ran around the perimeter of the pit and nervously tied the end of the rope to one of the huge, jungle trees. He threw the other end of it down into the pit where the crew continued sinking.

One by one, the crew climbed the rope and made it to the surface again. Captain Van Russel, Ranjit, Orville and the others jumped around, thrashing and shouting, as they tried to rid themselves of the remaining bugs that climbed through their clothes and on top of their heads.

Lothar walked up to Augustus. "Next time, tie that rope faster," he snarled, "and what are you looking at?" he shot at Jeremiah, who was clearly disgusted with his attitude towards Augustus, who had just saved his life.

Ranjit came up to the swabbie next. "For once, a good job," he said as he slapped Augustus on the back. He looked around to the crew. "Captain?"

"Yes, Ranjit?" Van Russel asked, his attention on the squished roach beneath his foot.

"Where's the rest of the crew?" Ranjit asked. Everyone had been so excited as they left the hole that they didn't pay attention to the number of crew that successfully climbed out. A head count ensued.

"Fifteen!" Van Russel gasped. "We've still got four men down in that hole!"

Everyone ran close to the edge and peered down, but no one was left waiting.

"I think I'm gonna be sick," said Augustus as he covered his mouth.

Jeremiah knew what happened. Those that didn't climb from the hole sunk down into the bugs and were either suffocating or being eaten alive. It was overwhelming to all, but Jeremiah and the others knew there wasn't time for mourning now and that they must push on. The fear of what might come out after dark was more than they wanted to consider, so they regrouped and moved with added speed up the hill.

"Looks like that rock wall is obstructing the path," one of the men said as they neared a small cliff.

"Maybe the trail goes around it," said Ranjit as he continued hacking at the vines blocking his way. He looked up at the rock face. The trail stopped completely — a dead end at the base of the sheer rock wall. "Why would I have expected any different?" he asked loudly. He backed up a couple of steps, scanning the wall in front of him.

Jeremiah walked with Van Russel behind them. He could see them looking skyward. Van Russel stopped and pulled the telescope from his pocket. He peered through it, scanning the cliff's surface.

"Quartermaster, there's a cave in the wall high up," he reported. "One of us will have to climb the wall and drop a rope from the cave."

Everyone looked at each other. None of them were climbers and there wasn't much at all to hold onto. Lothar turned to Ranjit.

"Want me to go?" Lothar asked.

"Think ye can do it?" Ranjit said.

Lothar hesitated.

"Never mind, I'll go," Ranjit replied, shaking his head. "Our ropes aren't long enough for the entrance to that cave… we're gonna have to tie a few of them together."

Orville had a couple of ropes on his shoulder and handed them to Ranjit. He worked quickly to tie the three ropes together.

"This should do, I think," Ranjit said. He coiled them, threw them across his shoulder and walked up to the wall. "If I fall, ye better go ahead and decide who'll try next," he said, starting to climb.

Jeremiah watched his muscular, Indian frame as he climbed quickly up the jagged, stone wall. There wasn't much at all to hang on, but Ranjit ascended the side of it skillfully, jumping from one hold to another, putting his weight on ledges that were only inches wide.

"Alright!" his voice echoed as he threw the rope down to the others. "The trail goes through the mountain up here. Those that can climb on their own come first! Those that can't hold up their weight must wait!"

The group turned to one another.

"Ye all go ahead… yer captain will make sure ye all get up first," said Van Russel.

Lothar moved to the rope. "I'll go." He pulled himself up it nearly as quickly as Ranjit had. Jeremiah watched as he disappeared momentarily into the small, black hole high above their heads and then peeked out from the mouth of the cave.

Within a matter of minutes, each person had their turn at either climbing the rope or being pulled by their crewmates. All the way up they went, with satchels on their shoulders and pistols and swords hanging from their bodies. Van Russel was pulled up last. He arrived at the top, to his crew standing in the semi-darkness, just beyond the light of the afternoon sun.

"So… where to from here?" Van Russel asked Ranjit, his voice echoing through the hanging, wet stalactites.

"Captain, shh…" Ranjit said. "Through there." He pointed down a dark tunnel waiting for them on the far side of the crew.

"Why are ye all standing around? Light a torch!" said Van Russel. His voice echoed loudly through the musty cavern. He seemed anxious to keep moving and yet he spoke before he thought.

Ranjit glared at him.

"What is that noise?" Jeremiah asked, turning to the others. He feared what was coming this time as the air began to rattle with an upcoming thunder.

"VAMPIRE BATS!" Patch screamed, hitting the floor fast. The rest of the crew dropped to the ground as well, throwing their arms above their heads. They curled in fetal positions as the swarming, black monsters screeched just inches above their heads.

"Captain, I swear… if ye call upon one more thing!" Ranjit screamed at him.

"Err… sorry crew! It was an accident!" Van Russel yelled through the maze of winged demons.

"Too late for apologies now!" Ranjit shot back.

Thousands of bats flew in twisting circles around the crew. The vibrations from their wings shook the ground and the nerves of the men that feared a nasty bite. Luckily for the crew, however, Van Russel's yells only startled the creatures and they soon poured from the mouth of the cave, emptying out into the evening sky.

"Captain, I'm gonna rope yer mouth shut if ye call one more thing upon us," Ranjit scolded as he and the others stood back on their feet. "This trip better have not been a waste of time. Already lost a good part of the crew and we haven't seen anything close to a treasure. The only thing waiting for all of us here is certain death."

Two torches were lit and Ranjit walked to the front. He yanked a torch from Orville's grasp. He drew his sword with his free hand and led the others slowly into the tunnel. Jeremiah kept to the rear, close to Van Russel, but didn't say anything to him. For once, he could appreciate Ranjit's anger — he too was agitated with the fact that the captain had yet again put them all at risk.

As they progressed through the tunnel, it spiraled downwards. It was cool, narrow and dark for those who weren't within range of the torches. Jeremiah could only see the man immediately in front of him and he inched his way through the tunnel with the others, listening cautiously for whatever might be waiting next.

Jeremiah turned to see Van Russel directly behind him. Water droplets echoed as they fell from the ceiling.

"We're approaching an opening," Jeremiah heard Ranjit tell the crew as they, one by one, walked into it.

Jeremiah and Van Russel were the last to arrive in the room and the crew's attention was on the gigantic hole in which they were now standing. They were far within the interior of the mountain and the crystal teeth that hung jaggedly above their heads must have been growing there for centuries. Jeremiah could see Van Russel's attention was upon the ceiling. He looked at the giant stalactites in awe, but he was the only one who was paying them any attention.

The rest of the crew, including Jeremiah, couldn't believe what they were seeing upon the floor in front of them. Most of them gazed upon the magnificent treasure trove with open mouths. The gigantic room was filled completely and as the flickering torchlight lit the room, a new air of excitement befell the entire crew. Everyone was careful not to scream out in amazement, but they grabbed each other happily, relishing their success.

The room glistened with the light of gold coins, gold bars, and gems that overflowed from hundreds of open chests. It was just as Daniels had written, "more than one man could ever imagine", and the sight alone was enough to make even the toughest man weak. Never before had Jeremiah seen, or even dreamed, of such an amazing, sparkling spectacle.

"Oh my," Van Russel whispered excitedly as he finally realized what was lying on the ground before him.

Ranjit turned back to him. "Congratulations, Captain — we've done it."

Most were speechless as they gazed upon the treasure.

"This much must have been collected over centuries," Van Russel said, his voice still near a whisper. "Oh, how I wish we could take it all."

"Greed will get every man here killed," Jeremiah spoke up.

"Yer right, cabin boy," Ranjit said. "We'll only take what we can get in the satchels. Crew, load the coins and load the gems. We can get more in our satchels if we only go for those."

Cautiously, Jeremiah and the crew took the satchels and walked around the room deciding which coins and gems to bag.

"How do you think the pirates got all of this up here?" Augustus asked Jeremiah.

"No telling… from what we've seen them do already, I'm sure it's not near as difficult for them as it was for us to get up here."

"And speaking of pirates, we'd better hurry. If they are that in tune with their treasure and know when it's been taken, they could return at any time… we don't need that," said Midget.

"I agree," Ranjit said. "Captain, any ideas after we get this treasure bagged up?"

Jeremiah and the others looked around.

"Captain?"

"Where is he?" Jeremiah asked nervously.

"Captain!" Ranjit called.

"What?" Van Russel replied, his voice echoing from the far side of the room.

Ranjit shook his head. "What are ye doing?"

"Finding us a way out of here," Van Russel shot back. He pointed behind where he was standing.

The crew quickly bagged up all the treasure they could carry and closed up the heavy, clanking satchels. They strapped them to their shoulders and lined up near their captain, who was waiting impatiently for them on the other side. There were thirteen satchels in all and each of them were so full that treasure dropped from them as the men walked.

Jeremiah was the first to reach Van Russel. He had a bag over each of his bony shoulders. "Find us a way out, Captain?"

"Aye," Van Russel said proudly. When all fourteen had reached the exit, he pointed out above the jungle trees. "There's our way out."

"Ye've got to be kidding," Ranjit said.

Tied to a rock in the mouth of their exit was a long, thin rope. It extended beyond the opening of the mountain and high above the jungle trees where it sloped downwards to a tree far on the other end of the green abyss.

"We're supposed to climb down that rope? Most of the men couldn't even climb up a third of that distance," said Ranjit. Jeremiah looked at the taught rope nervously.

"Climb it?" Van Russel asked. "No... we're gonna ride it," he said devilishly as he picked up a set of chains on the ground by his feet. "Yer captain has made enough mistakes on this voyage. So, I'll go first." He wasted no time. He threw the chains over the top of the rope, grabbed both sides, and jumped.

Jeremiah watched in amazement as Van Russel slid all the way down, across the top of the jungle, to the end of the rope near the water's edge.

"Well, for once, the good captain did it," Lothar commented. "Now, how are we gonna get back to the ship?"

"The captain is on the beach now... we'll follow it around to our boat," said Midget.

"And the chains? There aren't enough of them," Augustus said.

"You can use your shirts. Take them off and throw them over the rope. I used to do the same thing back home," said Jeremiah.

Ranjit raised a brow. "Very good, cabin boy... ingenious thinking thar. Men, take off yer shirts... yer gonna ride them home."

Those that didn't have a set of the broken chains did just that. They ripped off their shirts, threw the satchels on their backs and one-by-one rode the long narrow rope back to the beach and their waiting ship.

CHAPTER TWENTY

A BATTLE
OF SOULS

Jeremiah couldn't believe what he was seeing. Sitting on the table before Van Russel, him and Ranjit were the thirteen satchels overflowing with Molodan's treasure. Even in the poorly lit cabin, the gems glistened with magnificent brilliance and the silver coins and gold doubloons sparkled radiantly. Several, oblong Spanish doubloons scattered the table below them.

"He'll come a looking for these soon," said Van Russel. He leaned back in his chair and propped his feet up on the desk as he re-twisted the ends of his mustache.

"We should be there by early morning," Ranjit replied. "What do ye want to do with all this treasure?"

"Lock it up here in the closet... all of it," Van Russel said. He pointed out towards the deck. "If we can keep the fight out thar, it should be safe in here. If we swap boats, we'll move it to the boat we'll be fighting on."

"Why not take it back to the town and hide it?" Ranjit asked. He took one of the coins from the desktop and flipped it between his middle and index fingers.

"'Cause he'll go back and hit Gordington again," Jeremiah said as he walked over to the desk to grab a coin for himself.

"That's right, Jeremiah. We must keep the treasure on the ship — he'll know where it is. And Gordington can't take another strike — blimey, it's about in ruins now." There was a knock at the door.

"Come in," Van Russel said. Augustus and Lothar entered.

"Wanted to come and have a look-see for ourselves. The swab thought he'd leach onto my side when he saw me coming," Lothar said arrogantly as he walked towards the treasure. "An amazing sight it is."

"Cap'n, Orville is headed west. He said to tell ye he'd have us there by early morning," said Augustus.

Ranjit glared at Augustus. "Swab, why don't ye tend to yer own duties and not worry about mine."

"Ranjit, give the boy a break. It hadn't been for him, ye'd have been eaten alive by cockroaches," Van Russel jeered. "Augustus, thank ye."

Ranjit turned away from the Captain as he scolded, but quickly shot his attention back to his beard.

"What?" Van Russel asked, noticing Ranjit's expression. He looked down at his beard. "Um… err… why's me beard moving?"

Van Russel pulled the long, braided strands of his beard apart and gasped at the sight. "Arrgh!" He pulled out two, gigantic black and red hissing cockroaches and threw them on the floor. They writhed around one another at the feet of everyone there.

"What are they doing?" Lothar asked, horrified. The others in the room looked equally disgusted.

"I think thar mating!" Ranjit blurted out before bellowing with laughter.

Boom! The cockroaches disintegrated into a thousand pieces.

"Not now they aren't," Van Russel quipped as he tried to regain his composure. A small stream of smoke trailed from the end of his pistol. "Nasty varmints... probably laid eggs up in me beard."

"Was that absolutely necessary?" Ranjit asked as he wiped his face.

Jeremiah and Augustus were choking back the laughter, but Augustus couldn't hold it in any longer. "Ha, Ha, Ha!" he exploded. Jeremiah too began howling at the sight of the two biggest thugs on the ship wiping the bug remains from the front of their clothes and faces.

"'Twould seem ye don't know when to hold yer tongue!" Ranjit screamed. But Augustus couldn't help it. He was nearly on the floor now laughing, and soon realized he had two others that were about to rip him apart. He took off for the door.

"Come back here, ye slug! I'll slit yer weasand!" Ranjit screamed as he and Lothar took off after him.

"Quartermaster, leave the boy alone!" Van Russel shot at him. But it was no use — they were halfway across the deck already. He turned to Jeremiah. "Lad, ye better get some rest. There's a good chance they'll be waiting for us when we get there."

"Who are you talking about, Captain?"

"Who?" he looked puzzled. "Who do ye think? The pirates!"

"What about the rest of the crew back in Gordington?" Jeremiah asked. He knew they couldn't go it alone with their current crew.

"Oh... err... sorry. Didn't realize what ye were asking. We'll go by Gordington first, but we'll moor far out and have a man row in to the others to alert them. Hopefully we'll have more volunteers than just our crew."

In the wee early hours of the following morning, the lights of Gordington were far out in the distance. Most of the crew was sleeping below, but the Captain, Ranjit and Lothar were still on deck. Orville was still manning the wheel.

"Ye want to take some more along with ya?" Van Russel asked as they walked over to the dinghy on the deck.

"Nope, the gunner and I will go, Cap'n. Let the crew sleep. They'll need it, no doubt," Ranjit said. He and Lothar cranked the dinghy up and lowered it over the side of the ship. "Think the pirates will show up before we return?"

"Well, I hope not!" said Van Russel. "Ye two row quick and get back out here. I don't want to have to fight these heathens all by me lonesome!"

"Of course," Ranjit said slyly as he started rowing the dinghy towards Gordington. "When we return, Cap'n, we'll need to wake the crew and start preparing."

"Bring back a big one with ye," Van Russel instructed. He needed something much larger than the sloop to fight Molodan and his crew. He watched as Ranjit and the gunner rowed out in the darkness until they were no longer in sight.

Ranjit and Lothar rowed up right beside the *Nante*. It was still in pieces and they couldn't tell that much at all had been done to it. They neared it with extreme caution; Ranjit had one hand on his sword and Lothar was lightly squeezing the trigger of his loaded pistol. All sounded quiet above on deck, but they were fearful they were about to walk straight into a trap.

They looked at one another as they heard a heavy knocking over the surface of the ship. It was moving straight in their direction. Lothar motioned to Ranjit and they prepared to fight. Lothar pointed his pistol upwards towards the deck and Ranjit drew his sword from its sheath.

But as quickly as the sound came, it silenced, confusing Ranjit and Lothar.

"Tally Ho!" said a cheerful face over the *Nante's* rail.

"Belcher! Ye crazy bloke! Ye bout scared me insides all over this little boat!" Ranjit shot up at him.

A rope ladder came splashing down in the water beside them. "Well, did ye do it?" Belcher asked excitedly as he lined the ladder up. "Did ye find the treasure?"

Ranjit began climbing the ladder and popped his gold doubloon at Belcher as he neared the top.

"Oh my! I guess that answers me question!" said the peg-legged cook, examining the gold doubloon in the minimal light. "Even this one seems like a grand treasure in itself." He reached out an arm to help Ranjit over the rail.

"How's the leg?" Ranjit asked, seeing that he was obviously still in pain.

"Better… still sore, but better. Hoping it'll be healed up completely in another month. And how did the rest of the crew make out?" Belcher asked, looking intently at the doubloon.

"We looted enough coin for a hundred lifetimes, but it cost us the lives of several of our men," Ranjit said sadly. "We paid for what we took, believe ye me, Cook."

"The Cap'n… and the boy? Did they both make it back alive?" Belcher asked.

"Aye, they're fine… waiting out thar just past our view," Ranjit replied as he pointed to the dark waters away from the town. "Now, there's the issue of which boat we're gonna take back out to fight these devils."

Belcher grinned widely.

"What?" Ranjit asked, cautiously. Lothar was climbing up on deck behind him.

"Yer looking at it," Belcher tried to be coy, holding his hands out in the direction of the *Nante's* busted deck.

"Have ye lost yer mind, Cook? We can't fight in this! I can't tell ye've done a blasted thing to it since we left a few days ago!"

Belcher found this quite amusing. "Alright, Quartermaster... that was just me idea of a joke... err... sorry." He slid two fingers in his mouth and whistled.

"What?" yelled down another voice high above them.

They looked up to see a small head poking over the galleon docked right beside them.

"Is that one of our men?" Ranjit asked, surprised. Lothar looked up in amazement.

"Aye, it is," Belcher said proudly. "Ye are looking at the substitute *Nante*... and the very ship we'll be fighting the pirates with."

"And how did ye obtain this?" Ranjit asked.

"After I lost me leg... and then couldn't go with ye all to the Miridian Mountains, I was rather upset. I decided to pay a visit to the governor meself. After all, I'd lost me leg and me crew — what else could he do to me?"

Ranjit laughed hysterically. "So, ye talked him into lending us a giant galleon?"

"Yep, and it's got thirty-two guns, a captain's cabin fit for a king, and sleeping quarters for the crew that are more than accommodating. In fact, the crew is all there now. I waited on the *Nante* just in case ye all decided to return tonight. Oh yeah… and, best of all, it's got a glorious kitchen." He flipped the gold doubloon back to Ranjit.

"Nope, ye keep this, Cook. There's plenty more where this came from — ye'll see." Ranjit handed it back to him. "How soon can ye get the crew ready to go?"

"As soon as ye say," Belcher replied, proudly.

"There's no time to waste. We must set sail immediately," said Ranjit. "The pirates could be here any time."

"Do we have any additional men?" Lothar asked, gazing up at the gigantic vessel.

"Aye, about fifty others from town have volunteered to help us — and they too are on the ship, sleeping." He whistled up to the deck of the galleon again.

"Yah?" the man said over the rail.

"Wake the crew, matey! We've got a fight that's awaiting us!" Belcher ordered.

"Aye, sir!"

Back on the sloop, Van Russel sat on the stairs next to Orville. "Helmsman, do ye believe we come back as something else in our lives to come?" he asked, thinking intently of his earlier conversation with Ozron, Jeremiah and the subject of Rousseau.

"Well, I surely think it's possible," said Orville.

Van Russel felt a little disturbed. "Do ye think we come back as people every time or do ye think we could come back as others things… maybe like those despicable cockroaches? I don't think I could tolerate reincarnating as one of those blasted bugs." He felt nauseated at just the thought of it.

Orville chuckled. "Well, Captain, I'm sure yer safe. I think we'd only come back as the like —" He was distracted by the sight bearing down on them. "What the —"

They both shot to their feet.

"Now that's more like it!" Van Russel yelled as he watched the galleon moving towards them. "Helmsman, go wake the crew… I believe it's time to switch ships."

"Aye, sir!" Orville replied excitedly.

"So what do ye think?" Ranjit yelled down to Van Russel as they approached.

"A fine job, Quartermaster. Ye've made yer captain proud!"

"Can't take credit for this one, Captain!" Belcher was standing right beside him and he slapped him on the back. "Ye can thank yer cook for that!"

Van Russel turned his attention to Belcher, who was now standing on a nicely fashioned peg. "Ye did it, Belcher?"

"Aye, coxed the governor meself for ye," he said proudly.

"The governor!" Van Russel said, shocked. "A fine job… and worthy of a raise, me thinks! And how's the leg?"

"Doing much better! Feeling a little better by the day!" he said as he knocked it lightly on the deck.

"Well, ye come on down here and drive the sloop back to Gordington. Think ye can do that by yerself?"

"Of course," he said, laughing. "Think I can handle a sloop alright. Tis not that far to Gordington."

The crew was woken and each was amazed as they walked the long, wooden plank onto the giant galleon. Everyone stopped and watched the spectacle as the thirteen jingling, treasure-laden bags were carried on board. A few of the gems dropped to the deck.

"Where's me Blessie?" Van Russel said to Ranjit as he boarded.

Ranjit pointed towards the new captain's cabin. "In there, Cap'n. I think she's asleep."

Van Russel walked over to the cabin and peeked through the door. Blessie wasn't sleeping as a parrot typically would — perched with her head under her wing. She was on the captain's bed, on her side, and snoring on his pillow.

"Ahh, that's me girl. Sleeping just like her captain does," Van Russel said proudly.

Blessie heard him and raised her head. "Captain?" she asked excitedly. She flew across the room to him. "Did ye find the treasure?"

"Aye, we sure did. We got enough that the captain may even buy ye a boyfriend!" he laughed.

Lothar came to his door. "Captain, the crew is ready."

"Very good, Gunner. Inform Ranjit and the helmsman that we are to set sail immediately."

It didn't take them any time at all. They set out for the horizon while Belcher steered the sloop behind them back towards Gordington.

"Alright me men!" Van Russel hollered. "Draw on every rag of canvas these yards will hold! Fetch up yer hook!"

"Ye heard the captain!" Ranjit yelled. "Lift anchor and make all sail!"

Slowly, the gigantic, thirty-two-gun galleon maneuvered in the water towards the horizon.

A couple of hours had passed when they came upon the spot where they'd found Jeremiah in the water — the same place that the pirates last opened the gateway. Every man aboard the galleon had guns drawn and swords ready. And there wasn't a man aboard that vessel that wasn't afraid. They had no idea what to anticipate should Molodan and his crew return again or what kind of army they would bring along with them. The crew on deck was silent and all eyes were on the water. They had taken a heavy chunk of Molodan's treasure and they knew he'd be back to get it soon.

"Out there, behind us!" one of the crew screamed. "Molodan is right behind us!"

No doubt he had already been on the water searching intently for the thieves that took his treasure. And everyone knew that not only would he be coming for them, he would be intent on exacting revenge. Molodan's cannons began blasting and the waters around the galleon were soon splashing as the cannon fire came within inches of the galleon.

"We need to get her turned around!" yelled Van Russel.

Orville struggled to maneuver the enormous galleon sideways with the little bit of wind available.

"Man yer stations! Prepare to fight!" Ranjit ordered. The men took their positions and loaded their muskets.

Jeremiah stood next to Van Russel. "Go hide in me cabin, boy — I don't want ye battling in this fight," Van Russel ordered.

"Sorry, Captain, but this is a fight I'm not staying out of," Jeremiah said.

Van Russel looked down on him proudly. "All right, lad. I guess the captain can't hide ye forever… and I guess ye've got yer own reasons for wanting to fight these bilge-sucking beasts!"

Down below, Lothar commanded the men manning the guns. "Thar nearly upon us! Man the guns! Load the powder! Load the guns! Ready?" The men nodded. "Fire upon em!" he screamed as he threw his arms about. Four of the cannon balls went hurtling through the air, smacking the pirate ship on the broad side and knocking one of their main masts square in its center. It crashed down upon the pirate deck.

But this didn't stop Molodan's ship. It came with even more speed towards the galleon, causing the men on deck to stop and watch in amazement.

"What are ye doing, men!" Van Russel barked. "Prepare to fight! Thar coming and thar coming strong!"

Molodan's crew shot across the night sky with tremendous speed. They manifested into pirates. Three of Van Russel's crew were immediately killed by the force of the pirates' swords. The others worked with all their might to fight them off.

Ranjit worked with great skill in deflecting their powerful blows, but as before, each time he tried to strike them, they would quickly turn to mist. Ranjit was left swinging at open air. He looked over at his captain who was having the same problem.

In no time Molodan reached the galleon. The two crews were equally matched in terms of number, but Van Russel's crew was at a disadvantage. Their strikes were hopeless and the pirates were slowing take them down.

One pirate began swinging at Jeremiah. Jeremiah ducked as the heavy pirate sword went crashing into the railing above him. While the pirate worked to free his sword, Jeremiah tried to escape, but the pirate's foot came crashing down in the center of the his chest.

Jeremiah screamed in terrible agony. This caught the attention of the rest of the crew, but they were too involved in sword-to-sword combat themselves and knew they could do nothing for him.

Then, something caught the pirate's attention. Directly above Jeremiah's head was a brilliant glowing light. It was vast enough that all on board the galleon could see it clearly. The pirate released his sword from the railing of the ship and brought it straight up in to the air with both hands. Just as he was about to thrust it through Jeremiah's chest, the light became even brighter. It came with such intensity that the entire surface of the deck glowed with an amazing brilliance.

The pirate was completely distracted by the site before him. Although he still pinned Jeremiah to the deck, his sword was suspended in the air.

"Get away from my son!" the spirit of Jeremiah's mother screamed. She raised both her arms and directed them at the pirate attacking Jeremiah. This sent a blast of energy towards the brute, hitting him in the chest. He disintegrated into nothingness.

Jeremiah looked up at her. "Mother?" She had a weary look about her.

"Yes, son, he temporarily disabled the only energy I had. Now get up and fight!" And with that, she disappeared.

The battle continued and Van Russel and Jeremiah fought back-to-back. "What are we gonna do?" Jeremiah asked.

"Think we're needing a miracle now," said Van Russel.

"WAIT!" Jeremiah blurted, motioning out to the distant waters. "There are more lights coming! We can't handle any more of them!"

Van Russel screamed joyously. "Those aren't pirates! I believe that to be help for us!"

Jeremiah looked again. "Yes!" he yelled. "I believe you're right!"

It was Ozron. It wasn't a large boat he was traveling on, but something smaller than a sloop. Jeremiah watched his glowing staff leading the way. He was racing quickly across the ocean's surface.

Jeremiah and the crew looked aghast when they saw what was accompanying Ozron. They were creatures unlike anything any of them had ever seen before. Rowing the boat were twenty or more dwarves, small bearded creatures with amazing strength. There were hobgoblins, short and scruffy creatures that had nostrils, but no nose. One minute they were seen on the boat and the next they'd vanish. And lastly, Ozron had a fleet of trolls. All were friends of Ozron, and inhabitants of his thicket, that had come to help.

They leapt onto the galleon and climbed up its side as if it was no effort at all for them. Jeremiah and the crew were quickly becoming exhausted and these creatures couldn't have shown up at a better time. The hobgoblins came with swords-a-swinging and gave Molodan and his pirates a taste of their own evil. When the pirates swung at them, they too would disappear, causing the pirates' efforts to be as futile as those of Van Russel's crew.

The dwarves and goblins fought off the marauders with swords fashioned from some amazing metal from deep within the earth's core.

Ranjit was in sword-to-sword combat with Molodan, but he was defenseless against the monster. Ranjit swung his sword and was able to strike him. Molodan laughed in his face. He kicked Ranjit in the chest, knocking him off of the front of the ship, causing his sword to drop at the front of the galleon.

Jeremiah witnessed this and panicked. He realized that although he had tried to explain the proper demise of Molodan, he was always interrupted or cut off. He knew it was up to him.

Jeremiah watched Molodan motion for the chest. His heart pumped, knowing what Molodan wanted to do. He'd open the portal and take Van Russel and his crew to the other side where they'd be defenseless. There was only one problem, however — one of his pirates in charge motioned to him from the other ship that it had been taken.

"It's in here ye scoundrel! I've got yer amulet!" Van Russel's voice yelled from the captain's cabin.

Molodan stormed across the deck, striking another of the crew in the chest with his sword as he went, and burst through the cabin door. But Van Russel was not there.

"Ark! That'll show you!" screamed the bird.

There sat Blessie with the amulet, which she'd stolen during the battle, in her beak. She dropped it on the floor and fled, mimicking Van Russel's laugh as easily as she had his voice.

Jeremiah was astounded at Blessie's brilliance.

Molodan grabbed the amulet, took long heavy strides across the deck and headed towards the front of the galleon where he started to reactivate it — he was preparing to send them all into the realm of the dead.

"No!" Jeremiah screamed. "He's going to reopen the portal!"

But there was nothing anyone could do. They were all fighting their own battle with Molodan's army — even the hobgoblins, trolls and dwarves.

Jeremiah ran to the front of the ship where Molodan was reassembling the amulet.

"Jeremiah! No!" Ozron screamed. But it was no use — Jeremiah was determined to stop him.

Just as he reached Molodan, the towering brute knocked him down with a forceful swing. His head slid into the rail and rendered him partly unconscious.

Molodan assembled the amulet quickly. As he flicked the outer shell of the amulet, a shrill echo emitted from it and a shockwave of energy blasted out from the front of the galleon. The portal began opening.

"Stop him!" Ozron ordered. "Don't let him open the portal!"

Slowly, the silvery doorway appeared. But Jeremiah was regaining his senses. Though barely consciousness, he could feel Ranjit's sword just within his reach. He grabbed it. With Molodan's full attention and energy focused opening the portal, Jeremiah lifted the sword, pointed it upwards, and drove it straight through the heart of Molodan.

BOOM! A massive shockwave rocketed out in all directions, knocking everyone off their feet and completely evaporating every last member of Molodan's crew. Molodan was the only one left standing there, but not for long. As he looked down at Jeremiah, his face shrunk in, and he dissipated and vanished. The silvery doorway quickly dissolved and both the galleon and the empty pirate ship were left floating in the water.

Van Russel's crew and Ozron's army looked around at one another. Most of them stood motionless with their mouths hanging open. They couldn't believe what they had just seen, especially the demise of Molodan. Although Molodan had been destroyed, some of his energy must have been left in the amulet, for the blue stone in the center started glowing. It continued glowing on the deck of the ship and began shaking violently. Jeremiah slowly made his way back to his feet, but as he did, the amulet exploded. The blast was so strong that it knocked him from the front of the galleon and into the water below.

"Yer mine!" Molodan moaned with a mile-wide echo as he quickly rematerialized, but his last remaining energy was only temporary and he vanished within seconds.

"Get him!" Ozron screamed as he pointed to Jeremiah's lifeless body floating in the water.

"I've got him!" Ranjit yelled, pulling the boy close to him. "He's still breathing!"

Although everyone was fearful for Jeremiah's safety, they knew he had done it. After two hundred years of countless deaths, Molodan and his crew of deadly assassins had finally been defeated.

CHAPTER TWENTY-ONE

An
Awakening

Nefron awoke from his slumber and rose up from the top of the wooden desk. He looked about the room. A smirk emerged on his green, elfin face and his wings perked up and slowly began oscillating. He fluttered about the room, pulling on the shirts of everyone there. He needed them to wake up now. He was overly excited — Jeremiah was moving and he needed them to see.

Van Russel was the most difficult to rouse. Nefron pulled on his jacket, but it had no effect — so he went for his beard. He grabbed the end of it and moved it up and down, but the captain just responded with some nonsense talk and swatted his hand across his face. Everyone else in the room was woken easily by the small nisse. They watched as the entertaining little creature struggled to wake

Van Russel. Nefron grabbed the small twisted ends of his mustache, stood on the captain's cheek and tugged — but still, it was having no effect. Nisse were typically gentle, pleasant creatures, but this one was becoming a little frustrated.

Ozron chuckled. "Captain!" he blurted.

"What! Huh?" Van Russel asked as he jumped up from his dream. Nefron let go of him and buzzed away.

Everyone in the room laughed — all but Jeremiah. He was slowly beginning to come to. Ozron sat at his side. Van Russel was at the desk with his feet propped up comfortably and Nefron and Blessie had both been resting right on top of the old wooden desk. Ebineezer was there the entire night as well, but had just left to visit the porch for his morning pipe and brandy. Everyone had been there waiting patiently for Jeremiah to open his eyes.

He was waking, finally. It had been two weeks since the peasant, who had started homeless, without family and as a cabin boy, had made the ultimate difference for so many people. He had defeated Molodan. Even with all the odds stacked against him, he had successfully done what no other could do. Maybe it was a hint of Rousseau still in his blood or just his willful desire, but it mattered not — he had done it.

During the past two weeks, he came in and out of consciousness, waking long enough to take some food and water — and then he'd be out again, unaware of anything around him. The blast of the amulet had apparently made more of an impact upon his body than all of the other rigorous events he had been through. Even all of the loud, banging reconstruction happening at the inn since they had returned didn't seem to affect him in the slightest.

Jeremiah began by slowly moving his limbs. His hands did a minute jerk or two, followed by his arms. His legs were next... they all watched as he slowly moved an inch or two below his covers.

His eyes opened, only a little bit. Within minutes he was opening them fully and looking about the room. "Where am I?" he asked as he scanned the room, blinking his eyes. The room looked vaguely familiar and he realized soon enough where he was. He did have his wits about him now and he looked around room number one.

"Ozron?" Jeremiah asked of the first one he saw.

"Yes, young one," Ozron said softly. "I'm here. Actually, we're all here."

Jeremiah rose up from the bed. He grinned intently when he saw the friendly faces about his room. Blessie flapped over to his bed and nuzzled her beak into the side of his face. "Blessie's missed you," she said to him.

"I've missed you too," Jeremiah replied warmly to her, with a hint of a giggle.

Nefron flew across the room to him. Jeremiah held up his hand and the nisse landed on it, smiling at the boy. He bowed to him.

"No need to bow to me, Nefron," Jeremiah said. "We couldn't have done this without you either."

"I think the little guy has taken a liking to you, Jeremiah," said Ozron.

Jeremiah looked to his little friend. "That would go for both of us." He noticed Van Russel sitting at the old, wooden desk. He was watching Jeremiah — a giant grin across his face. "Captain, so glad you're here. Everything all right?" he asked him.

Van Russel jumped up from his chair and sat next to Jeremiah on the bed. He placed his arm around the boy and pulled him close. "Lad, the captain is quite proud of ye. Ye gave me quite a scare right there at the end too."

"Sorry Captain," Jeremiah giggled. "Didn't mean to do that again."

"Well," said Van Russel, "Ebineezer will surely want to be here for this… let me go fetch him." He rushed off to the porch below where Ebineezer was enjoying the beautiful morning. The innkeeper had been feeling better on this day with no fits of blood coughing or persistent hacking.

Jeremiah displayed a puzzled expression as he heard sawing and pounding on the old structure. "What is that noise?" he asked.

"The pirates nearly destroyed the inn completely," Ozron replied. "The carpenters and coopers have been working on it the last two weeks while you've been in your slumber," he joked.

"Oh yes, I remember now. It was in a state when we left."

"And they're coming along with it well," Ebineezer added, just coming in the room.

He went to Jeremiah and embraced him. Jeremiah moaned. The innkeeper was hugging him so tightly he could barely breathe.

"Oh, sorry Jeremiah," Ebineezer replied, loosening his grip. "We're all very proud of ye, boy. Ye have made a difference for so many people."

"It was all of us," Jeremiah assured him. "Not just me."

"That's right," Van Russel added with a dignified look. "We all defeated that scoundrel."

Two more had arrived and were standing in the doorway, but Jeremiah hadn't noticed them. A pleasant, female voice called to him. "Ah, the amazing boy has finally awoken! How good to see you doing better!"

Jeremiah turned to her. "Madam Karla," he remarked, "so glad to see you too."

"I've got someone else with me that I thought you may want to see," she said proudly.

But Jeremiah was confused. He didn't want to be rude, but he had no idea who this frail, older gentleman was standing at her side. "I'm sorry, but…"

The man smiled at the boy. "I wouldn't expect you to know my face, Jeremiah," he said.

The color drained quickly from Jeremiah's face.

"Oh no, he's going out again!" screamed the anxious captain.

Ozron rose. "Van Russel, you nincompoop, calm down!" he blurted. "Jeremiah, are you alright?"

Jeremiah said nothing. He remained with mouth open and staring.

"Amazed at my escape?" he said jokingly.

"Um, yes… but, how?" Jeremiah asked.

"Well, after you escaped, you left the keys in your cell door. I snagged them and did the same as you after we came back through the portal to the side of the living. Seeing where you went out was easy enough," he laughed. "After all, you couldn't miss the giant hole you left in the side of their ship. Which they weren't too happy about, by the way." All laughed. "I figured after a lifetime aboard their ship as a slave, it was worth immediate death just to try once. You inspired me." McKinley smiled at the boy, and Jeremiah was overjoyed for him.

He explained how he had held onto a small exterior edge, far beneath their line of sight on the ship's hull for two nights and a day. He rode all the way into Gordington, where he escaped during the great battle.

He reported that when he snuck behind the Wharf, he found a rather large man propped up on the ground next to a building behind it. He was dead, with a cannon ball resting in his arms. He had an atrocious look on his face. McKinley could have sworn as he walked by him that the man was boasting about something… even in death. At any rate, he walked past him and didn't pay him any more attention.

"We just came from Madam Karla's amazing shop," McKinley said. He reached down into his pocket. "She wanted me to bring this to you when you woke," he said, handing Jeremiah another small, green candle.

Jeremiah laughed. "You all know this is an amazing candle, right?" he asked as he took the candle from McKinley and looked at Madam Karla. She winked at him.

"What's so amazing about it?" Van Russel asked.

"I'm sure there's an amazing tale behind that too, isn't there?" asked Ebineezer.

"Yes," Jeremiah laughed, "and I'll tell you all about it sometime."

There was another knock at the door. Jeremiah turned to see a small Chinese man standing in the doorway.

"Doc Hazleton," Ebineezer said, rolling his eyes. "Good morning."

"Good morning to all of you," the man said in his American-Chinese accent. "I hear the boy has awoken."

"Aye, but a few minutes ago," Ebineezer said to him.

The doctor walked over to the bed. He sat his little, black medical bag on the covers and opened it. He looked at Jeremiah. "Been feeling alright today?" he asked.

"Yes, sir," Jeremiah replied.

The doctor put his ear up to his chest. "Hmm…" he said as he listened, "everything seems to be in working order. What about the spots and scabs?"

"Spots and scabs?" Jeremiah asked, horrified. Everyone else in the room seemed to be equally horrified. "I haven't had any spots or scabs that I know of."

The local physician obviously didn't hear him though, as usual. "Well, I've got a special concoction that'll clear those right up." He searched inside his bag again and fumbled around. Small, clinking vials of glass could be heard as he continued searching. Jeremiah and the others looked at one another, confused and speechless.

Ebineezer rolled his eyes. "The good ole doctor at it again," he mumbled under his breath.

"Yes, here we are," said the doctor as he pulled two vials from his bag. "The first is a mixture of sassafras bark and catnip tea. Mix this with a cup of warm and drink it slowly. It will help with your nausea and will cleanse and most definitely move your bowels." He handed it to Jeremiah, who appeared evidently mortified. "This other is a powder. It contains lye. You'll need to mix one third of this with a warm tub of water for three days. And soak your feet in it for two hours. This should make you good as new," he said. He handed the other vial to Jeremiah and closed up his bag and headed for the door. He stopped and turned. "Ebineezer, how's the cough?"

"Oh, great Doc… it's doing much better. Thank you," he assured him, smacking himself on the chest.

"Any of you feeling the same ailments as the boy?" the doctor asked.

They were all very quick to respond. "Oh no! We're great! No problems here!"

"Alright then. Good day now," the doctor said as he exited.

"Good day," they all replied, happy to see him leaving.

"The good doctor," said Van Russel, "thinks he has a case of small pox." All burst out in laughter.

"So what do I do with these?" Jeremiah asked, still horrified from his diagnosis. He held the two vials in his hand, confused.

"Give those to me. I'll put them to good use," Van Russel replied. He took the vials and dropped them in his pocket. "Now if yer up to it, I'd love to show ye the *Nante*. We've been working non-stop on her now for the last two weeks."

"It's quite amazing," Blessie chimed in from her perch on the desk. When Jeremiah gazed in her direction she wasn't the only one back there. He noticed some other odd-looking presence, unnoticed by everyone else.

At first glance, he was just an obscure form near the rear corner of the room — almost like a shadow. However, when he saw that Jeremiah took notice of him, he manifested into more of a human-like shape and waved. He said nothing.

Jeremiah looked to Ozron. He could see that he too was watching Daniels. Ozron said nothing though. Jeremiah knew he wanted him to have his final moment with Daniels.

Daniels extended a shadowy hand and waved goodbye. He waved back to the ghost and as quickly as he had noticed him there, Daniels's shape moved closer to the dark spot on the floor and dissolved into it, disappearing completely.

"What are ye waving at?" Ebineezer asked, looking behind himself. He noticed Jeremiah waving towards the direction of the dark colored spot. His eyes widened greatly. "Oh me! Ebineezer is going to return to his pipe. See ye all downstairs!" He took off for the door.

"Oh, think me stomach is going back into another fisherman's knot!" Van Russel blurted when he noticed what had just happened. "Jeremiah, ye ready to have a look-see at me ship?"

"Yes," said Jeremiah. He rose from the bed, laughing.

McKinley walked over to him and shook the boy's hand. "Jeremiah, I'll be seeing you again. Thank you for everything." They looked at one another and smiled and McKinley turned to walk away.

He started towards the door, but Jeremiah yelled, "Wait!" McKinley turned and Jeremiah ran up to him, touching his neck. "Where did you get this?" he asked as his eyes filled up with tears.

"What? This old necklace?" McKinley asked, startled.

Jeremiah nodded anxiously. He could hardly speak.

"From one of the slaves aboard Molodan's ship. He asked that if I was ever to come back here, to find his son and give this to him. But he never had a chance to tell me his name. They removed him as he was giving this to me." McKinley thought for a moment and then it hit him. "Oh my! Was that your father?"

Jeremiah went limp and dropped to his knees. Ozron ran to him and helped him back to his feet. "It's alright Jeremiah," he encouraged. "McKinley, tell me. Is the boy's father alive?"

"Yes, at least… he should be." McKinley responded, now upset too as he watched Jeremiah's reaction.

Ozron gazed intently at the former slave. "Then tell me…
where is he?"

"Where all the others are. In the lands of Abaddon — the
realm of the dead."

"My father is alive!" Jeremiah screamed. "We must go get
him!"

"Calm down, calm down," said Van Russel. He too had a tear
running down his cheek. "We'll get yer father… and the rest of
them. This will take planning."

"For once, I agree with the good captain," Ozron said. He
placed his hand on the boy's back. "Don't you worry… we'll do
whatever we have to do to find him, Jeremiah. Give us a little time
to work this out."

"But the only way there was with the amulet," said Jeremiah.

"It was destroyed during the blast, wasn't it?" Madam Karla
asked.

"It was, but we'll have to retrieve it and see if we can restore
it," Ozron said. "The waters were shallow and we know where it
was. We should be able to find the pieces."

Nefron rose from his place on the desk and flew to Jeremiah's
shoulder. He nuzzled up against him, trying to console him.

"I know I've got you by my side," Jeremiah said to him, smiling.

Jeremiah believed his father was still alive. He wasn't killed
in the storm, but was captured by Molodan and his crew… just as
many others were. All were full of excitement in the hopes that he

was waiting on the other side. But there was an underlying level of fear within all of them too. Journeying to the realm of the dead would be no small feat.

McKinley returned the necklace to Jeremiah, who took it proudly for both of his parents. As he reattached the necklace around his neck, he had a new look about him. It was one of strength — so much different than what he had displayed upon first arriving in Gordington. There was only one objective in his mind now, and that was to find his father. There would be no stopping the determination now running strong through his veins.

When they reached the *Nante*, Van Russel walked flamboyantly across the deck showing off his ship. "Jeremiah, what do ye think?" he asked, raising both arms and pointing about. He was grinning from ear to ear.

"Quite amazing!" Jeremiah said as his eyes scanned the new-looking brigantine. It was quite impressive. The sails had all been replaced with newer, white ones and the masts holding them up looked to be of the freshest, strongest wood. All of the minor detailing work had neared completion, even the rails and spindles, which were now ornate in design.

Jeremiah watched as the crew surfaced on the deck and townsfolk gathered near. They clapped and cheered and the sound of it grew in such enormous size that chills ran down his spine. He smiled back to all of them, waving. And the more he smiled and waved, the louder it became. He knew they were proud of him and because of his amazing efforts they were now free of any future worries from the pirates.

Jeremiah saw Ozron standing at the front of the crowd. On both sides of him stood Jonah and Arien. Jeremiah looked to the horses and to the old man holding them — he knew they'd be fine.

The deck of the *Nante* filled completely with the crew and when Jeremiah turned around from the crowd towards them, he saw three of his closest friends in the front.

Augustus was first. And he was full of smiles. He hugged Jeremiah. "Great to see you back," he said.

"It's great to see you too, Augustus."

"I've been in your room more times than I can count the past couple of weeks, and the captain and Ranjit were in full agreement of me taking time off from my chores. They said company would be good for your healing," Augustus added.

"Even Ranjit was alright with it?" Jeremiah laughed, looking at him. He was standing in the near distance, not too far from Van Russel. He was clapping along with the rest of the crew and nodded to Jeremiah when he looked his way. Jeremiah knew he had earned a little of Ranjit's respect. Lothar stood at his side, but said nothing; clearly jealous of the attention Jeremiah was receiving.

Midget, Belcher and Orville were standing up front next to Augustus and were overjoyed to see their friend return.

Startled, Jeremiah noticed Belcher's missing leg. He knew of the accident, but hadn't seen the result. "Belcher, how are you?" he asked.

"Doing better now," he said smiling. "It's still tender, but much better. The night we swapped boats I must have walked right past ye loading on to the galleon. It's good to see ye again, boy."

"Yes, it's good to see you again too. And Midget, how are you?" Jeremiah asked, looking over to the cooper.

"Oh, I'm great Jeremiah. Especially now that we have the ship completed. If I can overcome a nasty case of scurvy, nothing much else is a greater challenge — not even some senseless pirates," he laughed.

Jeremiah grinned at Orville. "Noticed your new wheel up there," he giggled.

Orville turned to the new, gigantic steering wheel they had replaced. "Oh yes, we can all thank Midget for that too. He fashioned it from oak and it's as sturdy as they come. Glad to have you back and I'm looking forward to the next game of coconut."

"Coconut… now that sounds great," Jeremiah smiled.

The crowd on the pier parted slightly to let a man through. He was holding a large, round box. He shuffled his way through the bustling patrons mobbed everywhere and managed to squeeze on to the deck.

"Ah, the tailor. The captain's been waiting for ye," Van Russel commented loudly as he made his way through his crew.

The tall, skinny tailor looked up to him. "Yes, Captain. Just finished it. Looks like I did just in time too." He handed the box to the captain.

Van Russel lifted the lid and looked inside. He grinned joyously as reached his hands in. It was a large, round, oversized hat with a magnificent red feather sewn neatly to the side of it. "Aye, an amazing hat," he remarked.

"Captain, isn't that just like every other hat ye own?" Ranjit asked in a loud voice. He seemed slightly disgusted.

"Aye, it is, but it replaces me hat that was lost in the storm." He placed it upon his head and indeed, it was exactly as his others — the same tailor had made the seven other spares he kept hidden neatly away in his cabin. Ranjit rolled his eyes and walked off as Blessie looked up to it... and then to her captain. "I know ye like it, don't ye girl?" said Van Russel.

Slowly, the crowd started filtering away and the crew resumed their chores and activities. Soon only Van Russel and Jeremiah remained standing there.

"Come with me. Need to give ye something," motioned Van Russel. Jeremiah followed him to his cabin. "Take a seat over there." Van Russel walked around to the other side of his desk. He started to reach underneath, but there was a knock at the door. "Come in," he said.

"Ah, Captain..." said Governor Addison. "Sorry I'm just now making it by. It's been a busy couple of weeks. I noticed all the commotion down here and figured I'd come have a look for myself." Van Russel said nothing and the governor turned his attention towards Jeremiah. "So, you must be the boy I've heard so much about."

"Yes, sir."

"Well, congratulations on your achievements with the pirates. I knew you could do it. It was, after all, my idea to send the *Nante* after them," he said with a dignified look. "I guess I should be taking credit for that part."

Van Russel rolled his eyes in disgust.

"Yes, sir... I guess you could maybe look at it that way," Jeremiah answered. He knew of the governor's antics, but hadn't had the pleasure of meeting the round, little man. He was respectful to him all the same.

"'Maybe' nothing!" the governor yelled with laughter. "If it hadn't been for me, we wouldn't be sitting here now."

"Actually Governor, yer not sitting," Van Russel quipped.

The governor gave him a scolding look. "Which by the way is partly why I am here. I heard you were able to obtain some of the treasure. I am here to collect my healthy share of it."

Van Russel scooted a small pouch across his table to the governor. "Um, yes. Here it is, sir. All that is left."

The governor looked down at it. A surprised and disgusted look came across his face. He picked it up, opened the pouch and dropped the contents of it into one hand. Nine coins dropped out of it. "Nine doubloons? That's it?" he barked. "My report of your pirate plundering was much more vast than this!"

"Sorry sir. I've given me men a few coins each for all their hard work and the pirates took back a great deal of what we had stolen from them. It disappeared into the abyss along with them when they were destroyed. Ye know though, nine doubloons is quite a treasure in itself.

The governor put them back in the bag and stormed towards the door, getting stuck in the frame. "Ah!" he yelled angrily as he popped himself free and stormed back towards his office.

"Oh Governor, wait just a minute!" Van Russel yelled to him, chasing him out the door. Jeremiah rushed to the door behind them.

"What Captain?" he sneered.

Van Russel reached into his pocket. I know how much ye love your afternoon tea. I've got a vial of herbs here that'll make it taste just dandy." He handed him the vials of sassafras bark and catnip tea.

The governor held them, looking them over closely. "Dandy, huh? Alright Captain... I'll give it a try," he commented as he stormed away.

"Now, back to why I called ye in here," Van Russel said, grinning as he walked back into the cabin.

Jeremiah kept himself from exploding with laughter. But he also felt confused. "Captain, is that really all that is left of what we took?"

"Of course not," Van Russel replied. He reached underneath his desk and grabbed one of the leather satchels. He picked it up and dropped it on the desk, causing hundreds of gold coins within it to jingle and ring. "Lad... this is yers." He handed the satchel to Jeremiah.

"Sir, I couldn't receive that much!"

"Don't argue with the captain. It's already been decided. Now, Ebineezer can help ye with the safe keeping of it. There's enough there for an entire lifetime… or a fleet of ships. But I'm not wanting ye to leave me."

Jeremiah took the bag. "Leave you? Of course not. And besides that, we have something else we need to do right away," he said as he looked out the window towards the open water.

They hid the coins in the cabin and walked outside. The crew had already prepared for the next mission and was anxiously awaiting word from their captain. Van Russel nodded to Ranjit who began yelling his commands.

Jeremiah walked to the front of the ship. Orville was at the wheel and called to Jeremiah, now standing off the bow with his foot propped up on the bowsprit.

"Where to Jeremiah?" Orville called to him.

Jeremiah pointed to the open water near the horizon. "Gentleman, you know where to go. Let's find my father."

SPRING,
1723

O ne couldn't have convinced Ebineezer that there had been a more beautiful day. The Saturday morning temperature felt incredible and the hustle and bustle on Banyard Street was just as it always had been. Even Mrs. Otterstein and her husband shunned him on their daily stroll through the middle of town. Everything seemed back to its perfectly normal self, as if the town had never endured anything strange, punishing or unusual.

Reconstruction had been taking place for three and half months and with the exception of the gaping hole in the wall of the Wharf, one would have never guessed what went on there. Another townsman assumed control of the Wharf's operations and everything on pier number three that was unjustly taken by the bartender had been given back to its rightful owner.

Ebineezer took a sip from his tankard and tipped his chair backwards. His pipe hung from his lips and drizzled a curling stream of smoke into the fresh spring air.

The last and remaining cooper who had been hired to help repair the inn came walking out. His tools were around his waist and he wiped the sweat from his brow as he approached Ebineezer.

"Mr. Drake, I think that'll do it. I spent the better part of last night finishing up the last of it. I believe you're as good as new now."

"Oh, thank ye… thank ye," Ebineezer said, lowering his chair and raising himself to his feet. "Ye men have done a fine job indeed."

"Well sir, if there's nothing else, I'll be on my way. My own ship is due to leave port any time now and I know they'll be needing me."

"Absolutely! Thank ye, young man… and send me regards to ye captain."

The cooper began to walk away and Ebineezer fitted his large rump back into his seat. He watched the man stop as if he had forgotten something. He turned to him with a troubled look upon his face.

"Cooper, everything alright?" Ebineezer asked.

"Oh yes, Mr. Drake. One thing I forgot to mention… I noticed some strange spots in room number one on the wall and the floor. I tried to clean them up when I was doing the repair work, but they were the darnedest things I've ever seen. The more I scrubbed them, the more persistent they seemed. I finally gave up, but I did think it to be a little odd and made note to tell you."

Ebineezer's mouth fell open, nearly dropping his pipe.

"Sir, everything all right?" the cooper asked.

"Oh yes, yes," said Ebineezer, regaining his composure. He gazed up, inconspicuously, to the window above him. "Everything's perfectly fine. Thanks... um... for letting me know."

"Alright then... good day now," said the cooper happily, setting foot for his awaiting ship.

"Good day now," Ebineezer called back, again glancing up to the window above him.

He rose from his chair and reentered the inn. He stood next to the bar for a moment and took a deep breath, turning his direction towards the dark, unwelcoming stairwell.

"Crazy innkeeper," he muttered to himself. "Get a grip on yerself." The unknown was killing him, however, and he made his way up to room number one. He turned the handle and took a deep breath as he opened the door.

He peered around the corner. Everything seemed perfectly fine. The shutters were open and daylight penetrated the old, musty room with a sort of welcoming friendliness. Nothing appeared out of the norm and he walked over to the window and peered outside — everything on Banyard Street was just as he had seen it minutes prior.

He looked down at the dark colored spot on the floor. He ran his shoe over the top of it, but nothing seemed any different. None of the darkness rubbed on his shoe nor made any difference on the floor. It was old and dried looking — the same as he had last seen it.

Seeing that everything was perfectly all right and back to normal, he turned for the door. He left the room, shutting the door behind him and relocking room number one. He left to return downstairs to enjoy his day of observing the patrons of Banyard Street.

But if one were to have looked through the small keyhole of room number one, they would have seen something remarkable with the spot on the floor. As the innkeeper walked away it began darkening… significantly.

It darkened and grew by the second. Even with the full light of day shining into the room, a small globular mass began rising from the spot and moved across the floor, taking on a human-like shape. It peered out of the window and down towards the innkeeper before moving quickly and disappearing from sight altogether.

ABOUT THE AUTHOR

Stephen Wren is a Registered Respiratory Therapist by education, a member of the SCBWI, and has always had a love for writing. In addition to creating middle-grade and YA fantasy novels, he also serves as the director of TN Paranormal and the radio producer for a paranormal talk radio program. He lives with his family in Tennessee.

CPSIA information can be obtained at www.ICGtesting.com
Printed in the USA
245321LV00002B/153/P